Great Eastern Land

D. J. Taylor was born in Norwich in 1960 and educated there and at St John's College, Oxford where he read Modern History. At present he works as a copywriter in the marketing department of a large London accountancy firm. He has contributed stories and reviews to the *Spectator*, *Encounter* and *P. E. N. New Fiction 1*.

GW00702889

D. J. Taylor

Great Eastern Land

A Novel

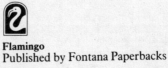

Flamingo
Published by Fontana Paperbacks

First published in Great Britain
by Martin Secker & Warburg Limited 1986

This Flamingo edition first published
in 1987 by Fontana Paperbacks,
8 Grafton Street, London W1

Flamingo is an imprint of
Fontana Paperbacks, part of
the Collins Publishing Group.

Made and printed in Great Britain by
William Collins Sons & Co. Ltd, Glasgow

Mike's

Ruth's

Contents

. . . and he had in the same temple an altar for the holy sacrifice of Christ side by side with an altar on which victims were offered to devils . . . This king Redwald was a man of noble descent but ignoble in his actions: he was son of Tytila and grandson of Wuffa, after whom all kings of the East Angles are called Wuffings.

Bede: *Historia Ecclesiastica Gentis Anglorum* ii:16 627 AD

The past is an infinitely more agreeable subject for speculation than the future.

From the *Notebooks*

What was the use of reading history unless the alchemy of literature had transcended the facts by the immortal presentation of them?

Compton Mackenzie *Sinister Street*

1. At Dr Feelgood's

They raided Dr Feelgood's at ten past three in the morning, by which time several customers were cavorting with the handful of Asian sluts and several others lying with their heads face down on the beer-stained table tops. Mr Mouzookseem said: 'Will you boys stop inconveniencing me in this way? Every time you bust down that door I'm losing good custom.' Later he said: 'This is a respectable house. And what do you think I pay that protection money for?' Later still he said: 'Two bottles each and the run of the girls, OK?' It was not OK. The police, inspired by a capriciousness that was attributable to boredom, to their district commissioner or (most probably) to some well-connected enemy of Mr Mouzookseem, were disposed to linger.

Dr Feelgood's lay at the western end of the village, slightly beyond the point at which the main street tapered off into suburbs of dust and scrub, down from the river and the Cree Wharf. It was inconveniently situated. Five years before there had been only the wharf and a patchwork of outhouses (and five years before that only the wharf) until the advent of Mr Mouzookseem who had arrived one morning, apparently from nowhere, in a cattle truck accompanied by an assortment of young women – 'daughters of my sister-in-law' – got up in print frocks and yellow headscarves. If Mr Mouzookseem claimed no provenance, was cagey about origins, rumour was scarcely less imprecise. He had come from the north; he had come from the south. He had escaped the clutches of the government; he was a government spy. Each speculation, honed to a fine point by reiteration, had its antithesis. He was a holy man who had been wrongfully imprisoned for predicting a flood. He was an Englishman travelling incognito (Mr Mouzookseem's face was the colour of bad tea) and possessed of a camera whose inspection he might permit after the payment of certain sums. He had farmed land east of the river until ruined by his brother and compelled to flee. He had ruined his brother, who farmed east of the river, and been compelled to flee by the weight of family opinion.

11

The one thing that could be acknowledged as fact rather than plausible hypothesis had to do with Mr Mouzookseem's entourage – 'daughters of my sister-in-law' – with their print frocks and strident voices. Evidently the connection was more tenuous, seeing that all were apparently of the same age and that at least one was black. Rumour, which had been merely interested in Mr Mouzookseem, was intrigued by his followers. They were chieftains' daughters, sold to Mr Mouzookseem after dishonouring their fathers. They were crossing sweepers' daughters who had been dishonoured (by Mr Mouzookseem) with their fathers' consent. They were orphans whom Mr Mouzookseem had adopted for the purposes of religious conversion. They were Mr Mouzookseem's daughters, the product of a variety of polygamous unions. As a matter of fact, they were just the sort of girls who could be picked up anywhere along the river by anyone with a little money and a little ingenuity. They rambled about the village, either in the print frocks or in more recondite attire provided by Mr Mouzookseem, affecting raffish attitudes. It came as no surprise when Mr Mouzookseem purchased the old shanty house down from the creek (in ready money it was said) stuck a tin sign on the door and a poster around the village announcing the mysterious word *cabaret*. It was generally agreed that this was a shrewd stroke on the part of Mr Mouzookseem. For a start, nobody knew what the word meant. Thus it offended no sensibilities, while encouraging the prurient. Mr Mouzookseem kept both his custom and his peace and quiet. Until now.

My visit to Dr Feelgood's that evening admitted no precise motive. It may have been for the brandy. Dr Feelgood's was the only place in the village where you could get brandy: pale, watery stuff that came out of vast, earthenware jars, but brandy nevertheless. Certainly it was not for the girls and for this reason Mr Mouzookseem regarded my presence as inexplicable. 'Why do you not like the girls? They are the daughters of the wives of my childhood companions. Is that not good enough for you?' Perhaps it may have been for Mr Mouzookseem, with his dusky, simian face and his fund of memorable anecdote. 'No, sir, I am *not* English. Neither was my father English. I have always hated the English . . . they are sharp fellows – no, sir, it is not permitted to pay for the girls subsequent to congress – always ready to swindle one, OK? Aisha, more brandy for the gentleman. You say you are an Englishman? I would not have realized, a thousand apologies. But yes, you have the face of an Englishman. Sir, I must beg you to desist from such unnatural practices – you are probably a spy.' It was fortunate that when there came the noise of boots on the concrete, whistles piercing the dead air and flashing lights beyond the window, he did not seek to cast me in the role of delator.

Yet Dr Feelgood's had attractions beyond anaemic liquor and simpering bazaar girls. It was infested with mice: fat, wanton mice who scurried unhindered along the wainscoting; flabby, overindulged mice who waddled sullenly over the coconut matting, constructed elaborate nests in cushions and beneath antimacassars. Possibly infested is too strong a word. Mr Mouzookseem did not seem to resent the intrusion. The establishment had once possessed a cat – a plump, farouche creature that had found the task too much and retired. It had never been replaced. Mr Mouzookseem occasionally made timid forays with poison beneath the floorboards, but it was plain that his heart was not in the business. The mice remained, their presence discernible in faint scufflings beneath the matting, the sight now and then of a tail slipping like a versatile eel behind a chair leg, the bead eyes on the stair. Of the traps – laid down occasionally by the Asian sluts, exasperated by the fouling of clothing – they took no notice whatever. It often crossed my mind that the mice might have a nocturnal existence unknown to the patrons of Dr Feelgood's. What did they do when the establishment was closed? I had a vision of sleek, overfed mice sniffing the night air on Mr Mouzookseem's alabaster table-tops, of squirmings and scuttlings and dainty, mocking rodent couplings. For who knoweth where the unregarded mice may linger, and who espieth the patter of their dextrous feet hither and thither in the afterhours, yea here and there over dusty staircases and forgotten rooms, establishing little mouse kingdoms, or little mouse republics – for are not mice democrats certain?

It was the mice that I watched, hiding behind the wicker door as the clock ticked on towards dawn, listening to the fine rain falling on the thin roof: (beyond the door the sound of Mr Mouzookseem attempting, with scant success, to make terms) tiny, inquisitive mice scurrying beneath the chairs and tables, burrowing beneath the shabby linoleum, lingering over crumbs, squabbling over the conical piles of cigarette ends. I had chosen a simple yet ingenious hiding place, a part of Dr Feelgood's known as 'The Cloakroom', although it was known that no cloak or in fact any other species of garment had ever been left there. A single, shoulder-high window led to the dark fields beyond – one could glimpse the dull ribbon of river in the distance – but for some reason I preferred to remain, watching the mice, monitoring the hum of remonstrance and counter-remonstrance from beyond the wicker door. Mr Mouzookseem was plainly having the worst of it: 'No, I am not a spy. I have been regular in my payments to the Commissioner. Such payments are illegal? Then I have not made such payments. No, I know nothing of opium shipments. No, I am not engaged in illegal activities. Why do you not search? It is not customary to search? I *demand* that my establishment be searched.' Yet the police were not inclined to search, which was curious seeing that there were at least six other of Dr Feelgood's habitués, some of them only partially clothed, distributed about the place in cupboards and bedrooms. The voices rose and fell. 'Precisely. You dare not search. You would find the husbands of your sisters, and the young men betrothed to your daughters. You would shame the honour of your families . . .'

Outside, the rhythm of the rain began to increase. It would fall until dawn. The voices settled down again into the quiet hum of remonstrance followed by counter-remonstrance. Already a certain inevitability had imposed itself on the evening. Mr Mouzookseem would end up in a regional gaol east of the river, consigned eternally to the company of leprous beggars and those suspected of the theft of goats. The Asian sluts – a less expendable commodity – would also go east of the river, to an establishment resembling Mr Mouzookseem's in everything but discretion. And Dr Feelgood's? That would become the property of a fat, well-to-do peasant from the flatland, shambling and ambitious, eager for a town house for his daughters, a venue for his adultery or – more prosaically – a warehouse for his corn. Only the mice would remain, inviolable and unchanging.

The cloakroom, illuminated by fitful shards of light beneath the door, was unprepossessing in aspect. Mr Mouzookseem was not an ostentatious man. He had been seen once, ruminative and a little afraid, in a frogged smoking jacket: there had been talk of a party that he was to have given for his intimates among the men of the village, of a juggler who was to be imported from east of the river to swell the entertainment, but nothing had come of it. Here in this tiny room, buttressed with discarded lumber, torn linoleum flapping underfoot, rustlings and scufflings beneath the tables, it seemed possible to investigate one aspect of Mr Mouzookseem's mind.

Mr Mouzookseem was an alien, but it had never occurred to him to forswear his heritage. Mr Mouzookseem was an illiterate but he had never discarded a peasant reverence for the written word. There was newsprint everywhere, hanging in wedges from the ceiling, piled up in jaundiced bundles on the floor, all of it bound and fastened with string, rather as if Mr Mouzookseem were worried about his hold on his heritage and considered that, unwatched, it might take corporeal shape and fly off out of the window. Directly above my head sheet upon sheet had been varnished to the wall. And what sheets! No newsagent, no matter how cosmopolitan his clientele, had ever assembled in the same shop what Mr Mouzookseem had together on his wall. There were copies of the *Straits Times*, the photographs faded away to nothing, with those queer typefaces they used to use in the days of letterpress printing. Some of these were as much as thirty years old. Some comparatively recent cuttings out of the *Lucknow Pioneer*, pasted on upside down, hinted at a previous base. But this was not the half of it. It seemed fairly clear (glossy German magazine covers) that at some point in his career Mr Mouzookseem had got as far as Europe. There was even – God knows how he had come by it – an illustration out of *La Vie Parisienne*, choc-a-bloc with wasp-waisted girls with shingled hair. I had a vision of Mr Mouzookseem, sullen and swarthy, gloating over it in some Parisian bar in the dog days of his youth, pocketing and preserving it in the memory book of his mind, a memento of happier times.

There were voices behind the door. 'Have the goodness to replace that table. I have entertained your Commissioner here on numerous occasions. I have a licence: there, what do you think of that? You cannot read? Then, my friend, we are united in our ignorance. What can I tell you? There is nothing I can tell you . . . no, Aisha, the gentlemen do not desire to be accommodated. You must excuse the daughter of my sister-in-law. She is an ignorant girl . . .'

It was the image of Mr Mouzookseem, an image that was almost certainly illusory, which lingered as the noises behind the door became steadily more raucous, the rain on the roof steadily more insistent. The past is an infinitely more agreeable subject for speculation than the future. Whereas Mr Mouzookseem's probable destiny stirred neutral, indifferent emotions, his past exercised a curious fascination. It is always the same. God invests the Mr Mouzookseems of this world with something of his own impenetrability. Silence betokens interest. Had Mr Mouzookseem been a garrulous man, had he imparted confidences, risen to coy references to the 'daughters of my sister-in-law', he would have been merely droll. As he did not, he beguiled. Now, despite the craven depositions coming from beyond the door, he seemed a man of infinite capacities.

But Mr Mouzookseem's past, splayed all over the ceiling in an orgy of reminiscence, prompted more than mild curiosity about his probable wanderings in Europe. For some reason, surmises about the past, however wild or idiosyncratic, always brought into my head a single, characteristic image. It was an image somehow associated with autumn, with smoky air, piles of leaves, wind careering over flat landscapes – an image of a man high on some east-coast cliff-top watching the waves of the North Sea, an image imprinted indelibly on my childhood, on my conception (and the two are naturally linked) of history.

My father had old-fashioned ideas about the teaching of history, had in fact old-fashioned ideas about a great many things, conceived of himself as a sort of spider maintaining a beady, proprietary eye on the web of the past. There was talk of thin red lines, enlightened despotisms. There were hints of decadent foreigners and the betrayal of monarchical prerogatives. There was also a curious little book called *A Child's Illustrated Guide To History*, full of whimsical encapsulations of the past: Raleigh, resembling one of Burne-Jones's young men, placing his cloak beneath the foot of a lissom Queen, (bad) King John gnawing his fingers in the company of a group of self-conscious barons. Yet the most evocative – that which impressed infant sensibilities with the ebb and flow of history – was captioned simply 'The Dark Ages loom'. It portrayed a man, bearded, clad in a garment halfway between a toga and a cloak (and reflecting nothing so much as the artist's incomprehension of his subject) standing in a somewhat self-conscious attitude on a cliff-top, hand shading his eyes, as beneath him a fleet of ships – again halfway between galleys and longboats – slid away across the horizon. Plainly the man was

16

intended to resemble a native of Roman Britain: the ships contained departing Roman legionaries, yet the scene assumed for some reason a greater significance than was warranted by my father's feeble remarks about the decay of civilizations, lingered obscurely as a metaphor. It suggested – I am sure that even as a child I had some conception of this – that the past has uncertainties as well, that it exists (at any rate partially) on the edge of things, is not amenable to docketings and filings, is not – in the last instance – assimilable.

Beyond the door Mr Mouzookseem, the assimilability of whose own past had prompted these reflections, indicated by a mounting crescendo of noise that his affairs were reaching some sort of crisis: 'If I were a younger man you would regret this intrusion . . . you are the sons of pigs . . . your mothers undoubtedly fornicated with diseased crossing sweepers . . .' The silence, and there had been silence apart from Mr Mouzookseem's righteous intonations, was suddenly broken by the sound of sharp, inquisitive movement. Somebody smashed a bottle. Somebody else, ostensibly Mr Mouzookseem, drew in his breath sharply. It was time to leave.

Through the window (a last glance at the sheaves of newsprint) into the dark air, through a backyard dominated by the angular shadows of piles of timber, on towards the wet grass. The glow of light from Dr Feelgood's grew smaller until it became a tiny pinpoint and then, as I turned left beneath an overhang of foliage, down in the direction of the river, disappeared altogether. Nearly dawn. In the distance the outline of the Cree Wharf formed an ungainly silhouette against the sky, wreathed in swathes of mist like ghostly cotton wool. Underfoot the ground was sodden. By the river the mist swarmed towards one in tangible swirls and eddies. Curiously, the image of Mr Mouzookseem still lingered, Mr Mouzookseem's fathomless past and probable future, down there on the edge of things. It brought to mind other associations, not merely the whimsical interpretation of the Dark Ages and my father's jingoistic view of history, but events nearer at hand. Reminded of this, and of other things, the virgin sheets of paper on my desk, the silent house, I sped off down the path. I wondered, quixotically, whether Caro had bothered to wait up for me.

Caro, of course, will not approve of this. He has a naive and somewhat misplaced belief that we have no secrets. Actually it was I who convinced him of this, quite a long time ago, some minor indiscretion having induced an unusually contrite mood. Poor Caro! Illusions should be kept intact. That is why I waited until he retired to bed before beginning.

As I write there is a sound of footsteps outside the door, a tugging at the door-handle which I had taken the precaution of locking. I pad from desk to door, unshackle the bolt.

'I could not sleep,' says Caro. 'I came to see what you were doing.' Below the hem of his nightshirt his pale legs shiver in the cold air.

'Letters, *Caro mio*. Only letters,' I say. 'I shall be along presently.'

'It is not usual for you to write letters at this time of night.'

'They must be done, and I am not tired.' (That is a lie. I can scarcely keep my eyes open.)

This seems to satisfy Caro. He smiles, runs his finger lightly down the side of his face until it reaches the point of his chin. 'Later then.'

'Later, *Caro mio*.'

Caro retreats towards the staircase. I return to the study and – being a prudent man – relock the door. Outside the dark air is still. I shuffle the blank pages, struck suddenly by the fact, self-evident but never considered, that I was Caro's age once, not that long ago; that thousands of miles away I must have felt something (*mutatis mutandis* of course) of what he feels. It is a pleasurable sensation. I look at the white sheets. I pick up the pen.

2. An Age Like This

It looks as if a considerable part of this is going to be about trains. I do not know why. Perhaps it is simply the result of logistics. After all, if you had lived where I lived you would know all there is to know about train journeys.

This afternoon there is no sign of Caro who is in the village buying groceries. He is an unobservant youth and, thus far I think, unaware of this activity. Or perhaps not . . . there was a nasty moment earlier during a conversation about the purchase of provisions from the bazaar. 'That will be all,' I said, 'but you must be certain not to forget the chickens.' 'And the ink,' says Caro. 'The ink? What about the ink, *Caro mio*?' 'For the *letters*,' says Caro mischievously. It is impossible to determine exactly what he means by this.

Travelling by train from Paddington to Oxford, in the evening, is neither a simple nor an expeditious business. Though I have journeyed extensively, indiscriminately even, from the Kashmir to the Russian steppe, from the North African desert to the Jo'burg veldt (in imagination if not in actuality) I have never ceased to be confounded by the questions it raises, by the decisive existential choices it propounds, never ceased to be puzzled by its insoluble ambiguities.

It is possible to see the journey from Paddington to Oxford, in the evening, as a metaphor for the entire human condition. I do not exaggerate. Consider the alternatives. Marvel at their complexity, shudder at the capacity for decisiveness they assume on the part of the itinerant.

There are exactly three trains heading in the general direction of Oxford, although one is scheduled to continue on towards Bristol and the West Country and another, impeded by a fallen sapling of whose existence nobody on Paddington station can possibly be aware, will very likely not get as far as Didcot. Already you see we are impinged on by contingent reality, which I shall ignore for the sake of cogency, for the sake of an *uncluttered text*. The train to

Bristol we can discount (though there is the possibility of course that somebody insufficiently diverted by the prospect of the conventional run-through to Oxford might choose to board it): it leaves at a late hour, performs a leisurely loop around the teeming underbelly of south-west London and demands that one change at Reading. The remaining trains, however, present an insuperable problem. Let us take the case of the 18.30. This leaves almost immediately (and I have been kicking my heels here since six o'clock, casting nerveless glances up and down the platform, seeking refuge in the rapt contemplation of cigarettes), yet arrives, after pausing at half the villages of Oxfordshire – fey hamlets with names like Radley and Appleford – only at 19.55. In contrast, the 18.50 arrives also at 19.55 (though not, presumably, on the same track), its speed, its pleasing haste, assured by the fact that it stops precisely nowhere.

The matter does not, unfortunately, end here. The villages of Berkshire and Oxfordshire are picturesque and not overabundant: it is pleasant to glance at them from stationary carriage windows. Yet it is already pitch-dark, so the pleasure would be instinctive rather than visual. The 18.50 then? But I, David Castell, being my father's son – the importance of this descent will be demonstrated only subsequently – am a pragmatist, not a philosopher. There is no guarantee, no absolute certainty, despite the assurances of timetables, that the 18.50 will ever depart. Who knows, in fact, whether I am not the victim of a vast cosmic conspiracy, or even a minor logistical plot, that induces me to linger in the hope of catching a train that does not exist.

('All this fine talk about contingent reality,' I can hear my father saying. 'There is a train. Get on it.')

So I, David Castell, being my father's son, and a pragmatist, standing in the dark hangar of Paddington station, the sky seen through the gaps in the rafters, a mass of crimson streaks tinted indigo, resolve to board the 18.30, offer my ticket to an official who, after examining it as if it were Monday's fish (how parochial, they will say, are his metaphors), allows me to proceed down the dusky platform, suitcase in one hand, parcel in the other, towards the waiting train.

As I write this Caro comes into the room, carrying a tray on which there are two glasses and a small amount of whisky.

'What are you writing?' he asks, knowing that it is neither to my mother nor to Sarah, both of which occasions are determined by the calendar.

'Nothing,' I tell him, placing my hand carefully over the corner of the page, 'nothing of importance.'

'A likely story,' says Caro, 'when you have spent the last half hour chewing your pen and staring into space.'

'And how,' I ask, mollified already by his interest, 'are you aware of that?' In the background I can hear the rasp of the generator, which further predisposes me in Caro's favour: innumerable are the evenings when he has forgotten to turn it on. Caro points mysteriously above his head.

'There is a skylight,' he says, 'through which I am accustomed to watch.' He makes no apology: I do not know if I expect one.

'As you have no manners,' I tell him, 'I shall not tell you.'

'Then I shall come in one day when you are out and see for myself,' says Caro negligently.

Thinking the conversation at an end (and most of my conversations with Caro consist of this opaque repartee) I hunch myself, rapt and crookbacked, over my desk. But Caro hovers in front of me, knowingness mixed with bewilderment.

'Am I in it?' he asks.

'Presently,' I tell him. 'Presently, *Caro mio*, you will be in it.'

This seems to satisfy him. At any rate, peering up ten minutes later through the dirty glass of the skylight I can see nothing but dark, empty air. The generator continues to hum.

And so: on. Past the outskirts of west London – Acton, Ealing and the Uxbridge Road – all wreathed in shadows and identifiable only by firefly lights high up on gaunt buildings, past desolate sidings where last year's graffiti gleam palely on viaduct walls, past Hounslow, past Hillingdon, past what appears to be the last strew of houses and lights, past Slough where the illusion of countryside is sadly debunked, past the limit of the London overspill where it is renewed.

And then: past a succession of somnolent country stations each so scantily lit that it is impossible to determine exactly where one is, past Twyford, where the train judders slightly as if weighing up the advantage of pausing and then ploughs on regardless, past dark

21

fields, past a herd of cows – luminous in the murk – still browsing with hectic diligence, past impenetrable hedges that swerve up to the track and shroud it in foliage, past another train, half-empty but harbouring neutral, aquarium faces, past a henge of industrial monoliths, their red brick illuminated by neon, past Reading, where the carriage thins out, is replenished and there are glimpses of rucksacks piled up in a breast-high corral on the platform.

And then: north, up, out, past a sudden stretch of open country where the moon simulacras up from the slate surface of a reservoir, past curious humps and hillocks (which daylight reveals as the haunt of herds of swine) past a tract of ploughed earth curving away sharply to the ridge beyond and dotted with silvery stones, past Didcot power station, where the chimneys thrust up like monstrous, craning phalli and you can see the roll of the downs beyond, past Didcot itself where the siding is choc-a-bloc with derelict rolling stock. Past Goring, past Appleford – where a courting couple, entwined on a bench, spend so long in extricating themselves from each other's grasp that they nearly miss their connection – past banks of firs and stunted larches at an ever-increasing rate, past Radley, where not even the station lights are working and the train disdains to halt, past the last silent stretch of fields, past more water (conscious of the fact that there are church towers in the distance, awash in coruscating light), past a graveyard full of sprouting tombstones, past a handful of tiny cottages with white stone walls, past the first platform signs, themselves past all memory . . . Oxford station.

In Oxford it is snowing. Snow everywhere. Snow on the pinnacles of Tom Tower. Snow massing in great flocculent drifts from the Cornmarket to the gates of St Hugh's. Snow rolling through the deserted gardens of All Souls, up South Parks Road to the river. Snow on the dome of the Sheldonian, empty now and gaping, for the Dean of Degrees has fulfilled his annual quota and having set loose on the world a battery farm of BAs in black gowns and mortar boards will not return until the new year. Snow whirling outside the great halls of the Oxford colleges wherein the young men console each other with thoughts of Christmas. Snow collecting on the kerbsides of the Woodstock Road, where it has already assumed an off-white tint in deference to the power of the smoky air. Michaelmas full term nearly over and the Christmas vacation upon us. And beyond. Snow lingering over the rooftops and chimneypots of the Cowley Road, whose residents knowing (and caring) nothing of the completion of university terms have registered nothing more than the fact that it is December. Snow blanketing Port Meadow and turning the river up beyond the Folly Bridge into a seething torrent, snow on the high ground above Marston and Headington, snow on the low ground beneath Iffley, snow drifting through the thickets of the University Parks and meandering on (as the wind drops and gives its passage an almost slow-motion quality) over Somerville and St Anne's.

And, nearer at hand, the streets from the station to the city centre brought into clearer focus by the sharp air that whips round David Castell as he pauses on the bridge above the canal, monitoring the white towpath and the houseboats draped in tarpaulins and huddled together by the bank. Umber slush banked up on either side of Beaumont Street and disappearing into the dark alleys that wind in the direction of Jericho. More snow in St Giles, gusting almost horizontal, slewing off the tops of the cars in the taxi rank, piling up on the rooftops of Balliol, obscuring and giving a slightly alien quality to three years' memories, an undergraduate career only recently concluded. Snow in the doorways of the colleges beyond the Martyrs' Memorial, where a single porter stands in the square of light, greatcoated and holding a trunk, staring pensively and with resignation at the white world, through whose gateway David Castell, his father's son, a pragmatist remember rather than a philosopher, slips, his destiny a lighted window high up in the first quadrangle.

Little Miss Knox goes about her business under the lowering sky. Up past Blackwell's (before whose lavish windows the cold makes it inadvisable to linger), along the Broad, sharp right into St Giles past a couple of skidding cyclists, Miss Knox, in a dainty camel-hair coat, a complicated arrangement of hat and scarf admitting no more than the tip of her nose to the piercing air. A word about Miss Knox as she picks her way carefully through the puddles of slush, and turns unobtrusively through the college gates. Her name, bestowed upon her by pious and scripture-saturated parents, is Sarah, but she realizes that there is scant chance, at any rate during her time at Oxford, of her being referred to as anything other than Miss Knox, this the result of a friend's delving into *Dombey and Son*, his discovery of the character of Miss Tox and of the comic possibilities inherent in that euphony. There is even a clerihew that goes:

Miss Knox
bears striking resemblances to Dickens' Miss Tox:
Prim and sedate
yet alluring of gait!

(all of which is patent nonsense. Miss Knox's gait being regular and unremarkable). It is not the name to which Miss Knox harbours objections, it is the associations, for within the Dickensian parallel there lurks a suspicion that Miss Knox is the exemplar of, how shall I put it, a certain oldfashionedness, a certain want of immediacy, a certain unresponsiveness to the ideas with which the collective brain of Miss Knox's acquaintance teems. Which is a pity, because Miss Knox is very much of the modern world, in for, and apropos. Her horizons, she is fond of remarking, have been widened literally as well as figuratively, her vistas expanded beyond the limits hinted at by age and background. She is very *echt*, Miss Knox, very authentic, compared to the shamanism of her contemporaries.

But her newness, her sense of being in the vanguard by chance rather than design, is assured rather than hectic, in which position she is very much a part of the modern world. She is fond, for instance, of discussing 'relationships', her own and others', mapping them out, plotting their course like a storm-hardened navigator, plumbing their idiosyncrasies with a thin scalpel of sensibility, but while her friends get pregnant, have messy abortions or are betrayed by shits, her own proceed calmly and logically to fruition or termination, to the stars or to the depths. There are no half measures about Miss Knox, never have been, except perhaps early on when she was less assured and by that definition, presumably, not Miss Knox.

There are no half measures either in her attempts to extend the bounds of her experience, to make herself quite definitely part of the modern world, in a physical as well as a spiritual sense. She is a great traveller, is Miss Knox, a great voyager to a succession of dimly imagined countries served only by makeshift airlines and of uncertain stability, each more arcane than the last. She is, by public

24

admission, a 'globe-trotter', a word then very much in vogue, though no one has ever been so ungenerous as to suggest that Miss Knox, with her dainty mien, had ever trotted anywhere. The last two years alone have seen her in a variety of locations, participant in a variety of tourism, but then 'tourist' is a word descriptive of blowsy American migrants, certainly not applicable to Miss Knox with her wide-brimmed sun hat, her cornucopic knowledge of local custom, her innate resistance to the more picturesque local diseases. Here, there and everywhere. To India, ensnaring and accompanying the shambling coastal trains from New Delhi to Bombay, to the nearer East, to Jedda, Beirut and the orange groves of Haifa, further afield to the sultanates and sheikdoms, west to Morocco and the Tunisian beaches. The world is Miss Knox's oyster, preserved lovingly in a shell of photographs and roseate memories, produced occasionally for the edification of Miss Knox's acquaintance.

And there you have another fact of Miss Knox's modernity, why she is so manifestly apropos her time rather than in pursuit of it. She has her cohorts, has Miss Knox; she is a chummy girl, a girl of cronies, in whose company she evinces none of the reticence which her upbringing, her position, if you like, in the scale of things (and Miss Knox is very much concerned with her position in the scale of things) might have been expected to inculcate: senescent parents and a traditional education have imposed no limitation which Miss Knox has not been able to transcend. She is a great talker, Miss Knox, a stage-manager of meaningful conversations, an impresario of revelation, a past mistress of the art of extracting confidences. She will talk to you about anything, about her sex life, about your sex life (more engagingly if the two conjoin), about D. H. Lawrence, about her father (for despite being inherently of, for, and apropos the modern world, Miss Knox has an almost Victorian obsession with her parents), about literature (her subject), the exotic (her passion), the commonplace (her bugbear), about God and about the joys of conversation. She will enjoy getting to know you better, even if she actively despises you, for charity is her strong point: enjoys – a key phrase, the touchstone of her modernity – *developing the relationship*.

Miss Knox. She is Madame de Staël and she is Columbine; she is the girl who captivated your mother when she came to tea but who never came again and whose reputation consequently remained inviolable; she was the girl who got the French prize, but she was the girl who told you what 'fuck' meant and lent you copies of *Lady Chatterley*, a bewildering conflation of styles, an immaculate whole, the girl who when you were very young and the urchins yelled obscenities at you, looked on with tolerant disdain.

'Oh', says Miss Knox, as they meet at the top of the stairs, contemplate together the scribbling pad on the door on which Miss Knox's callers are requested to write their messages, 'you.' 'Me,' says David Castell, unsure momentarily, as Miss Knox folds into his embrace, both of motive and response, of authenticity and subterfuge. But it is pleasant to feel Miss Knox's breath on his cheek, pleasant to grasp Miss Knox's bare hand in his gloved one, pleasant to watch Miss Knox's eyes, like darting fish behind her aquarium spectacles, regarding him as she searches in her pockets for the door key.

'I missed you,' says Miss Knox, as the key turns complicitly in the lock. 'I missed you too,' says David Castell, as he follows her into the room, satisfying each other that they have demonstrated once again the compatibility, where and how they fit in, that their position in the scope of things remains unaltered.

Miss Knox's room is unfamiliar, its accoutrements remembered: the playbills stuck on one wall, the Indian broadcloth hanging from another, the photographs of Miss Knox's parents on the desk, the photograph of Miss Knox about to board the Bombay express by the bed, the English texts in the bookcase . . .

'Wow,' exclaims Miss Knox, removing the camel-hair coat, emerging in sweater, jeans and leg-warmers, fanning the empty air. 'Good journey?' 'Slow train out of Paddington,' says David Castell, divesting himself of his greatcoat, handing it to Miss Knox who smoothes it, places it dextrously on the bed. 'You should have taken an express,' says Miss Knox, shrewdly alive even to the provincial idiosyncrasies of travel. She bustles around the room, plumps cushions, infuses tea, swoops on confidential items of lingerie hitherto unobserved, stows them away, stopping occasionally to exchange shrewd, affectionate little glances.

. Yet, the tea brewed, the ice broken, the certainties re-established, they sit together on the sofa, Miss Knox grasping her mug in both hands and gazing at it intently as if demanding from it the secrets of the past. And it is pleasant again to sit on the sofa in the glow of the gas fire, to sip tea, pleasant again to exchange news of the where-abouts of mutual friends, the adornments of merchant banks, graduates condemned to the lurching tumbrils of accountancy, pleasant again – these preliminaries having been dispensed with – to proceed to the real business of the evening.

'Take your glasses off,' says David Castell, and Miss Knox takes them off, so that the room dissolves (in acknowledgement of Miss Knox's chronic short sight) into a blur of light and shade, a kaleidoscope of unfocused images, and places them gingerly on the table before her. Miss Knox gives a swampy smile, as if there is something about the simple act of removing her spectacles that is morally beneficent. Without them she looks oddly vulnerable. It is this image, more than any other, that will remain.

Outside there is silence. The snow has gone to fall over Banbury or Didcot, or hastened on towards London, leaving behind only a legacy of vanished gardens and rooftops, slushy water coursing down Cornmarket as if it presaged a second flood and it would not be wonderful to see an ark drawn up outside Frewin Court, the stones in the graveyard by the station simply a succession of white humps pushing up the surface of the ground, like the vertebrae of some monstrous skeleton hidden under a blanket.

This is not a novel about Oxford, which has been done before and better, if indeed it can be done at all. Neither is it a novel about the difficulties of writing a novel. Even I, David Castell, more con-cerned with the workings of my generator than literary ideology, am aware that fiction is cognate with the verb 'to feign' and also of the highly original critical notion that all novels are in the crudest sense telling stories. But I (my father's son, remember), as I sit here pruning my paragraphs, sharpening my similes, shuffling my sub-clauses in a ceaseless transposition of type, have a cavalier attitude to the ambiguities of my craft. There are darker tales to tell, subtler truths to elucidate, wider canvasses to spatter. There is more to tell you, not to put too fine a point on it, *more to tell you about me*, about *my* place in the scope of things, my curious ancestry, my puzzling destiny. All of which will presently become apparent. (For the moment remember that there are darker tales to tell.)

There are certain questions that a great many of you will be posing by now, certain self-evident and purposely self-evident conundrums that doubtless require solution. My father would, I imagine, already have cast this aside out of boredom, fascinated nevertheless by the references to himself. Who is this Mr Mouzookseem, you will be asking, and why this absorption in his tenuous ancestry? And what of Caro? I can see you would like a more adequate explanation of *that* relationship. Not to mention Miss Knox. You will want to know more about antecedents, about *how it happened*, and why.

Here, fortunately, our interests coincide. Because this is a novel about the past, though not your sort of past, with its continuities, its spaghetti threads twisting back to a bedrock of explanation and motive. So where did it start? And why? To which the answer is – a conventional answer I regret – far away and a long time, a very long time, ago.

3. Great Eastern Land

In Norfolk. Norwich. Norfolk *and* Norwich, as the founders of hospitals and the secretaries of local archaeological societies style their catchment areas, in a satisfactory conflation of *rus in urbe*. Prosaic names. Historic names. Scratch the back of the red earth and you find axe-heads, a bone or two, out towards the Breckland, inland near the Roman settlements. You can find 'Norfolk' in charters from as far back as 1043. *Pagus Sulfochi*, alas (neighbourly rivalry predated the conquest) is ninth century. *East Anglia*.

Consult any map of Southern England and you are confronted with the outline of a prone yet supplicating angel – for some reason I have always visualized my geography in theocentric terms. Yet it does resemble an angel, despite the lump arising out of its back and the pinioning nets of latitude and longitude; feet, the cloven toe of the West Country; hands; curve of the throat below the Thames estuary; head, its brow furrowed by the wrinkles of the coast, East Anglia. So called because of the East Angles, of whom more later, from Frisia, from Holstein, Schleswig, unknown Saxons from out of the dimmest part of Dark Age Europe. Try to summarize East Anglia in that dimly imagined pageant of English history you have somewhere in the back of your head, a procession of thesis and antithesis, lord and peasant, Cavalier and Roundhead, Whig and Tory, and what is there? The Danes perhaps? There would be no East Anglia without the Danes: longboats in the Yare; Danish encampments in Norwich Cathedral Close. But a little later? Bigod's rebellion? Yet that is but a footnote, a mere bagatelle to Anglo-Norman history. The prosperous years, the wool-rich middle ages, when Norwich was the second city in England, the merchants built themselves the draughty mansions that dot the county to this day and the pious erected the finest parochial church architecture in Western Europe.

We are a God-fearing people and we have been here a long time: Sir John Fastolf, stuck in his gloomy hall at Caistor as the wind rushes over the flats, pondering the wide expanse of sky and field;

Parson Woodforde marooned in his vicarage at Western Longeville by the snow drifting on the Norwich road, reaching uneasy, unspoken compromises with his creator as he trawls back and forth under the wide East Anglian sky. But it is Norfolk I am talking about, the true East Anglia, not the more debatable lands to the west, not the fens, not Cromwell country, nor yet Suffolk, the land of Constable. Norfolk. The North Folk, such is the derivation, from a harsher land.

It is a wide, flat world, this uppermost half of the angel's head. Travel towards it out of Liverpool Street through the outlands of Essex and Suffolk and you are travelling – presuming that the contour map does not lie – through valleys, where the hills dip occasionally out of view, where there is variety: the Chelmer, the Colne, the Stow flowing beneath you and alongside you. Then on, through Stowmarket, through Diss, where the land falls away on either side, the houses recede from the track and there is nothing but you, the train, the fields and the great wide sky. It is a land of vast horizons, out beyond the Acle strait between Norwich and Yarmouth, where you can gaze for miles over wet fields, going on forever like the squares in a patchwork quilt, dotted with windmills, and in the distance the sinewy curve of the Breydon Water.

And there is antiquity here, all around you, staring you – to use a cliché – in the face, falling away beneath your feet. Walk along the cliff-top down from Southwold, Walberswick, and you can see the skulls spilled on the beach from the crumbling Dunwich graveyards. Let me tell you about Redwald, about Wuffa . . . but no, I think Redwald and Wuffa (who gave his name to a dynasty but one of which you will never have heard) had better wait until a more appropriate introduction can be arranged. No, I think I had better start by telling you about *me*.

Although one side of my family, my mother's, had lived in East Anglia for longer even than genealogy could demonstrate – and we possessed what I am now inclined to regard as a rather fanciful family tree – the other had less reassuring origins. My father's family came from Northern Ireland, three generations back and in obscure circumstances, a descent that was possibly reflected in shortness of temper and a sympathy for the more raucous forms of Ulster Protestantism. Yet, queerly, it was my father who, for some purpose of his own, was concerned to appropriate and exploit our maternal ancestry. It was he who demonstrated that there were Spaldings (my mother's maiden name) in the Tribal Hideage – seventh century who proved incontrovertibly our connection with the tribes Spaldings who lie in St Nicholas's, Great Yarmouth, and the graveyards of Northern Suffolk.

Perhaps, in retrospect, it was this tunnelling in the mines of genealogy – my father's discovery of what my mother *was* – that established what might otherwise have been a precarious relationship. The unkind, seeing only my father's idiosyncrasies and my mother's slightly *distrait* acceptance of them, often wondered how it was that they had got married, but as a matter of fact they had a great deal in common. Their strongest tastes were negative. They were, or so it seems with hindsight, dull people. They liked dull books and dull pictures, enjoyed dull conversations whose comfort lay in their predictability. This placid acceptance of the mediocre extended even to landscape: hence dull Sunday afternoon drives, on which I was constrained until my late teens to accompany them, in search of what they imagined were picturesque views. Initially, I imagine that I resented this attitude. It was only later that I discovered distinct and definable virtues in dullness.

But my father . . . it is odd how people are defined by certain actions, how – to put it more plainly – their past is redefined by a single act. Thus, at school, boys of mediocre intellect who squeezed against odds into the university found their childhood potential elevated into an article of faith. Similarly, all my father's previous interests and avocations vanished entirely – as if they had never existed – once he had become beguiled by our family history, or in fact the history of a region. By degrees (there was even a suspicion that he had fabricated suitably decrepit notebooks) my father managed to create an impression that he had *always* been interested in this obscure hobby, that it had been the diversion, practically, of a lifetime.

It was with these thoughts already taking nebulous shape in my head that I returned home late one Saturday afternoon in the autumn, I think, of my fifteenth year, to find my father entertaining a visitor. That there was anybody in the house at all came as something of a surprise. My parents usually devoted this part of the week to shopping trips or to some activity tenuously connected with sport. My father was in the sitting room talking to Mr Mortimer.

Smoke hung in the air, drifted obscurely over the trees – now leafless and sentinel-like – at the further end of the garden so that my mother, hovering, rake in hand, over a badly constructed bonfire, emerged only at intervals from the murk. This relatively unusual spectacle had escaped the notice of neither my father nor his guest.

'Your mother,' said my father as I came into the room, 'is burning leaves.' His voice had a reproachful air but conveyed a hint of diffidence, as if he were partly responsible and therefore unable to condemn outright. The probability was that he had constructed the fire himself (I could imagine him, unaware of the need for ventilation, happily piling leaves into vast, unburnable blocks) and then left the lighting of it to my mother. 'I wonder,' said my father, peering out into the garden with a somewhat theatrical air, rather as if he were a rescuer about to leap into a smoke-filled building, 'that the neighbours don't complain. I know *I* would.'

My father was leaning against the fireplace, in which a small fire burned – a characteristic pose. One foot was crossed over the other. Though he wore a shabby tweed jacket and stained check trousers, the belt sagging uncomfortably, the effect was impressive. Greying hair, parted anachronistically in the middle, and a habit of speaking his mind gave my father an old-world air. You would have thought him a bookmaker or, perhaps, a publican. In his left hand he held a book, the cover a gritty brown, which he continued to tap – emphasizing, presumably, a point which had been made before I came into the room.

'There does seem to be a lot of smoke,' said Mr Mortimer.

I had met Mr Mortimer on a number of occasions, though he had not yet become an habitué at my parents' house, and found that each remark tended to demand a reappraisal of his character. He was a small, obscure man, yet dapper – fond of gaudy waistcoats, old-fashioned bow ties which he liked to whip out of his pocket at intervals (he habitually went about tieless) and make up in front of mirrors. He was practically bald, which gave his skull a frail, delicate quality. A single blow, you thought, would be enough to make it cave in like an egg shell.

The remark about the smoke discomforted my father. As Mr Mortimer addressed another remark, this time to myself and I think connected with my schoolwork, he interrupted in an insistent, high-pitched voice, apparently with reference to some previous remark.

'No, you are quite wrong about Edmund. Demonstrably wrong. Yes, I know there is that late Anglo-Saxon illustration. I am aware that it is not portrayed. The flight of the arrow into Harold's eye at Hastings isn't portrayed. You don't allow primitive artists the degree of licence they extracted from their patrons. But I've had a look at the sources' – here he tapped the book and held it before him like an escutcheon – 'and there is no doubt that in Denmark at his time there existed widespread acceptance of the cult of the Spread Eagle.'

This outburst, initially bewildering, was in fact a summary of an old argument. My father and Mr Mortimer had for some time been conducting a dispute over the exact circumstances of the death of King Edmund the Martyr, a ninth-century East Anglian king killed after his defeat in battle by the Danes. Mr Mortimer held to the view that he had been tied to a post and shot full of arrows. My father, who had a host of unorthodox views of this sort knocking about in the back of his head, rather thought that he been subjected to the ritual of the Spread Eagle; that is, that his ribs had been torn out of his chest with axeheads. My father had advanced several proofs of this opinion, not all of them very efficacious.

Looking at my father as he rocked back on the fender, his face a wattled, beetroot colour, and then across to Mr Mortimer, who had removed his spectacles and begun to examine a fissure in one of the rims, I was impressed by the incongruous nature of the encounter and, ultimately, by my father's ability to transcend his milieu. He was not by nature a scholarly man, had left school at the age of sixteen to work for the insurance company that still, forty years on, employed him. Self-taught and with the dogmatic passion of the amateur he made an impressive performer.

'Of course,' said Mr Mortimer, unperturbed, 'it's hardly my subject.'

Mr Mortimer, standing now in front of the window, his feet planted squarely in front of him, was an Oxford don though I could not then have told you at which college he taught or even which subject. In retrospect I am inclined to think that my father was similarly ignorant. References to Mr Mortimer's scholarship hinted at a fairly nebulous tutorial appointment. 'Your sort of area?' my father would say – it might be of a Bewick print, an étude, or a volume of Trollope – and Mr Mortimer would nod his head amiably and with the precision of a metronome.

I was never very sure where my father had picked up Mr Mortimer. They may have met, somehow, when my father went to Oxford on business. A stronger possibility was that the aquaintance derived from freemasonry: my father was an inveterate collector of invitations to lodges all over the country. But the difference in taste, background and standing was not in itself remarkable. My father knew a great many people – some of them very queer indeed – in a great many walks of life. He was a collector of persons. Indeed his attitude to Mr Mortimer, his habit of prowling round him as he talked casting appreciative little glances, was that of one who has stuffed something under a great glass cage and is now at pains to observe it.

'Where are you staying tonight?'

'Brooke Rectory,' said Mr Mortimer, who seemed to have clerical friends in half the incumbencies of East Anglia.

'Just a brief visit then?'

'It has been a most enjoyable day,' said Mr Mortimer, who seldom bothered to answer direct questions. 'I spent the morning in Holt, where I examined a delicious little church, ate lunch at an enchanting village whose name escapes me, before proceeding here. Tomorrow I am promised an early celebration of Holy Communion – such a change in these decadent days – and a lurid rood screen. It is most diverting.'

Here I rather expected an answering remark as my father was, or claimed to be, an authority on rood screens. However, he had turned once more to examine the smoking lawn.

Picture this, my readers, as a portrait of my adolescence! No doubt you enjoyed more conventional diversions; no doubt – as Mr Mouzookseem might say – you fornicated with the sisters of your friends and made unseemly purchases at the bazaar. No doubt you succumbed to the fashionable teenage neuroses, neglected your schoolwork and had complexes over the size of your genitalia. Adolescence makes self-important fools of us all. And if so, think of me, David Castell, my Saturday afternoons beguiled by paternal discussions of myth and history, or history and myth. My father, the thoughts tumbling out of his head like a waterfall, seizing a book, jotting a note in its margin, seizing another, making a tiny, significant emendation in its margin, consulting again his copy of Ekwall's *English Place-Names* or Bede's *Historia Ecclesiastica*. My father the note-taker, the compiler of scholarly addenda, the author of scrawled notes on forgotten pages, the sifter of evidence in ancient controversies, my father the abstracter of the dead past, the filcher of *myth*.

It was instructive to examine the spectacle of my father and Mr Mortimer together in the same room, each immersed in his private thoughts, yet painfully dissimilar. My father was ill at ease, even in his own living room. Mr Mortimer seemed eminently at home and, while my father shot nervous glances at the smoky gardens and at the carpet, examined – with a kind of resolute compassion – an engraving of the battle of Culloden.

'I think,' said my father eventually, 'that my wife will be bringing us some tea.' The reference to 'my wife' was characteristic. Mr Mortimer accepted it with an elegant little bow.

'Ah yes, your wife,' said Mr Mortimer, as if he had just had his attention drawn to a scholarly footnote, 'and how is she?'

'Well,' said my father heavily. 'And how are your undergraduates?' This was spoken with considerable tension, my father wondering if he were sufficiently *au fait* with university affairs to chance such an enquiry.

'They also are well or rather have chosen not to bring any of the disgusting diseases from which they suffer to my notice. After all,' said Mr Mortimer, 'I am an intellectual, not a moral, tutor. Do you know,' he went on, 'the undergraduates are entirely beyond my comprehension? I simply fail to understand them. It takes me back to when I first began teaching. Twenty years ago they all wore sports jackets of inferior cut and talked about Sartre. One could understand that – it meant that they came from good homes and were stupid. But one could forgive stupidity. In fact in some ways it seems to be a very enviable quality. Ten years ago it was all sit-ins and student rights – whatever they were – and dismal sexual misdemeanours. And one could understand that as well: it meant that they were bored and impressionable – and still stupid, of course. Grubby sweaters and beards, oh yes.'

'But presumably,' suggested my father, 'they are still stupid?'

'Oh dear me no! That's why I can't understand them. These days they all write horribly clever essays and worry about their careers. Careers! I ask you. In my day they all went off to teach in third-rate private schools – it was considered bad form to get a good job. And they're not stupid at all. Derrida. Foucault. That's about the long and short of it these days. *French criticism.*'

My father, not aware of Mr Mortimer's expression of mild enquiry, and knowing nothing of Derrida and Foucault, remained silent.

'Trollope and the idea of the gentleman,' Mr Mortimer went on. 'That was more my sort of subject. Do you know, I think I rather preferred sports jackets and *La nausée*. At least one could regard them in the light of a civilized aberration.'

Thereafter the conversation lapsed, not to be renewed until after my mother had brought in tea on a trolley. As I say, Mr Mortimer had on several occasions been a visitor to my parents' house, but it was not until now that I regarded him as a person of any consequence. It may have been the air of imperturbability, the faintly ironic treatment of my father (accompanied by sly winks to myself) or merely the outward composure which my parents did not possess. Tea consisted of scones and a heavy spongecake. Mr Mortimer received each item as it was handed to him with a kind of benevolent wonder, even going so far as to examine the first scone between finger and thumb as if he had never seen one before. He drank three cups of tea, rather to my father's annoyance.

(Why these oblique strokes of the pen, I ask myself. Why these nuances? Why do I not simply tell you the truth about Mr Mortimer and myself? There are a number of reasons. Because I want you to work it out for yourselves. Because Mr Mortimer's role in all this was not at the time immediately apparent to *me*, so there is no reason why it should yet be apparent to you.)

After tea my father and Mr Mortimer played Scrabble with quiet intensity. 'A capital game, Scrabble,' said Mr Mortimer as he shuffled the pieces dextrously in the box-lid. 'Like all the best games, a matter of chance *and* skill. Fate ordains the materials. What you do with them is a matter of your own ingenuity.' Whatever the workings of fate, Mr Mortimer's own ingenuity was not in question. My father swiftly conceded defeat, though he did not do this until my mother had left the room to do the washing-up.

My mother's attitude to Mr Mortimer was unusually complex. As a general rule she did not care for my father's friends. There were too many of them; their relation to my father was inexactly defined, and there was about the majority of them an undeniable air of raffishness. They came to her house, driving vulgar cars and wearing vulgar clothes, called her 'dear', drank her sherry and scattered cigarette ash across her carpets: all this my mother was prepared to tolerate. She was not, however, prepared to like them. In fact, the thought of liking them scarcely crossed her mind. Mr Mortimer was a rather different proposition. Though his relation to my father was inexactly defined, his relation to the world was not. My mother thought university dons, even those as unworldly and out of date as Mr Mortimer, eminently respectable. And, though she was not deceived by it, my mother rather admired his deference, enjoyed being addressed as 'Mrs Castell' or, through my father's agency, as 'your wife'. There was no element of hypocrisy in her enquiries after his welfare.

Outside, the streetlamps shone dully beyond the undrawn curtains. Mr Mortimer made several premonitory signals of impending departure, stowed a handkerchief away in his trouser pocket, declined my father's offer of a drink. I caught his gaze fixed on me a number of times.

'And now,' he remarked, 'what about this young man?'

'What about him?' demanded my father.

'Fifteen are we?' questioned Mr Mortimer. (We were.) 'And what plans have we?'

Although adolescence is punctuated by these enquiries about one's future I was still young enough to find them intensely irritating. However, I knew that my parents quite liked the spectacle of these question and answer sessions.

'A levels,' I said, 'but not for a couple of years. And then university. Oxford, if they'll have me.'

'Not much doubt about that,' said my father, who venerated my intellect.

'Possibly not. But where do your interests lie?'

I think it was at this moment that I began to conceive an intense dislike of Mr Mortimer, irrational – because his questions did not differ markedly from those of a score of other people. But there was about them a faintly proprietary air and more than that, a shrewd appreciation of possibilities. Besides, how is one to answer such a question? Impossible to tell Mr Mortimer of Smollet, Thackeray and Gissing and other, darker figures lurching through my consciousness: Redwald, Wuffa and Edmund, Parson Woodforde and Margaret Paston.

'Local history, mostly. Churches and so forth. My father will tell you.' My father positively bridled, but Mr Mortimer shot me a look of devastating penetration, as if to say that though I could deceive my parents I must not go so far as to suppose that I could deceive him.

'Oh indeed. Do you know,' said Mr Mortimer, whose intention was plainly to throw up an elaborate piece of camouflage, 'I find it distinctly refreshing to discover that the interests of parents and children continue to coincide? *So* reassuring. *Such* a challenge. One hears such shocking stories. A friend of mine at college, an authority on Donne – I met his son the other day, reading Mechanical Engineering and appeared never to have read a line of poetry in his life.'

'I don't see that that's such a bad thing,' said my mother, somewhat naively.

I thought this might provoke some comment from Mr Mortimer but he did not seem inclined to argue. In any case, my father, who seemed able to endure only short bursts of his company, hurriedly suggested that snow had been forecast and perhaps he ought not to linger. There was a brief round of handshaking (Mr Mortimer's hand had the texture and consistency of dead fish). Afterwards I went upstairs to my room.

Emerging ten minutes later in search of a book I discovered Mr Mortimer standing at the top of the stairs, carefully shutting the door of the lavatory behind him in a way that suggested he had been lingering there for some time.

'Can I help?'

'Oh indeed,' said Mr Mortimer, dipping his shoulders, so that the light gleamed on his bald head. 'Brooks of Sheffield to be sure' – and as I turned to go – 'A word with you, young man.'

Mr Mortimer's eyes, viewed behind his spectacles, were pale and agile; darted like fish as he spoke. Despite a cloak of affected self-possession I was more than a little afraid of him. 'This local history business. Most amusing. And by no means unprofitable. But,' he went on, 'your evasiveness did not go unnoticed.'

'There's rather more . . .'

'You are an intelligent and by no means unpromising young man,' said Mr Mortimer blandly, 'and I am sure you would not do me the discourtesy of interrupting. Now, because you are an intelligent young man I am going to give you a piece of advice. No, let us use a stronger term. I am going to give you a *warning*' – there was something unaccountably sinister about the way in which Mr Mortimer said this – 'yes, a warning. Your father. Yes. The most admirable enthusiasm, vigorously prosecuted. Something of a rough dimond, shall we say? But I should take what he says – and I have no doubt that you are the most dutiful of sons – with a pinch of salt. Because,' said Mr Mortimer, 'if there's one lesson you ought to learn before any other it's that one doesn't take liberties with the past.'

Any amplification of this curious remark was forestalled by a shout from the foot of the stairs. Mr Mortimer and I exchanged a clammy handshake. Presently the sound could be heard of his car negotiating the gravelled drive. I went downstairs and listened to my father, voluble now and self-confident, telling my mother about a seventh-century Mercian abbot who had tried to purchase a brace of nuns from an East Anglian convent. I knew already, knew without the slightest shadow of doubt, that I hated Mr Mortimer.

I enjoyed a strange childhood, my readers, here under the wide sky and the distant horizons. Perhaps, in retrospect, it was not a childhood at all. Perhaps, in your own past, you knew the sort of boy I was, the whey-faced swot who sits at the back of the class suffering the taunts of his contemporaries in the certain knowledge that eventually he will have his revenge. My childhood, or so it now seems, was bounded by books, by my parents and my suspicion. None of these pillars encouraged extroversion. There was talk from my father of 'advantages' which I was alleged to possess, presumably in the field of education, of corresponding opportunities which I would be foolish to overlook. The implication – that these advantages had not been available to my father – was a reasonable one but proved, on inspection, to be a characteristic piece of subterfuge. Our educational backgrounds had not merely been similar; they were identical.

But what is one to do? I was a dutiful child. I did not repine.

4. The Jigsaw Feeling

In the event, Mr Mouzookseem's impending release from the town gaol was rather more than a nine-days' wonder. In fact it was seen as a portent, a symbol of some climacteric in the affairs of the gods, and a number of stockbreeders, fearing floods, moved their cattle to higher ground. The news, originated by a passing street vendor, relayed by gaping passers-by, spread through the bazaar like a forest fire, progressed – refined by the gossip of idlers – to the further edges of the town and subsequently to outlying fields so that even the *dirzi*, lost in rapt contemplation of a blade of grass, scooped up his mat and came running into the market-place prepared to tell fotunes (in the light of this momentous occasion) and solace the discomfited. By eleven o'clock a large crowd had gathered outside the door of the gaol.

There was, however, no sign of Mr Mouzookseem – an unforeseen occurrence which gave rise to various speculations. Mr Mouzookseem had indeed been released, but such was the extent of his injuries, sustained at the hands of the Commissioner of Police himself, that he was unable to rise from the floor of the cell in which he had been confined. He had not been released but in fact had escaped, disguised as a washerwoman, and was now, as a means of throwing the authorities off the scent, practising his trade in a laundry not far from the bazaar. And then, questioned that part of the crowd which inclined to the former view, what was the reason for this act of clemency on the part of the Commissioner of Police? Mr Mouzookseem had friends in the government who had interceded on his behalf. He had offered himself to the Commissioner of Police in the role of pimp. He was the Commissioner of Police's uncle by marriage, a relationship of which the Commissioner of Police had only lately become aware, and which had stirred in him such remorse that he had not only released Mr Mouzookseem on the spot but presented him with the gift of a donkey and a goat.

Midday came but the crowd showed no inclination to disperse. The street on which the gaol lay became impassable to traffic. A small boy who had climbed into a tree, the better to monitor developments, fell from its branches and broke an arm, whereupon the *dirzi* clicked his tongue and assured several pregnant women that this portended childlessness. Rumours concerning the indignities wrought upon the person of Mr Mouzookseem continued to multiply. He had lost an eye in the ferocious struggle necessary to convey him to gaol. His leg had been amputated, either out of malice or medical necessity. He had broken several teeth after persistently gnawing the bars of his cell.

Given this pitch of speculation Mr Mouzookseem's eventual appearance, leaning on the arm of one of the Asian sluts, was something of an anticlimax. A little bruised about the forehead, a little uncertain in his movements, he was nevertheless whole. The crowd fell silent. The prison guard who had accompanied Mr Mouzookseem to the door slipped back behind him into the gaol. Mr Mouzookseem looked about him, sniffed the air almost, like some beast that had just emerged from hibernation. There was a low buzz of talk.

'I see no crutches. Where is the amputated leg of which you spoke?'

'I said nothing of amputated legs. It was Ali, drunk on bazaar gossip, who spoke of amputated legs.'

'But he is blind. See, he blinks. He cannot focus his eyes.'

'Neither could you, brother, if you stood in direct sunlight.'

Plainly, the crowd expected Mr Mouzookseem to speak. The expression of their solidarity, as it were, demanded some explanation. Yet Mr Mouzookseem stood shuffling his feet, raising his eyes now and then to monitor the urchins in the tree tops, the bazaar women collected in little knots beneath them, an expression of mild bewilderment on his dusky face. A rumour circulated, initiated by the *dirzi*, maintaining that his tongue had been cut out as a means of stifling abuse of the Commissioner of Police, only to die as Mr Mouzookseem turned and said something in an undertone to the Asian slut.

How long this confrontation might have gone on – Mr Mouzookseem perplexed and absorbed by the presence of the crowd and (it was possible to speculate) something else sputtering away in the back of his consciousness, the crowd bewildered by his apparent dismissal of their enthusiasm – was anybody's guess. A warder came out of the gaol to examine the spectacle but seeing that no criminal offence was being committed thought better of it and ambled disconsolately away, swinging his stick against the iron bars of the gate.

Dust swarmed across the road, stinging one's legs, collecting in shoals beneath the shade of the trees. There was a thin, acrid smell in the air, suggesting smoke a little way off. All at once, as in one of those speeded-up monochrome films, things began to happen. Mr Mouzookseem shrugged his shoulders, spat decisively in front of him. There were sounds of movement at the far end of the street. The *dirzi*, detecting a change in the atmosphere, aware, possibly, of the plume of smoke rising over the distant rooftops, set up a high-pitched keening.

'Ai! The bazaar is on fire!'

The crowd stirred uncomfortably. Mothers remembered their children, left to play beneath the wide arches of the bazaar; nephews, their uncles engaged in vending the latest trinkets imported from across the river; girls, their young men whose habit it was to stand gossiping beneath the high canopies of sail cloth. The *dirzi* recalled that the wells were dry and that the rubber of the town's single water-hose would almost certainly have perished. Mr Mouzookseem, a figure now of only marginal attention, stood still on the steps of the gaol like a great, fleshy idol, a little forlorn but half-amused. One gathered that the irony of the situation rather appealed to him.

The rumour of a fire in the bazaar was not, of course, a novelty. There were always such rumours: the Commissioner of Police had been known to manufacture them as a means of keeping his men alert. Mischievous children frequently had recourse to them as a means of enlivening dull afternoons. Often they were rooted, in an oblique way, in reality. A cooking stove overturned on tinder-dry kindling, a box of sulphur matches accidentally detonated – small conflagrations, quickly extinguished – would be enough to empty the market-place for hours on end. The village physician had not treated a burn for twenty years.

Smoke trailed high overhead, fell in wispy skeins beyond the tops of the trees. Inherently credulous, the crowd, confronted at last with something tangible, was strangely disbelieving. A few stragglers detached themselves from the throng and loped away.

Mr Mouzookseem, who had been brooding, head on his chest like a giant, ruminative bird, suddenly began to speak:

'This is an ignorant people – a stupid, superstitious, ignorant people. If a cloud obscures the sun at dawn they fear for the safety of their oxen. Though they fornicate with . . . with the daughters of my sister-in-law' (the Asian slut rolled her eyes at this unusual description) 'still I say they are an ignorant people.'

At this, faces gape in the crowd, knuckles are held up to eyes, so you might have thought Mr Mouzookseem a conjuror producing rabbits out of a hat. 'A prophet,' one hears mothers saying to their children, 'a prophet, for all your father says that the age of the holy men is dead, got up by the *dirzi* who is too idle to work.' And even I, David Castell, edge nearer, transfixed by the novelty of the spectacle, curious, unaccountably curious, to hear what Mr Mouzookseem will say next. There is thick smoke now, billowing above us.

'Ignorant. But listen to me and you will learn knowledge.' Mr Mouzookseem's tones were curiously muffled, as if there were little rivulets of speech washing to the front of his mouth, bursting forth, only to be drawn back in. 'You will learn . . . of the indignities committed on my person, gross indignities. I have friends who will hear of this, powerful friends.' The sentences stuttered on, a series of muttered nouns, reiterated and qualified by appropriate adjectives: 'Lies . . . egregious lies . . . damage [whether to property, person or reputation] . . . wanton damage.'

Throughout this denunciation the crowd stands strangely still, like a hutch full of rabbits mesmerized by a luxuriating snake. There is silence, apart from the occasional cough (a result, most probably, of the smoke), the odd comment or exclamation indicative, as Mr Mouzookseem shows no sign of ceasing, of divided loyalties.

'Ai, we must hurry. There is no knowing what might have happened . . . Anand, who I left playing near the stall of the vendor of sweetmeats.' 'Please not to worry sister. Anand is as safe as if you had left him in my own care . . . and this is a prophet, surely.' 'In your care! A fine mother you are to your children. Besides I see no prophet. I see a fat gaol-bird of a brothel-keeper, but no prophet.' 'Lies, lies. At least I has *children*. You has only one, and that not your own.' 'Slut . . .'

There are further desertions, a handful of children scampering down the street, an old woman fearful of the safety of her husband's bazaar stall. Even the *dirzi*, anxiously casting his eyes this way and that, at the smoke, at Mr Mouzookseem – caught like Burridan's donkey between the water and the corn – decides that his talent for fortune-telling might be better expended elsewhere and scurries away. Mr Mouzookseem, aware of this diminution in the size of his audience, reaches his peroration.

'But I have a reason for speaking to you in this way. I give you' – Mr Mouzookseem paused a moment, his hands extended before him – 'a *warning*.' At this, wavering attention was redirected – apart from the Asian slut who was making strange signalling motions with her hands to somebody on the outer reaches of the crowd – weary, smoke-filled eyes refocused. Gloom is proof of prescience.

'A warning,' repeated Mr Mouzookseem, quivering like a statue, altogether oblivious of the Asian slut who was now performing what seemed to be a complicated series of physical jerks at his side. 'There is . . . evil coming. Do you hear me? There is evil coming, from east of the river – who knows? There are many things happening east of the river, things unknown to you or to me, things of which your soothsayers, who think they can predict the future by holding straws in the breeze, are altogether ignorant. So listen to me, you credulous, senseless people, because I *know*, I know,' Mr Mouzookseem repeated, as if the thought had only just occurred to him, 'what this portends.'

My attention was distracted by the advent of Caro, sidling through the crowd with the agility of a snake to stand at my side. He seemed rather flushed: his shirt appeared to be torn at the elbow.

'There is trouble in the bazaar,' he remarked, having first examined Mr Mouzookseem with an air of mild enquiry.

'What sort of trouble?'

'There is a *fire*,' said Caro sagely, showing the whites of his eyes. 'There are also rumours.'

'There are always rumours.'

'That may be so' – Caro peered back over the heads of the crowd, back the way he had come, where there seemed to be some disturbance – 'I wonder what is happening *there*? But it would be advisable to leave now, I think, unless you want several months without the leisure to assemble your pretty pieces of paper. There is—'

44

'I must just see the end of this.'

For the reason for the disturbance at the back of the crowd now became quite apparent. A small cart was approaching through the throng of people, who grasped superstitiously at its sides, drawn by two oxen and garlanded with flowers. Seated upon it were the remainder of the Asian sluts, got up in their best frocks, several of whom now began to beat small goat-skin drums, creating an insistent, throbbing rhythm.

Plainly Mr Mouzookseem's departure was to be elaborately staged. He stood stock-still on the steps of the gaol, staring up at the sky as the cart drew near. The sluts threw flowers over the heads of the silent crowd. The smoke continued to billow. It seemed, despite the inclination to impose patterns on a past event, that there was a certain symmetry about the proceedings, a slotting in of segments following some obscure formula into a prearranged whole. There was a logic in the coincidences of Mr Mouzookseem's warning and the plumes of smoke, and in the moral dilemma imposed on the observers, a hint that one had witnessed something memorable, that Mr Mouzookseem's words would echo through the years – a jigsaw feeling.

The sound of the drums rose to a crescendo. Mr Mouzookseem, looking neither to right nor left, waddled down the steps to the cart. Such was the impression created by his demeanour that there was a ripple of applause, a pounding of feet in the dust, a low murmur of remark. Stationed in the front of the cart behind an inscrutable driver, Mr Mouzookseem raised his hand in front of him, a single finger extended. One of the Asian sluts cast a garland around his head, which lodged askew about his eye. The comical effect went unnoticed. Surrounded by a listless flow of people who ambled woodenly beside and in front of it, the cart moved off, accompanied by the sound of drums, the squalling of the sluts and, in the distance, the sound of running feet, excited voices. I watched it for a long time, until the cart – Mr Mouzookseem still statuesque in the prow – was the size of a beetle and all that remained outside the gates of the gaol was a litter of crushed flowers and a handful of children playing intently in the dust.

Subsequent enquiry allowed a partial reconstruction of the day's events. There had, it transpired, been a fire in the bazaar – this much was incontrovertible. A paraffin heater, overturned by a small boy, had set light to some straw which in turn had set light to a tray of cooking fat. But this was not all. Investigation revealed that the ground near the paraffin heater had been doused with petrol, that there had been cans of fuel hidden beneath awnings and under tables. Moreover, attempts to put out the blaze had been hindered by the discovery of a dead goat wedged in the aperture of the adjacent well.

Fortunately, casualties were slight. The small boy lost most of his hair. An old woman had been trampled on by the crowd and a policeman sustained a sprained ankle trying to recapture a brace of chickens. Material damage was more extensive, although here information varied. A number of traders who alleged complete destruction of property were thought to have taken it away in the confusion and hidden it, in the hope of compensation. It was known, however, that two trestle tables and green baize cloth had perished in the blaze, although this last item was disputed by the Commissioner of Police.

The hurt done to person and property was, of course, only a secondary consideration. Of more immediate import was responsibility. Who had done it, and why? The small boy, now bald and snivelling, was taken away and spanked but it was felt that the matter could not be allowed to rest there. Paraffin heaters! Petrol! Dead goats in wells! Responsible opinion – that is, the Commissioner of Police – felt that it had been the victim of a plot. The suspicion that a number of market traders had conspired to do it for the insurance was entertained and reluctantly dismissed. The suspicion that the Commissioner of Police had done it in pursuit of a private vendetta was not even advanced. And then somebody recalled that, at the same time as the flames had smouldered in the bazaar and the smoke climbed above the tall trees, Mr Mouzookseem, a gaol-bird no less, had been prophesying doom from the back of a cart only half-a-mile away. That of course was that. The small boy was brought back and ordered to admit that Mr Mouzookseem had bribed him with confectionery and a detachment of police was sent to Dr Feelgood's.

There was nobody there. The doors were shut and barred, but smashed open revealed only empty rooms and of course the mice who, unimpressed by police officers, swarmed wantonly over the

46

chairs and under the linoleum. The tin sign had disappeared. Of the Asian sluts there was no sign, except for a strew of clothing in one of the rooms on the upper floor. Whereupon the Commissioner of Police, oppressed by the silence and the fog swirling up from the river, ordered his men to destroy several tables and retired home to devote himself to speculations of the most disagreeable nature.

5. Wehha, Wuffa, Redwald . . .

And in the beginning there was a king named Wehha. And Wehha begat Wuffa, who gave his name to a dynasty . . . But that is not, strictly speaking, the beginning (one must be precise about these things), only the beginning with which *I* am concerned; and I share my father's concern, every historian's concern, to impose artificial barriers on history. It is this – a handful of dates, added to a picturesque idea of costume – that makes our conception of history a sort of glorified wall-chart, where the world changes with almost mechanical precision. 1499 – the Middle Ages are still with us, knights in their castles, churls in their huts; Chaucer, Gower and English demotic. But turn the clock forward to 1500 and you are in something called the Renaissance. Elegant gentlemen in abundantly coloured hose are composing sonnets; there is news from intrepid explorers of new worlds existing where before there was only sea, and whispers from Europe, of what? Of the infidel at the gates of civilization, of dark heresies, the wicked despoliation of mother church. It is a *bourgeois* world, instantly assembled, artificially complete.

The passing of the years – history – is a ragged business. Nobody knows exactly what happened in this part of the world in this part of time. We know that there was a king named Wehha, who begat Wuffa, who gave his name . . . or at least we think we know, although we have only the evidence of a couple of chroniclers – who may have been whimsical and imaginative men – as proof. And, in any case, what came before them? Because, in whatever way history proceeds, it does not proceed out of a void. And so my history, *our* history, East Anglia, is to do (as is much other history) with the Romans, or rather the fact of their absence. For the Romans had gone, after four hundred years or so of enlightened despotism, arrow-straight roads and public works, gone long before that epoch-ending date of 410 when the Empire fell, when the fires burned on Capitol Hill and there had not been for some time – it was in any case a negligible office – a count of the Saxon Shore.

But the Roman interest in East Anglia, examplified in Caistor castle and the coastal forts, had long since flickered and waned, or so we learn from numismatists and archaeologists, since the end of the fourth century at least. A race of native imitators wrought an existence of a sort here among the flat fields, under the wide sky, inland from the unprotected coast. They struck barbarous copies of Roman coins. When their villas crumbled and fell about their ears they used the stone to construct shoddy, imperfect replicas. It was an ersatz culture, introspective but dimly aware of what was happening in Europe; that the tribes were moving west out of Asia to Eastern Europe, out of Eastern Europe to Central Europe, that they might soon move further west, that the world was in flux, that the certainties of four hundred years of complacent servitude had been irrevocably disturbed, here in the fifth century when there were other fires burning (on the Suffolk coast, these ones) and the longboats nosed out of the Scandinavian fjords into the Yare, the Chelmer and the Colne.

And it was from Scandinavia, we think – and the evidence is painfully, wantonly dim – that these first invaders came, from Uppsala, and that there was some remote connection with the Scylflings, that is, the Scandinavian royal house. They were pagan of course: they believed only in the dark, plangent gods of natural phenomena, and they found Christian notions of charity inexplicable. (The Christians found them barbarous and uncouth but that is another matter.) In the manner of most invaders they were characterized by their industry. They had colonized most of Southern Suffolk before the inhabitants were properly aware that they were being invaded. And being people who set great store by custom, and in the manner of their forefathers of the Scandinavian forests and fjords, they established, by about 520 AD, a royal line which began with Odin – a piece of whimsy with which I will not detain you – continuing until it reached . . . until it reached more familiar names. And in the beginning there was a king named Wehha. And Wehha begat Wuffa, who gave his name to a dynasty . . . the *Wuffingas*.

We must not emphasize their singularity. All over England at this time, beyond the frontier of the Trent to the border, southwards through Channock Chase to the Charnwood, other Wehhas were begetting other Wuffas, establishing other mini-dependencies, dealing out summary justice to the defeated. Though the geography varied, the route lay westward: across the Pennines to Cumbria, across the Peaks to Wales, beyond the Parret to Devon. The Wuffings, having only the bare sweep of the Fens and the Breckland to encroach upon, made short work of the process of expansion. Whereas the kings of Northumbria and Mercia, kings of tenuous nobility and abstruse ancestry, foundered in the quicksands of tribal warfare, were besieged on Bamburgh Rock or embarrassed by Picts, Wuffa and his descendants wrought a more prosaic conquest: another hamlet, another group of resigned villagers swearing reluctant fealty, another altar cast down as a means of propitiating darker gods, another addition to the new nomenclature of place and legend.

Bear with me, please, because the history lesson is nearly complete. And we can move on from what is at best informed speculation – a phrase I am chary of – to something which is nearer fact, to a world whose lineaments are more narrowly quantified, to Bede, Augustine and iconoclasm. For, at the very end of the sixth century, in this cranny of time, things in this part of the world have begun to quieten down. The age of the great migrations is over and only the north wind blows down from Jutland: though the thatch is disturbed, gusting air is preferable to fire arrows. Where formerly there was imposition and subjugation now there is assimilation. You cannot, after all, stop people marrying. And though conqueror influences conquered, the business is reciprocal. And time, remember, is passing. It is a long time, seventy years, since there was a king called Wehha, who begat Wuffa, who gave his name . . . Redwald, their successor, is a different proposition, not a tribal chieftain but a monarch, not a sheep-pilfering local brigand but a *diplomat*, you understand, a man of authority, and there is a royal palace at Rendlesham. The great clinker boats (apart from the odd, atavistic raid along the Lincolnshire coast) lie idle in the deep-water creeks.

And still the world, even this faraway, imperfectly reconstructed world, is changing. Even paganism, the dark, censorious gods of an older mythology, is no longer safe. To put it plainly, England is being invaded again, by spiritual warriors, ever since Augustine came to Kent in 597 and converted the Jutish royal house, and there are new currents abroad (or rather very old ones) of whose existence

50

even Redwald, sitting in his draughty hall on the Suffolk coast, pondering his precarious position, cannot fail to be aware. There is the White Christ, this White Christ who has so beguiled the King of Kent as to cause the overthrow of every heathen temple from Maidstone to the Weald. There are monks abroad, rumours from the north of a new magic, more efficacious than the gods of sky and sea and field, and Redwald, who has spent decades being a political opportunist, is quite prepared to be a religious opportunist as well. Emissaries are sent back and forth. Tokens of good will are exchanged, rumbling in ramshackle carts down the dusty Kentish roads and that, as far as Redwald is concerned, is that. Or not quite. There is a process, a process both ancient and reputable, known as backing two horses in the same race. And so Redwald, who has a heathen wife, ancient scruples and a thoroughly modern conception of insurance to prod his consciousness, keeps a pagan temple (festooned with idols) next to his Christian altar at Rendlesham – or so we learn from Bede, whose pious sense of principle was mightily affronted.

We are a people of compromise. Perhaps that is uncharitable. Let us say that we are a people unconvinced by certainties.

6. A Rough Music

Life at Oxford stirred questions about role, about identity, that had previously – at school and during whatever one did in the intervening period – lain dormant. Possibly this was the result simply of the outward relaxation of constraints. Adrift from the attentions of teachers and the admonitions of parents (no small consideration in my own case) one was able to do pretty much as one chose: to fornicate diversely, to get drunk with impunity, to do as little work as was necessary. Curiously, the absence of formal restraints brought no change in my behaviour, the result I suppose of habit, timidity and sheer indifference. There is, after all, little point in stealing from an empty shop. Outward signs of undergraduate licence – the Somerville girl leaving at eight a.m., the empty bottles outside the door – served only to discourage emulation; a case of freedom generating only sterility. Given the opportunity to do anything, one wanted only to do nothing. Probably it was this contradiction which produced the peevish feeling of resignation I have always thought characteristic of my university life.

It was Page who first put this sense of obscure dissatisfaction into words, sitting in my college rooms late one afternoon in autumn. Noises from the darkening quadrangle hinted at the recent completion of sporting activity: sounds of boots scraping the cobbles, of hockey sticks flung into corridors, good-humoured shouting on the stairs. I had never been a sportsman myself. On these occasions the idea of loping after a rugby scrum on misty, riverside pitches, the subsequent cameraderie, had a vague kind of allure.

'The problem about this place,' said Page, bending over the gas fire to retrieve an unlit cigarette, 'is that nobody really cares what you do while you're here.'

The gas fire flared. Outside the window, beyond the garden, the scaffolded underbelly of Trinity chapel was draped with mist. As with most of Page's statements, denial seemed the best way of prompting explanation.

'That's not quite true. They can chuck you out.'

'In extremis.' He began to fumble in my desk in search of matches. 'Certainly, if you threw bottles at the porters, or burnt down the chapel, then doubtless they could make it pretty hot for you. But I'm not talking about that. I'm talking about licence, not licentiousness. Dons aren't schoolmasters, and more's the pity. As long as you don't do it conspicuously you can do practically anything you like. Which although it might suit the multitude' – a wave of the cigarette in the direction of the window – '*I* find rather enervating. I liked being at school. I liked being told that I shouldn't do this but ought to do that. I liked petty regulations which I could find ingenious ways of subverting. Besides, take away proscription,' said Page in a tone that suggested he was not being entirely serious, 'and you take away most of the reason for doing anything. But I suppose I'm simply being whimsical.'

I supposed it, too. Meanwhile, if our position in this nervous, post-adolescent milieu gave cause for anxiety there were compensations to be found in surroundings. Traditional illusions of grandeur – architectural and intellectual – waned when confronted with wintry reality. Fog which rolled up from the river across adjacent playing fields gave journeys down the South Parks Road a slightly fantastic air. Corridors were liable to be rendered impassable by burst water pipes. At some stage during my first week in Oxford I incubated a cold which did not go away for a whole year. I also incubated an unreasonable dislike of nearly every one of my contemporaries of which – we were a large, prosperous, strident north Oxford college – there were about a hundred. We were a curious, heterogeneous group, coralled only by intellect. The range of background and experience was wonderful. There were public school boys from the home counties with short hair and orthodox opinions. There were wild-eyed convent girls bent on dissipation. There was a girl from Ireland who became a recluse, locking herself in her rooms and receiving meals from a tray left outside the door; stolid chemists from ghoulish comprehensive schools beyond the Trent; clever, insouciant boys of mean origins who would get firsts; stupid, overdressed girls from the fashionable London schools who would get thirds. Taken as a whole they were unlikeable. Ambitious or not, complacent or resolutely dissatisfied, they did not improve on the company of books. A handful of eccentrics, detectable not so much by dress as by an unpredictability of manner, seemed the only resort for society.

Page himself would not have relished this description. In some ways he was a very ordinary young man, had enjoyed a grammar school education and applied himself with erratic enthusiasm to his subject, which was ancient and modern languages: when the worse for drink he could sometimes be persuaded to declaim Pindaric odes. Enquiry disclosed more unusual attributes. He had, for instance, been expelled from his school – no mean feat in these tolerant days – for reasons which, though obscured by conflicting information, seemed to have something to do with a catalogue of practical jokes. This much was hinted by schoolfriends – inscrutable and rather sinister young men – who occasionally visited him at weekends. In an undergraduate society where eccentricity was usually the result of a single, marked aberration, Page was notable for a number of tiny idiosyncrasies whose cumulative effect was impressive. He wore a moustache and at one stage sported a beard (not then so fashionable as it had once been). This, shaved off badly in front of a roomful of onlookers, had contributed unreasonably to his reputation. But there was a great deal more: the pipe, the tea-drinking, the irrational dislikes (foreigners, Americans especially), the curious enthusiasms. A person – amid the kaleidoscope of new yet uncannily familiar faces – who it seemed was worth knowing.

Page, among other more or less nominal appointments, held some office in the university Wagner Society in which his duties consisted chiefly of writing letters of complaint to the authorities about various members of the committee. As a result we tended to hold our conversations to the accompaniment of strident music.

'Hadn't you better turn that thing down?'

With affected reluctance Page adjusted the record-player so that the noise was reduced to an acceptable hum. He seemed ill at ease about something, prodded at the bookcase so that a copy of Stenton's *Anglo-Saxon England* dislodged itself and fell onto the floor. Looking at him as he bent down to retrieve it, shoulders hunched, pushing his hair back over his forehead, it was possible to discern echoes of an earlier age. One saw him, perhaps, as a victorian student labouring interminably, yet with transparent enthusiasm, at some thesis in the British Museum Reading Room.

'I saw that man again this afternoon,' said Page, slotting the book back into its resting place. 'He wanted an essay on Herodotus. But that proved impossible. So I did him one on Thucydides. He didn't seem terribly pleased.'

'He didn't seem terribly pleased last week.'

'There is a want of enthusiasm,' said Page in an unnaturally cracked voice. 'There is want of application, of method and embellishment. Bastard! Pedant! I pointed out that I'd spent a lot of time on it and perhaps he hadn't read it properly, but he seemed unimpressed.'

Page seldom got on with his tutors. Quiet, articulate men, they examined his manner with the same disinterested air that they examined his pageant-like essays and detected only flippancy. Three had refused to teach him. Two he had preempted by refusing to be taught by them.

'This cannot go on,' said Page. 'So they're sending me to somebody else. Somebody called Mortimer.'

Far from coming as a surprise, this announcement struck me on reflection as inevitable. One grew used in Oxford, more so than in other places, to the past impinging on present reality: the knock on the door bringing a school friend not seen for five years, the girl who had known one's cousin. There was nothing one could do about such encounters. Accepting them as logical made them somehow assimilable.

'A bald little man with spectacles?'

'A fat, bald little man in spectacles,' corrected Page. 'In fact, positively globular. I went to see him this afternoon. Very correct. Very formal. Like a little clergyman in Trollope. Asked me to come to a tea party next Sunday at the Catholic Chaplaincy.'

'Is he a Catholic then?' Somehow the idea of Mr Mortimer at Mass, genuflecting before a high altar, did not correspond to previous notions of his character.

'I don't think he's anything much. You know, one of those dons who've read about Anglo-Catholicism, Ronnie Knox and so forth, and write little articles about Pusey because it's all so quaint and so terribly Oxford. Mortimer, I gather, makes quite a name for himself out of it – goes to tea with nuns and amuses them all with stories about Cardinal Manning.'

Though I had not, during my two-and-a-bit years at Oxford, so much as set eyes on Mr Mortimer, not even glimpsed him in the street, I knew all about him. He was one of those people who appear unfailingly, and without obvious effort, in the public eye. A student sit-in or related misdemeanour brought well-publicized chidings.

The visit of some dignitary, a world-famous novelist for instance, meant a photograph of him and Mr Mortimer, pictured in Blackwells bookshop, in the university newspapers.

'Don't you know him from somewhere?' suggested Page, remembering some comment long ago on one of Mr Mortimer's public performances.

'In a way. He was something to do with my father.'

'*Something to do with your father*. My dear David, you make it sound as if the two of them ran a little shop with white-washed windows and were daily in receipt of parcels from Sweden. Ought I to go to this tea party at the Catholic Chaplaincy? Will you come with me?'

'I might. As long as you don't start abusing smiling nuns.'

Page, who was not by nature the most tolerant of people, carried his distaste of Roman Catholics to fanatic lengths. I had heard him maintain, with apparent seriousness, that 'recusants' ought to be compelled to report to police stations on Saturday afternoons.

Outside, on the further edges of the quad, a bell began to toll, heralding evensong in the college chapel. Obscurely, the effect was galvanizing. I began in a rather perfunctory way to tidy the strew of papers on my desk. Page lounged for a moment in front of the gas fire, hands in pockets, and then carried the coffee cups off to the tiny sink in my bedroom.

'What are you doing tonight?' he demanded abruptly.

'Seeing Sarah.'

Page did what he called his Etruscan orgy face. This consisted of narrowing his eyebrows, composing his lips in a grotesque pout and affecting a horrifyingly glazed expression. He looked rather doleful.

'Evenings are becoming hell,' he said.

'This one in particular?'

'I suppose not. The Wagner lot are coming round,' said Page, 'for a play through of *Tannhäuser*. A regular collection of perverts and child-molestors. I shall enjoy myself enormously.'

He went out. I settled down to wait for Sarah.

The past, combed for similar situations and states of mind, provided much to admire but little to reassure. Parson Woodforde, in his vicarage at Weston Longeville where the elements contrived each winter to keep him, taking his greyhounds out coursing at the first sign of spring, was resolute in his celibacy. He was not a marrying man; he found the society of women irksome. This much the diary conveys with a kind of oblique diffidence, though an exception was made of his niece, save when the Parson's Somersetshire relatives came to stay and he considered her to be 'confederate with them against me'.

The detachment is impressive, all the more impressive for being not quite complete. For there had been someone once, though the Parson is reluctant to commit very much about her to paper, a certain 'sweet-tempered' Betsy White back in Somerset, of an amiable disposition, or so we learn . . . from a handful of scattered references, a sentence or two of uncharacteristic musing on might-have-beens. The marriage never came off. Betsy White met a Mr Walker who had five hundred pounds and much else, doubtless, to recommend him, and married him instead. Parson Woodforde, who chanced upon the couple out walking one Sunday afternoon, had the satisfaction of cutting them dead. 'She has proved herself to be a mere jilt,' he confided to his diary and there, on paper anyway, the matter was ended. Henceforth, he reserved his chivalrous devotion for Mrs Custance who sent him little gifts and was solicitous of his health. A tolerant man, even of the Custance family foible of keeping mistresses, because the Parson was quite prepared to acknowledge that other people had peccadilloes, even if he had none himself, here at the tail-end of the eighteenth century, under the wide East Anglian sky.

I was never afterwards able to remember where I met Miss Knox. I say 'met' in the sense of being formally introduced: our acquaintance – given that we lived in the same college and had rooms on adjacent staircases – was longstanding. One of the disadvantages of life in an Oxford college is that everybody more or less knows everybody else. Possibly it was the library, where I was an habitué, though an earlier tête-à-tête may have occurred over a sheaf of poems Miss Knox had submitted to a university magazine I helped to edit. The poems, undistinguished to a line, were quickly dealt with. Their author seemed to demand less cursory treatment. Miss Knox struck one initially as being incurably serious. A small, slim girl (there were rumours of anorexia nervosa, lately overcome) her pebble spectacles gave her a wistful, permanently inquisitive air. Her acquaintance, a collection of persons of obscure religious beliefs and impenetrable shyness, was less promising. Calling at her room one might find a monk from the Catholic theological college, a heavy-lidded girl bent on suicide, a garrulous American penfriend. One found it hard to believe that they were all quite as interesting as Miss Knox maintained. Like my father, with whom there was no other resemblance, she was a great collector of persons, as Page had once unkindly suggested, a sort of emotional philatelist. This too demanded investigation, even if the memories it stirred were not agreeable. The Sunday at home, the visitor in the front room, the indigestible salads, the radio playing safe Light Programme music in the kitchen – it was a scene on which Miss Knox, like a previously unknown face in a painting, seemed to have made an appearance.

Purposeful steps on the flagstones outside give way to a double knock at the door, which opens to reveal a small figure carrying an assortment of books and box files. A sticker, Sellotaped to the topmost file, proclaimed, 'If All Else Fails, Give Up'.

'Sorry I'm late,' says Sarah. She places the pile of books carefully on a windowseat and sits down in one of the armchairs, clasping her knees up in front of her.

'It doesn't matter. Tea?'

'Just a quick one.'

It is a characteristic of Sarah's to give the impression that she has continually to be elsewhere. Initially disconcerting, the affectation becomes tolerable as long as one knows that it means very little.

'Bloody Lawrence,' says Miss Knox, referring presumably to the afternoon's sojourn in the library. 'What did you do today?'

'Work. Page came round. He seemed rather depressed.'

Sarah accepts this without comment. Presently she replaces the teacup on the wooden tray by the hearth and begins to prowl round the room. This too is characteristic. Watching her as she moves aimlessly, yet still with a sort of purposeful intent, stirs conflicting emotions. I am still reluctant to take women seriously, Sarah especially, disillusioned by the absurd pronouncements, the obsessions – foreign travel, religious apologetics – so transparently marginal. Yet still there persists a kind of allure, rationalized admission of infatuation. The more absurd the pronouncements the more enthusiastic the response.

I have not at this time slept with Sarah. I have not at this time

58

slept with anybody: a rigorous, self-imposed (one liked to think) chastity of which I was not especially proud. Why not? Because I was a solitary child. Because I lacked the necessary self-possession. Because women scared me and, of course, because I thought them trivial. Because of the inevitable guilt.

Sarah continued to prowl, stopping now and again to examine a postcard on the writing desk, a new invitation tacked to the wall. It is possible that she has some conception of what is going on in the back of my head, a dilemma that has occasionally been aired on the long, Sunday afternoon walks, during the late-night, post-library conversations.

'I wish,' says Sarah, sitting down in the chair by my writing desk, 'that you wouldn't mope.'

'I don't.'

The allegation has been made before, remains unrefuted. I stare at her as she curls up into a small, foetal ball peering at me over knotted arms. Another pang of indecision is replaced – buoyed by the knowledge that Sarah is waiting for something to happen – by a stirring of resolve. Miss Knox. There are passages from the Paston letters floating around in my head, ghostly *imprimaturs*. 'I shall think myself half a widow because ye shall not be at home,' Margaret wrote to her husband John, 'ye have left me such a remembrance that maketh me to think upon you both day and night when I would sleep.' Sarah raises her head from the symmetrically layered arms and legs, smiles. I place my hand on her arm. 'And she desireth, if it pleased you, that she give the gentleman ye know of such language as he might feel by you that ye will be well-willing to the matter that ye know of.' Sarah does not look up but allows the hand to stroke the back of her neck. At such moments it is her habit to go into a sort of hypnotic trance so that each action has an almost slow-motion quality. Rising slowly from the chair she allows herself, guided in the manner of a blind man, to be propelled in the direction of the sofa. I pad to the door and extinguish the main light, reassured by the silence in the passage, the glow of the gas fire.

Sarah reclines on the sofa, one arm thrown down to the carpet. She has tiny, yielding breasts on one of which I now place my right hand. Somewhere outside in the passage there are remote footfalls.

'Don't stop,' says Sarah. I insert one hand inside her sweater so that it rests on her bare back. She shifts nervously: marshy kisses are

59

exchanged, spectacles removed. 'I knew,' says Sarah, 'that this would happen.' I murmur something about prescience. Close up her face has a curious pear-shaped quality, cheeks overlarge, forehead disproportionately small. I am obsessed still by the vision of flat fields going on forever like the squares in a patchwork quilt. 'Is there anything the matter?' asks Sarah. I shake my head. There is a further interlocking of mouths, the unfastening of straps, more placing of hands on breasts. Sarah pulls the sweater over her head.

'And you,' she says. I unbutton my shirt, remove my tie in a single snatch. Sarah is wearing, apart from the sweater and the brassiere, a pair of jeans, shoes and socks. I decide to remove the last items myself. There is a pause. Sarah trails her fingers along my arm. Remember . . . the Paston line is extinct; only the gulls inhabit Caistor Castle. And here am I, David Castell, an East Anglian child, falling into the ancient trap, the eternal dilemma. What is one to do? Sarah shakes her head from side to side. Left hand touching her right breast I begin to undo the waistband of her jeans.

And so Parson Woodforde, Margaret Paston, Edmund and all the saints, Miss Knox writhing beneath me, two starfish, and where will it end . . . 'God, oh God,' says Miss Knox, and there are waves crashing in my head, a surge of distant water, far away. After this there is silence. Quite a long silence.

7. Collapsing New Buildings

As I write this Caro comes into the conservatory carrying a tray on which there is a small slip of paper. Having handed me this, and looked sullenly over my shoulder at the neat piles of foolscap, he asks if I want anything else. I tell him to go away. I am afraid I have little time for Caro at the moment: It is not simply this, the business of trying to assemble my thoughts on paper, but . . . that matter of the inkstand, which I later discovered in the bazaar and had to buy back at an extortionate price. In any case he has formed a liaison with the gardener's boy which takes up most of his time. I see them occasionally, sitting in the shade of the acacia tree, holding hands. From time to time Caro catches my eye and glares stonily. I am rather sorry for the gardener's boy who, being terrified of both of us, is placed in an invidious moral dilemma.

Meanwhile, the note, once unravelled, smoothed down and deciphered (for it is written in thin, febrile handwriting) turns out to be from Miss Cluff and proposes afternoon tea. It does not mention any date. I summon Caro back, watch him loping over the grass, not caring for the moment about the silence caused by the absence of the generator.

'Did Miss Cluff say on which day she proposed to call?'

'She said she would call today. She said she would bring fruit.'

In the distance, near the bushes at the edge of the grass, I can see the gardener's boy regarding us incuriously.

'I do not want her to. I hope you told her so.'

'I told her nothing,' says Caro inscrutably. 'What are you writing?'

'That is none of your business.'

He goes away again. The gardener's boy steps forward a few paces from the bushes to greet him and they clasp hands. One day I will tell Caro what I am writing. I shall confide in him, tell him what is to be found in these curious pages, tell him what it means. But not yet. The difficulty is that Caro cannot read himself, regards the business of writing as a quite incomprehensible activity of almost occult significance.

And now this perplexing note from Miss Cluff. I suppose one should feel a certain affinity to the only other white person for twenty miles, but somehow I have always felt constrained to repudiate Miss Cluff's advances, such as they are. Miss Cluff lives in a large greystone bungalow about a mile down the river past the Cree Wharf. Her arrival, about a year ago, though less dramatic than Mr Mouzookseem's, excited no less comment and took place in circumstances practically as obscure. She had come from the north. She had come from the south. She had taught English in an academy for young ladies. She had been the mistress of a government minister but had compromised him and been compelled to live quietly in the country. She was a famous prostitute, the madonna of the bazaars, who having amassed a fortune now wished merely to retire to a discreet and respectable existence in a region where her former activities would be unknown.

The subject of all this profitless speculation was, apparently, a mild little woman of about forty, unspectacularly dressed (strangely enough this was held to substantiate the rumour of the brothel madam living incognito) who could be seen occasionally wandering through the village, turning over items on display in the bazaar stall trays but never buying anything. She was not known to receive visitors, although the *dirzi* had called one afternoon in the hope of reading her fortune. Curiously the incident had served only to heighten conjecture.

'She is a terrible woman, a she-devil,' the *dirzi* had pronounced after he had emerged, pale and shaking, from the bungalow half-an-hour later. More than this he would not say. Neither would he say anything about Miss Cluff's fortune or the manner of its extrapolation, though the village idlers said a great deal. Henceforth Miss Cluff was regarded with disquiet, verging on suspicion. When three spindly cows strayed one night from their meagre grazings and were found next morning dead in a ditch she was hissed in the bazaar, and a crowd of youths, bent on stoning the bungalow, were forestalled only by the charitable dissuasion of the *dirzi*. Gradually she came to be regarded with an awe usually associated with the more obscure local fetishes. Mothers forbade their daughters to pass her house (which as it lay on a main road led each afternoon to the spectacle of a procession of girls picking their way with evident discomfort through the thorny scrub). In the bars and louche drinking shops, haunts of adventurous young men, it was considered daring to think her good-looking. Miss Cluff seemed unaware of this intense interest in her affairs, perhaps fortunately.

Meanwhile, I had other things with which to occupy myself, in particular a copy of the local newspaper which Caro had brought back from the village that morning. Entitled the *Sentinel*, jelly-graphed on four sheets of vile, burnt-ochre paper, it contained little factual information – being largely given over to the pro-nouncements of the Commissioner of Police and character assassinations of local officials arraigned for speculation. The current issue devoted most of its front page to the picture of a woman who had just given birth to her seventeenth child and, of more interest, an article headed 'Disturbing Rumours'. This in itself was not unusual. 'Disturbing Rumours' was the sort of headline that the *Sentinel* kept permanently set in type, along with 'Rainy Season Brings Fear of Floods' and 'Cattle Die in Drought'. Quaintly written, italicized in the manner of Queen Victoria's journals, the article ran thus:

Our readers will doubtless be aware of the closure of a *certain establishment*, scene of activities of the *utmost depravity*, thanks to the prompt action of persons known to have the wellbeing and *integrity* of the community at heart. [It was a fact that the Com-missioner of Police paid the salary of the editor of the *Sentinel*]. All right-minded citizens will applaud this vigorous defence etc. etc. Yet reports have reached us of the activities of a *certain person*, whom modesty and regard for the sensibilities of our *discreet readers* forbids us to name, which we feel it our duty to record. It is known that this scoundrel has long been at work to undermine the sense of wellbeing that exists in our *cheerful community* both through his *nefarious trade* and by other more sinister means. Many are the ruined daughters, embarrassed husbands, illegitimate children etc. etc. But there have come to our ears disturbing rumours, hinting at the further activities of this *au-dacious villain*. New buildings have collapsed scarcely an hour after the bricklayers' mortar was dry. Livestock has perished in the most *mysterious circumstances*. Rivers have risen, wells have run dry. Is it not remarkable that these *shocking outrages* should follow the release from prison – his rightful place we may aver – of

63

someone so *eminently fitted to instigate them*? May we suggest that *steps* be taken to secure the incarceration of this *gross seducer M z m* at the *earliest opportunity* etc. etc.

There was a great deal more of this, of course; speculations about droughts, forecasts of floods, hints (the *Sentinel* was a family newspaper) of an epidemic of syphilis. One could only guess at what had prompted this spectacular animosity. Equally, as was demonstrated by the article, one could only guess at what had happened to Mr Mouzookseem. The probability was that he had merely transferred his activities twenty miles downriver, created an establishment identical to Dr Feelgood's in everything but location: the same worn linoleum, the mice burrowing beneath the antimacassars, the tired faces of the Asian sluts, the same air of enervated glamour. Village gossip, however, had an aversion to probability. It was stated for a fact in the bazaar that Mr Mouzookseem had obtained a government appointment east of the river, that he had sold the Asian sluts to a wealthy and libidinous landowner, that he was training a guerrilla army out in the scrub, that he had died of malaria.

Yet, whether or not one linked rumours with the silent hand of Mr Mouzookseem, it had to be admitted that all was not well. There was something in the air, these days, something of which even I, David Castell, preferring solitude and the company of sheets of paper, could not fail to be aware. Looking out occasionally into the middle distance, late in the afternnon, one could distinguish puffs of dust along the horizon, suggesting the movement of vehicles. Who was driving out there in the scrub? What was their purpose? Ours is not a region characterized by an abundance of motor vehicles. In fact the only car in the vicinity was owned by the Commissioner of Police and that did not work. Then again, there were the distant lights that could infrequently be seen at dusk far away down the river, lights of various shapes and hues which winked, extinguished themselves and were relit with logical persistence. Were they beacons? An indication that persons unknown were signalling to each other out there in the flatland, communicating silent messages of which we were unaware? Uneasy times. Uneasy times, my children, agreed the *dirzi*, shrugging his shoulders and glancing sideways at the straws he held perpendicular in the wind. But who knows? There must be uneasy times, or we would not appreciate the good, and there will be corn in

64

the fields again, and water in the wells. The birds were flying south, great unidentifiable birds intent on obscure migrations, so that one grew used each morning to the sound of the beating of wings, high above, and the shadow cast by vast flocks moving at a great pace through the empty air. The village idlers conversed in low, anxious voices, casting occasional glances at the feathery sky, wondering perhaps what it portended.

And then, Miss Cluff . . .

There are preparations to make, designs to set in train. I do not wish Miss Cluff to think that I live like a hermit. I shout for Caro several times, fruitlessly, until he comes stalking round the side of the conservatory. There is a large, purple bruise just above his eye, a displeased expression on his face.

'And how, *Caro mio*, did you come by that?'

'These things happen when one is in love.'

That may be so. They did not happen to me. 'Did he hit you?'

'I do not wish to talk about it.'

'Very well. But there are one or two things that I wish to talk about. Miss Cluff is coming to tea. You had better make a seedcake.'

'I have made it,' says Caro, meaning that he will make it.

'And we shall need fruit. You had better go down to the bazaar and buy some.'

'You will get no fruit in the bazaar this afternoon. There is a rumour going round the village that it is all poisoned and the bazaar is to be inspected by the Commissioner of Police.'

No fruit and the seedcake not yet made! Caro and I regard each other warily for a moment. Over his shoulder I can discern the figure of the gardener's boy, watering can in hand, bending over a bed of scarlet flowers, oblivious to Caro, to me, to everything except the thin stream of water that pours unwaveringly onto the dry earth. There is a noise of movement down by the gate. A white dress, flickering the tips of the grass, sun hat teetering slightly as its owner steps to avoid an overhanging branch; the sound of ungainly footsteps. Miss Cluff . . .

Now that Miss Cluff has departed I want, obviously, to record my impressions of her before they recede from memory. She is my first visitor for some weeks, so it will be an interesting exercise. You think this is a curious undertaking do you my readers, this wish to pin people down on paper as if I were some sort of lepidopterist? You are probably right. But I have always done it. Barely had Mr Mortimer left my parents' house, Miss Knox replaced her clothing or Page wandered out into the night in search of diversion than I reached for my pen. It was a reflex, quite involuntary. And so with Miss Cluff.

This was the first occasion on which I had spoken to Miss Cluff, but an exchange of nods, a wave or two as we passed in the village, seemed to have imposed a spurious intimacy on the meeting. There was an exchange of greetings, supervised by Caro who, impressed by the arrival of a visitor and also, it was possible to speculate, by the fact that the visitor was female, wrought upon us a seedcake of enviable texture and consistency.

'I meant to bring some fruit,' said Miss Cluff, without enthusiasm. 'But when I got to the bazaar they said they'd been told it was all poisoned and they daren't sell me any until the Commissioner of Police had said it was all right. I asked, what did the Commissioner of Police know about it, and how could he tell? – short of sampling every orange in the bazaar – and that I'd take my chance on it being poisoned. But it didn't do any good.'

There was about Miss Cluff an undeniably farouche air, suggesting some deep-seated grievance whose redress had been placed permanently in abeyance. As she drank a cup of tea, nibbled half of piece of seedcake (the other half of which, thrown on the floor, was retrieved by Caro and replaced on her plate) she seemed scarcely aware of my presence.

'I expect all this sort of thing seems entirely commonplace to you,' she went on, 'but let me tell you I regard it as infuriating. I didn't know it was possible to be so credulous. One old woman eats an orange and has a stomach-ache and the next thing you know it's all round the village that some "enemy" has poisoned every piece of fruit in the bazaar. Do you mind if I have a cigarette?'

'No. Was that what happened?'

'How should I know? You haven't got a match by any chance, have you?'

I despatched Caro to the house for a box and for an ashtray. Miss Cluff removed her sunhat and placed it on the table between us, prodding the butt-end of the cigarette softly against the lining. Hatless, her face framed by uncombed brown hair, the effect was not

66

prepossessing. Somewhere beneath the make-up and the creased skin there lurked the memory of a fresh complexion. Her voice suggested formative years somewhere in the English home counties, somewhat distorted by another idiom, possibly transatlantic. This straining after accent was not lost on Miss Cluff.

'English as well. Not difficult to work out, I suppose?'

'But somewhere else?'

'Sure. The States. For ten years. I got married,' said Miss Cluff, assuming that some explanation was needed, 'to an American when I was eighteen. Cue ten years of Texas – and other places – TV dinners and tubby little redneck cowboys pinching your backside. Do you know, I hated that country so much I could have reached out and smothered it.'

The return of Caro, carrying matches and ashtray, signalled a gap in the conversation. Miss Cluff lit the cigarette with long, curving fingers, blew one or two dextrous smoke rings. The effect, curiously, resembled a painting I had once seen in an exhibition of early Victoriana in which a votary, watched by a pair of neophytes, celebrated some abstruse, mystical rite.

It was excessively hot here in the conservatory, surrounded by virid foliage. The seedcake, even when moistened by tea, stuck to the roof of one's mouth.

'I suppose you're wondering,' said Miss Cluff, 'why I came over here this afternoon?'

'Not especially. People often drop by. I'm usually quite happy to receive them.'

'Sure. Boy, the things I hear about you. Strange things. I thought I'd come and see for myself. Just you and him is it?' – she gestured at Caro who could be seen, through the glass, ambling disconsolately towards the bungalow – 'who live here I mean?'

I nodded, decided to let Miss Cluff make of that what she would.

'Sure. He's cute. But what do you do? I mean, why the solitude? Do you write or something?'

Thus phrased, the question seemed obtuse, verging on the indecent. 'One or two things, occasionally.'

Strangely, this studied piece of indifference brought what could almost be described as a tone of animation into Miss Cluff's voice. 'Hey, d'you know I used to write myself? At school. And then in the States. Bobby used to let me do this creative writing course at

UCLA. Poems mostly, but I wrote a short story once that they broadcast on Dallas radio. Hey,' she enquired, 'you ever hear of Stanley Weinstock?'

'No.'

'I guess not. He was my course tutor. Wrote a novel called *Dance This Mess Around*. You ever hear of that?'

'No.'

Despite my lack of response this exchange seemed to infuse a warmth (metaphorical rather than actual) that had previously been wanting. Miss Cluff ceased to pick at the skin beneath her fingernails, gave me a look that mingled shrewdness and awe.

'You been here long?'

'A year or so. Gradually you get used to the fact that there's no one worth speaking to for twenty miles, or rather' – for suddenly there came a glimpse, in the manner of the image of a die appearing on metal, of Mr Mouzookseem's dusky face and quaint locution – 'hardly anyone. Eventually solitude becomes rather enjoyable.'

'You can say that again. When I left Bobby at the airport and headed east I didn't want to see anybody again for a thousand years.'

It became possible to reconstruct some sort of picture of Miss Cluff's recent movements. Presumably she had accompanied her husband on some business trip (and what did that make her husband?) and a new environment, the prospect of richer diversion, had done the rest. I had been prepared to dislike Miss Cluff intensely. Oddly, the accent, the self-possession, the listless demeanour – tedious in anyone else – were redeemed by a sharp, piercing humour.

The light was beginning to fade. The gardener's boy wandered across the distant grass, a spectral figure, his face made luminous by the tip of his cigarette. Lights were on inside the house, flicked off. A mile away, beyond the trees and the river, somebody was lighting a beacon, a tiny pinpoint of light that grew intermittently larger and more ragged. Miss Cluff leant across the table.

'Anyway. About why I came over here this afternoon.'

'Something more than a social call presumably?'

'*A social call*,' repeated Miss Cluff, in what might or might not have been an attempt at mimicry. 'I don't make social calls. I want to know,' said Miss Cluff sharply, 'just what the fuck is going on? Lights over the river. This crap in the paper. And the cars out in the bush. Sometimes I go to bed in that bungalow of mine and I think, fuck, there's strange things happening out there, on the edge of things you know? So what do I do about it?'

'Don't do anything.'

'Is that what you do?'

It was remarkable how newcomers, even relatively civilized ones, began by deploring peasant superstition only to end up by emulating it. I shook my head. Miss Cluff chewed her lower lip, removed her hand which had lain an inch or two from my own.

'Time to go,' she remarked, stumbling slightly over her chair as she rose from the table.

'I'll see you to the gate.'

'Don't bother.' There was a definitely hostile tone to this injunction, almost as if Miss Cluff rather regretted her former confidences and wanted me to infer disingenuousness. I watched her thread her way back along the path to the gate – stooping now and again to avoid the branches, giving an angry little squeal when her foot caught a protruding root – then turned back to the house, anxious to speak to Caro.

Caro, questioned on his return from the village, was able to give some account of the afternoon's events in the bazaar. Miss Cluff's summary of the situation proved to be substantially correct. What had happened was this: an old woman, having eaten three blood oranges, complained of stomach pains. Normally this would have excited no disquiet. However, as the old woman was the aunt by marriage of the Commissioner of Police it was thought that some sort of cursory inspection ought to be made. The *dirzi*, called upon to examine the old woman, in whom the suspicion of poison had induced palpitations, turned up her eyelids, squinted at the soles of her feet and looked grave. The Commissioner of Police, called upon to examine the spectacle of his aunt undergoing this examination, became very angry and went so far as to kick the *dirzi's* scrawny backside. However, he also visited the bazaar and in the midst of a kaleidoscope of onlookers ordered that every available orange be assembled before him.

This measure had unforeseen repercussions. For a start, the presence of the Commissioner of Police was seen as a corroboration of rumour and numerous people who had purchased and consumed oranges went away to induce vomiting fits. Then again, as the Commissioner of Police watched the trays of oranges being laid out in front of him, eyed the procession of wheelbarrows, monitored the growing pile of empty sacks, he began to feel distinctly uneasy. A single orange can easily be proved unwholesome. A tray can be examined and given some sort of *imprimatur*. But a row of trays? A wheelbarrowful? The Commissioner of Police picked up the nearest orange – a fiery leviathan about four inches in diameter – and eyed it unhappily, bit into it, winced as the liquid sprayed over his face. The crowd watched expectantly. The bazaar traders stood around, wearing disgruntled expressions.

But the Commissioner of Police, having ordered this display of produce, having assembled two thousand oranges in various states of freshness and decomposition, was determined not to lose face. 'Bring me a knife,' he demanded. It was brought and the Commissioner of Police, having drawn up a small table and placed the fiery leviathan on it, cut it neatly into quarters. After which he examined them, sniffed them almost in the manner of some high priest extrapolating entrails and then shook his head. A subordinate, at a wave of the Commissioner of Police's hand, brought a fistful which he placed on the table. Again they were sliced neatly into quarters. Again the Commissioner of Police examined them minutely. There was nothing there. Oppressed by the murmurs of the crowd the Commissioner of Police picked up one of the quarters, held it between finger and thumb for a moment, and then ate it. Experiencing no immediate aftereffects he picked up another quarter and ate that.

The afternoon wore on. After an hour, when the Commissioner of Police had eaten eighty-seven orange quarters and the ground about the bazaar was awash with juice, pips and peel, it was thought politic to call a halt. As the Commissioner of Police was about to depart in search of some emetic he was stopped in his tracks by a subordinate bearing a half-eaten orange which he had been sucking simply for purposes of refreshment. Sliced, diced and squeezed it was found to contain traces of white powder. Inspection of the rind revealed several small holes through which, it was speculated, the powder had been injected. Prudently declining to sample the powder himself, the Commissioner of Police directed that it be smeared onto a piece of meat and fed to one of the town dogs. What would happen? The dog, tied to a stake in the middle of the bazaar, scrutinized for twenty minutes, emitted a few mournful howls, lurched ataxically in decreasing circles round the stake and then fell dead. The Commissioner of Police shrugged his shoulders, retched a little at the overpowering smell of pulped orange and stumped disconsolately away.

Later this evening I stumble upon Caro sitting in the corner of the library, a book propped upon his knees. His eyes have a peculiar heavy-lidded look. The book turns out to be an edition of Samuel Butler's *Notebooks*.

'What are you doing?' I ask him.

'Learning to read,' says Caro matter-of-factly, regarding me vacantly. He does not seem disposed to talk. I leave him there, crouched in the half-light, staring at the page with vague concentration.

8. Mr Fowler's Good Influence

Dull afternoons, Sunday afternoons usually, when the remainder of the day gaped before one like a chasm, could usually be enlivened by visits to one or other of the college eccentrics. Consequently, this particular Sunday, having extracted from Sarah a promise that we might meet later in the evening, I set off to find Fowler. The college, though practically deserted, bore all the signs of winter torpor: the leafless trees in North Quad festooned with lavatory paper (a week-old prank, still unrectified), a few earnest young men, box-files tucked under arms, striding self-consciously in the direction of the library, a pile of leaves, improperly stacked on the grass, blowing in ones or twos over the flagged path. I was already oppressed with the certainty that Fowler would not be in.

As befitted a college eccentric (a distinctive category and by no means unrespectable) one could never be entirely sure of his movements or availability. Three o'clock on a Sunday afternoon might find him about to go to bed, about to get up or, if not in his room, practically anywhere. At an anarchist 'happening' in North Oxford, at a Buddhist tea party in the Iffley Road, at a transport café near the station or further afield, in Sussex (where he was alleged to have relatives), in Cardiff (where he was known to have a girl). Even if you found him at home you could never be certain of his response. He might give you two seconds of his time or two hours. He might offer you coffee or ask you to go and do his washing, discuss his research thesis at inordinate length or ply you with questions about some unknown girl that he had met in the street.

Beyond the back gate of the college a path led between high garden walls to a small road, nominally a public highway but cluttered with building materials and mounds of sand, its exit barred by a sort of gate composed of packing cases. On either side of the pavement, flights of steps led up to high Victorian houses, four-storied and newly painted, as if somebody had thought that by doing this, attention might be drawn to the squalor of the road. You could tell at a glance that students lived there: the rows of doorbells, milk

72

cartons resting on window ledges, the glimpses, through alleyways and windows, of wild little gardens fantastically overgrown, as if there had been a competition for negligent college gardeners and these, lined up in rows awaiting judging, were the result.

Walking through the doorway of the house in which Fowler had a bedsitting room you were immediately conscious of a smell not exactly of food but of something vaguely resembling it. There was a general air of unwashed frying pans and sour milk. Somebody – probably Fowler – had attached a poster to the back of the door (which it was impossible to avoid seeing as you closed it) advertising a university arts magazine. Reaching the top of the house (three stair-flights) it was reassuring to hear music, although Fowler was quite capable of going out while leaving his record player on as an example of what he called 'a diversionary tactic'. A knock at the door – on which had been inked the words 'Is Your Journey Really Necessary' – produced a diminution in volume and the muffled sounds of movement.

'What the fuck do you want?' said Fowler, as I entered the room. He was sitting cross-legged on the carpet, his back to the door, prodding gingerly at the suspended arm of a record player, and then, turning to examine his visitor: 'Oh, I'm sorry – thought it was going to be someone else.'

He was one of those people who achieve most of their reputation by being rude to other people. With Fowler this idiosyncrasy had been raised practically to the level of an art form. He was rude to his tutor, who could never quite work out whether he were a genius or a charlatan. He was rude to women who inexplicably, were fascinated by him. He was rude to his friends who were either too tolerant (Page) or timid (myself) to reprove him.

I sat down on the room's single chair as Fowler continued to effect some obscure repair to the record player. Fowler, seen in his room, represented a revealing juxtaposition of character and environment. He was a tall, thin boy – so thin that it was almost the first thing you noticed about him – with protuberant eyes and black hair combed back very tightly over his scalp. At the time he would have been about twenty-four, but one imagined that he had always looked and would always look the same, an impression reinforced by his clothes. These rarely varied but although he affected negligence in matters of dress it was clear that he chose his garments with some care. On this occasion he wore a pair of tight black trousers – which had the effect of making the lower half of his body appear virtually atrophied – and a white shirt buttoned up to the neck, but there were other items that were equally characteristic: the PVC jeans, the herringbone overcoat. These, added to the lemur eyes and the permanently truculent expression, gave him an air of desperate intentness.

'Look, make yourself some coffee or something,' said Fowler, giving an odd little tap to the record player. 'It's bloody inconvenient,' he added, either referring to my appearance or to the malfunction. I began to hunt for the electric kettle, a task rendered comparatively simple by the fact that the contents of the room consisted only of a table, a chair, a bookcase and the record player. The kettle was run to earth beneath the table.

It was said that the chairman of the English Faculty Research Committee, when the subject of the renewal or the extension of Fowler's grant arose, had asked, 'But what does he do?' It was a question that had never been satisfactorily answered. Nominally he was writing a thesis on erasures in Donne (or as he put it 'the bits that Donne crossed out or the bits he might have put in but didn't') but remained evasive as to its progress. There were standard editions of Donne, thick with dust, on the top shelf of the bookcase wedged up against critical works by Barthes and Foucault, a hint, possibly, as to his true interests. What Fowler's tutors made of all this was anyone's guess. For the last three months he had been conducting a sort of guerrilla warfare with his current supervisor, a shy, shabby arts don from Keble. It was a savage, no-holds-barred sort of struggle – and one-sided, as the supervisor was not really in the same league as Fowler when it came to petulance. Requests for written work, or explanations of its absence, were countered by illiterate postcards or messages deploring the fact that the supervisor had not bothered to get in touch as Fowler had something particularly interesting to show him. They seldom met, and had not done so since the occasion on which Fowler, seeing his supervisor in the street, had affected to mistake him for the college medical officer.

Curiously, the stratagem worked. The arts don, reduced to a state of nervous terror, wrote personally to the English Faculty chairman supporting the renewal of his research grant. It was another link in the chain of legend that had begun to accumulate around him, most of which had to do with characteristics which in a less unusual person would not have excited remark. His voice was cold, almost to the point where it became metallic, but with a suspicion of irony. It was obvious that he realized and derived amusement from the fact that most of his incidental remarks were incomprehensible to cretinous colleagues. Then there were his relaxations. His favourite pastime was chess, sometimes against Page, whom he trounced with contemptuous ease (though it may have been that Page allowed him to win), occasionally against a computer, whose logical brain was no match for his devious stratagems. When he did lose (rarely) the pieces were thrown on the floor and the board out of the window. There was none of your light nonsense about Fowler.

Eventually Fowler finished tinkering with the record player, rummaged briefly amid the detritus of his desk, and thrust a sheet of foolscap into my hand.

'Here,' he said. 'I did this this morning. I knew you'd be interested to see it. Just a photostat, but,' he added darkly, 'it's about time we got the fucking thing out.'

I examined the sheet of paper, whose grey tint suggested that it had only lately emerged from the photocopier. Across the top, in bold Letraset, ran the words *Radical Review* and beneath, in smaller type, 'New Critical Strategies'. There followed a list of authors and their subjects in which I discovered the names of Fowler, Page and myself.

'I thought,' said Fowler, seizing the sheet and jabbing his forefinger at the white space that separated title and by-lines, 'of putting a drawing of a brick in here, and sticking the word "Culture" on it. With a "K" of course.'

'Of course.'

The *Radical Review* had been occupying Fowler's energies for some time. Normally a rather indolent person, the prospect of running his own magazine had spurred him to prodigious industry. Friends had been harassed for contributions (I myself had written a piece entitled 'Spritual Equivocation in Saxon East Anglia', which hardly constituted a new critical strategy). By dint of persistent and outrageous lobbying Fowler had managed to acquire a grant out of some obscure college fund. Publication now seemed assured.

'We'll do a thousand,' said Fowler, rising stiffly from the floor and moving back to his desk, 'and we'll saturate the bloody place with them. Sales campaigns in the women's colleges. Flog it in the streets – American tourists, taxi-drivers, anyone.'

This pitch of enthusiasm, so rarely manifest, was a little disturbing. Watching Fowler as he bent over the proof, made corrections in the margin with a fountain pen, it was possible to imagine the idiosyncratic sales campaign he might conduct. Nevertheless, the enthusiasm was infectious.

'We ought to have a launch – some sort of party.'

Fowler regarded me with the look of one who indulges a backward child. 'I thought of that. It's in a fortnight's time. I've done the cards.' He fumbled in the pocket of his trousers, produced a grubby piece of pasteboard on which it was announced that the editor and directors ('That's *you*') invited the bearer to a grand launch party, that the hour was nine, and that dress was to be 'uncompromising'.

'How uncompromising?'

'We'll see what people wear and decide then. We can always chuck out anyone we don't like.'

It was growing dark. The room, its curtains half-drawn, admitted only pale shafts of half-light. This crepuscular setting seemed vaguely appropriate. Fowler crouched once again upon the floor, his knees up to his chin.

'Hilary will be around in a minute.'

'Do you want me to go?'

'No.'

Plainly some thought had just occurred to Fowler which he was not at present in a position to formulate. I ventured another question.

'The contributions are all in?'

'Most of them. Page did a piece on abstract music. At least,' said Fowler, 'we might get the Wagner Society to buy a few. But there's something else I wanted to talk to you about – about the contributions, I mean. I had a letter from a don – Mortenson, Morterman, something like that.'

'Mortimer.'

'That may well be it. I suppose you know him or you wouldn't have said?'

'Sort of.' For some reason, as with Page, I felt disinclined to admit the extent of my connection with Mr Mortimer. It was obvious from the enquiring look on Fowler's face that he felt some explanation to be in order. As I considered the problem of Mr Mortimer, his inexplicable involvement with people I knew, there was a sharp knock at the door.

Curiously, this had an effect on Fowler that could only be described as unsettling. Bawling 'hold on a minute' he disappeared into his bedroom, returning with a brightly coloured sweater which he unfurled and flapped at arm's length before him, rather in the manner of somebody shaking a mat, considered it for a moment and then finally hung it over the back of my chair. The knock was repeated, whereupon Fowler disappeared again into the bedroom.

The door opened to reveal a small, pale girl with a shock of dirty yellow hair. She was carrying a pile of records clasped to her chest. Prompted less by politeness than by a nervous urge to move, I stood up.

'He's here, I suppose?'

I was used to encountering indifference or even derision from the more obscure of Fowler's acquaintance, but the tones verged on hostility.

'In the bedroom.'

The girl glanced fiercely in the direction of the bedroom door but, seeing that I was unable to offer any further explanation, came into the room. I supposed that this was Hilary, whom I had not previously met but of whom I had heard a great deal. A very great deal. In a university each undergraduate year throws up, with unfailing persistency, a number of people who are in some way exceptional or notorious, or a combination of the two. Hilary – her surname was I think Charteris – rather fell into the second category. Looking at her as she stood in the centre of the room, staring furiously at the bedroom door, the pile of records still clutched to her body like a breastplate, it was possible to reassess this reputation for subtle acts of depravity. She wore a shapeless, flowered garment, rather frayed about the edges, that extended almost to her ankles. The hair had been tied up, using blue ribbon, into arbitrary bunches that were now beginning to come apart. Yet the most marked characteristics were facial: dark, almost bruised eyes and a jutting chin combined to produce an expression that was both sullen and intransigent.

Fowler came out of the bedroom, where it seemed possible to deduce that he had been combing his hair.

'Quite a little party,' he observed. 'David, this is Hilary.'

'Hello.'

Hilary, her attention drawn to the fact that there was somebody else in the room, seemed surprised and somewhat displeased.

Glancing briefly in my direction she tipped the records out one by one onto the floor.

'You've eaten I suppose?' she demanded.

Fowler appeared to be disconcerted by this. 'I had a spaghetti at lunch.'

'You wonder sometimes,' said Hilary, 'whether Italy has been responsible for anything except pasta, cowardice and the fiction of Alberto Moravia. Well, I haven't had anything. You'd better take me out and buy me something.'

'Don't let me disturb you.'

'You are not disturbing us,' said Fowler, with a certain amount of uneasiness. 'Look, Hilary, I've got a few things to talk about. I'll be with you in a moment.'

In a gesture that might have indicated acquiescence Hilary brought out a tobacco tin and, sitting down at the desk, began to roll a cigarette. Fowler fetched her an ashtray, holding it gingerly in both hands as if it were some sort of curious beetle he had just found under a chair. After this lapse, conversation, understandably, took some time to resuscitate.

'This Mortimer,' said Fowler eventually, 'this fucking don or whatever he is, writes me a letter saying he's heard about this enterprise – that was how he described it – and can he write us an article?'

'What sort of an article?'

'Christ knows. The Gnostic Gospels. Jesus the First Rotarian – if I know the type.'

'Not if I know the type. Anglo-Catholic ramblings would be more his line.'

'In that case,' said Fowler, who had long ago abandoned any idea of editorial impartiality, 'I shan't even take it out of the envelope. He says he knows you.'

Once again, I had a queer, premonitory feeling of unease, a suspicion of design, even intrigue, rather than the simple workings of chance. 'He's right about that. What else?'

'Something about a party, a fucking *tea* party,' said Fowler, with infinite disgust. 'And will I go? I think I will. Can't stand Catholics – it's at the Catholic Chaplaincy – but God, can you imagine it? Horse-faced women with crucifixes and how many angels can dance on the head of a pin.'

Fowler, like Page, had some curiously old-fashioned ideas about Catholicism.

'You'll find they've moved on a little from there. It'll all be birth control and is soixante-neuf absolutely forbidden by the college of cardinals.'

'In that case,' said Fowler, almost with glee, 'I shall certainly go. It sounds as if we have a fuck of a lot in common.'

This outburst infused in Fowler a sense of vitality, of purpose, that had been previously lacking, for all that its core was sheer malice. He jumped to his feet. 'Time to go.'

Hilary did not say anything. I made some remark about a drink we might or might not be having the following evening but Fowler declined to be drawn. As I closed the door I caught a glimpse of him bent on his knees, shuffling the pile of records back into some sort of order, as if he were making a supplication to the gaunt unsmiling figure before him.

Descending the steps of Fowler's house your view was immediately dominated by the back of the college, row upon row of rooms, their sides composed entirely of glass, rising in hexagonal tiers to distant rooftops. From the topmost windows there were lights shining. The effect of this vast, Brobdingnagian structure was unnerving, prompting one to move quickly down into the street, between the piles of sand, pale and vaguely amorphous in the murk. It was about half-past-five. On the other side of the road, beyond the builders' apparatus and beneath the college wall, there were a few figures moving in the shadows, some of them recognizable. Pious girls hurrying back to chapel. Entwined couples returning from walks beyond Godstow to early hall and further entwinings. Solitary postgraduates, dazed by an afternoon's scrambling for facts, and now emerging for air. As I watched a figure came striding out of the gloom, clad in a mackintosh and carrying an umbrella, peered briefly in my direction, stopped for a moment and then moved hesitantly towards me. It was Page. Drawing nearer he drew the umbrella up to the level of his chest and, stretching his left leg back in the manner of a fencer, made stabbing motions at my head. Page was always doing things like that.

'I've been looking for you,' he said. His face, luminous in the shadow, hair flowing backwards in the wind, seemed distinctly aquiline.

'I'm gratified.'

We set off along the passage, back in the direction of the college gate, past a couple of girls wearing gowns and wheeling bicycles off to a formal dinner somewhere in North Oxford. It had begun to rain, gently yet persistently, so that a fine spray obscured the beams of light thrown by the street lamps. Above us in the accommodation block a light suddenly went on and there was a slither of curtains. The college was settling down for the evening.

'How was Fowler?'

'Hilary arrived in mid-conversation. I thought it unwise to stay.'

'That,' said Page, 'is an extremely, a severely unappetizing young woman. Typical, however, of Fowler.'

It seemed unnecessary to review previous associations. The one who had (temporarily) converted Fowler to an obscure oriental religion, the one who had smashed up his rooms, the one who had produced two children and a husband, the one who liked being beaten up, the one who liked beating him up. Fowler's experience of women, like Sam Weller's knowledge of London, was extensive and peculiar.

At the back gate of the college where there was a sort of porch leading through into the quadrangle a porter stood smoking a cigarette. Page paused indecisively, torn by the conflicting attractions of the library, his room and the dining hall.

'It's no good,' he said. 'I shall have to go and spank Perseus. Seeing Mortimer tomorrow. I told him I'd go to his party by the way. Remember, there'll be girls. I told him you'd go too.'

'I suppose you told him Fowler was coming as well?'

'Practical jokes are out with Mortimer. No I didn't.'

'Well, he seems to be invited.'

'In that case,' said Page, 'we shall have an excessively interesting time. I shall see you later.'

I watched him disappear up the nearest flight of stairs before turning back to retrace previous steps: over North Quad, where tattered pieces of paper still hung in the tree tops, past the chapel into which a disconsolate group of choir-boys was now proceeding, back to my room.

9. Searching for the New World

I begin to find myself increasingly disconcerted by this attachment of Caro to the gardener's boy. This is not simply due to the inconvenience, which is massive, the irregularity, which is forgivable, but owing to what it may or may not portend. I see them sometimes, early in the morning, in the sickly yellow light, emerging furtively yet with a certain ostentation out of the conservatory. Invariably the gardener's boy wears a slightly bemused expression, as if he cannot comprehend the attractions of his society, wonders occasionally what solace Caro derives from his dusky limbs, his vacant eyes. Often Caro, aware perhaps that I watch them from my desk, will snatch his hand and cradle it within his own, only for the gardener's boy to snatch it back, hold it in front of his face as if it has been in some way contaminated. I know for a fact that the gardener's boy – his name is Aziz – has taken to washing himself in the mornings with rainwater out of the tank. Possibly this is because Caro, who is a fastidious young man, has impressed on him the need for hygiene. More probably, however, this frenetic cleansing has an exclusively symbolic basis.

But the inconvenience . . . Caro was never a very good cook, but at least his productions in this line had a certain elementary consistency. Now all has changed. Meat either falls unhindered from the bones or clings obstinately to them in a welter of blood and sinews. Last week I *broke a tooth* on what was supposed to be a pie-crust. It will not do. Then there is the business of the laundry. It is a regrettable fact, but unquestionably true, that the sheets on my bed have not been changed for upwards of a fortnight, also that I am down to my last clean shirt. Furthermore, small but significant items of my wardrobe have actually begun to disappear: handkerchiefs, a tie or two. Yesterday I discovered Aziz wearing a pair of brightly coloured ankle socks. Obviously the suggestion was not his as I caught him looking at his feet with a kind of horror – as if he had sprouted fur or begun to grow flippers. Caro, reproached with these thefts, is evasive.

'They are Aziz's socks,' he maintains, 'knitted for him by his grandmother.' 'They look very like a pair of mine.' 'That may be so. I shall punish Aziz for stealing them.' 'But are you sure you did not take them?' 'You have too many socks.' And so on and so forth. It is fatal to engage Caro in one of these question-and-answer sessions. Years of duplicity have given him a talent for deflecting unwelcome enquiries.

Meanwhile, he is neglecting his duties in the house. There is dust everywhere, crouching in great flocculent balls under chairs and beneath sofas. The damp patch above the bookshelf in my study has still not been dealt with. The kitchen is a wasteland of flies, greasy plates and blocked sinks. Something, clearly, will have to be done. What if Miss Cluff should visit again and propose a tour of the house? What if . . .? At any rate a house should be clean, whether or not there are visitors. Caro is unimpressed by this piece of logic.

'Nobody comes here,' he says. 'What is a little dirt? There is only you and I and we have other things with which to occupy ourselves.'

What he means by this is anyone's guess.

The business of the poisoned oranges did not die down in a week or even in a month. Its initial repercussions were quite startling in their variety. On the following day six policemen, working in relays and superintended by the Commissioner, disposed of the remaining one-thousand-nine-hundred-and-seventy-seven oranges, watched by a gaping crowd. Three further specimens were found to contain traces of the white powder, though such forensic tests as the Commissioner of Police was able to apply were unable to determine whether all the powder was of the same type, what sort of powder it was, whether it were harmless or whether injurious. Three further dogs, chained to stakes and fed lumps of meat on which the powder had been smeared, displayed conflicting symptoms. One declined to eat the meat at all; another barked insanely for several minutes, rolled on its back and was assumed to be dead until three hours later, when it woke up and was proved to have been asleep. The third did die, but this evidence was held to be inconclusive as the owner attested that it had been ailing for some days.

The atmosphere in the bazaar became hysterical. A suggestion that the market's entire stock of fruit – bananas, pears, pineapples – should be similarly chopped into segments and examined was only narrowly dismissed. As each orange segment joined the glistening mound of pulp the crowd set up a low moaning noise, halfway between a sigh and a threat. A merchant who complained at the destruction of his property was spat upon and stoned under the very noses of the police. Meanwhile, the Commissioner of Police wandered about the bazaar with an abstracted air, brushing aside the stream of villagers who knelt in his path to invoke aid. It was generally felt that the Commissioner of Police ought to act decisively, make some bold stroke, unearth both culprits and design and dispense summary justice. Even the *Sentinel*, sensing the strength of public opinion, printed an editorial advising that 'the unremitting attention of our *devoted* servants be focused on the *heinous crime* as a matter of the utmost urgency'. This was one in the eye for the Commissioner of Police, especially as the *Sentinel* then printed a list of the illegitimate children the Commissioner of Police was alleged to have fathered in the previous six months.

The Commissioner of Police bore all this with apparent stoicism. This was not the first occasion on which his abilities had been called into question. An outbreak of swine fever, the suspicion of fowl pest, a few robberies in the bazaar – these were usually enough to prompt murmurings about his usefulness. Not that the Commissioner of Police cared, even if he knew. The Commissioner was a swart, globular little man of forty, so heavy that when the etiquette of public ceremony demanded that he be borne aloft on a chair it took three men to lift him. He owed his position to an uncle who was something – no one, least of all the Commissioner of Police, quite knew what – in government. The government, having appointed him, took no great interest in his activities. Once a month a government official trekked down the dusty road to the village, accepted a glass of whisky, asked a few perfunctory questions and departed, bearing with him the Commissioner of Police's good wishes to his uncle. Three times a year a large pink form arrived on which the Commissioner of Police was asked to list all the robberies committed, investigations prosecuted and criminals incarcerated in the district. The Commissioner of Police, who was quite illiterate, usually threw these away but lately he had taken to pasting them to the door of his bungalow as a tangible proof of his authority. The villagers were awed. Had the pink forms failed to arrive, or had they been suitably completed and sent back, he would have forfeited a considerable part of his respect.

But the Commissioner of Police, though he shared his living quarters with a goat and a number of hens and believed sincerely that if he seduced a woman when the wind was in the east the issue would be a girl, was not a stupid man. The god – a remote, clangorous deity – who had advanced his standing in the affairs of men had invested him not only with his own inscrutability but with a degree of wisdom. Wisdom enough to realize that the crimes of the last few months, the bazaar fire, the poisoned oranges, represented a new development in the affairs of the village. Their singularity stemmed from the fact that not only had no culprits been apprehended, but that nobody had even made any plausible allegations. This was most unusual. Normally the slightest suspicion of iniquity roused a tumult of accusation and denial among the villagers. A stolen cow, later found to have strayed a few fields away, would bring the owner, a list of suspects, a troop of bribed witnesses and half-a-dozen rival farmers anxious to swear their innocence before they were accused. The poisoned oranges – if poisoned they were – brought nothing at all.

Or rather, they brought nothing tangible. They brought rumours, of course, but rumours so nebulous that even the Commissioner of Police felt inclined to ignore them. The prime suspect, at any rate according to the rumours current in the bazaar, was Mr Mouzookseem. It was said that he had been lurking at nightfall on the outskirts of the village. It was alleged that a bazaar trader, acting as Mr Mouzookseem's confederate, would be prepared to swear that he had been bribed to inject the oranges with cocaine. Yet no witnesses could be brought forward and the bazaar trader, if he existed, kept silent.

Obviously Mr Mouzookseem had acquired the status of a popular ogre, someone who could be blamed for extensive and peculiar depravity in default of any other candidate. Thereafter, attention transferred itself to more plausible miscreants. Miss Cluff had a rotten pineapple thrown at her in the bazaar and a stone hurled through the window of her bungalow. Yet even here the response was instinctive rather than considered. Though the stone shattered a pane of glass, broke a vase and injured Miss Cluff's servant, it was not thrown with any heart. The Commissioner of Police, disillusioned but patient, turned his gaze elsewhere. Not unnaturally, he turned it towards me.

The Commissioner of Police's visits follow a familiar though by no means unamusing pattern. I see him from the conservatory, usually in mid-afternoon, making his way clumsily along the path that leads from the gate. He brings with him a tall, silent assistant who remains at a distance beneath the trees, Aziz watching him with vacant curiosity. The Commissioner of Police has a nice sense of protocol. though he can see that I am sitting in the convervatory, and though we will occasionally exchange nods, he makes a point of going into the house to ask Caro if I am at home. Subsequently, there is a sound of movement and two sets of legs, oddly juxtaposed (Caro's gazelle-like, the Commissioner of Police's like bandy tree-trunks), approach across the grass. Caro comes into the conservatory, unnaturally subservient.

'The Commissioner of Police. To see you.'

'You had better tell him to come in. Would he like anything to drink?'

'I have asked him. He says no.'

So the Commissioner of Police is bowed into the conservatory. Examined close-up he appears even smaller than casual sightings have suggested. He is crammed into a nondescript brown garment which may or may not be a uniform and only emphasizes the plunging curves of his belly. He is monstrously fat, and not a little proud of the fact. Popular prejudice tends to equate obesity with virility. Certainly when he speaks he has a habit of resting his hands, plump knuckleless trotters, on his stomach in the hope – invariably realized – that my attention will be drawn to this vast frontier of flesh. The effect, a combination of the bald, inscrutable head and the pear-shaped body, is oddly disconcerting, as if a squat yellow idol had somehow got hold of a suit of clothes and wandered away from its temple in search of diversion.

The Commissioner of Police is painfully ill-at-ease during our conversation, fixes his gaze on the ground or at a point somewhere between my chest and my left shoulder.

'There is trouble,' he says. 'Trouble in the bazaar.'

'I am sorry to hear that. Can I be of any assistance?'

This offer of help flummoxes the Commissioner of Police entirely. He looks over his shoulder to where the silent assistant is standing perfectly still, beneath the trees.

'They say that you are responsible.'

'You know perfectly well that I am not responsible. What would I be doing poisoning oranges in the bazaar?'

'That is a question I have asked myself. You must realize that it is necessary for us to investigate this matter properly.'

'Obviously I realize that. Will you not have something to drink?'

The Commissioner of Police shakes his head in a slow, metronomic motion. Plainly, the refusal of hospitality is a point of principle with him.

'It is very kind. No. You will not mind if I look at your house?'

'I will not mind at all.'

We wander slowly over the grass towards the back door which, according to custom, Caro has left open. The Commissioner of Police is engrossed in private thoughts, refuses to raise his head as he steps onto the stone patio, trails disconsolately behind me as we walk into the house. The sun glints on the high windows. Looking back I can see that the silent assistant has composed himself cross-legged beneath a tree and lit a cigarette, sending smoke up into the air in an unwavering, vertical line.

Inside the house there is a strange, sweetish smell hanging in the air. I follow the Commissioner of Police into the kitchen where the flies buzz and a week's plates lie choc-a-bloc in the sink. He views the squalor incuriously, pauses only to tug open the door of the refrigerator, examine the trays of rancid butter, the rotting meats, and then closes it. On the kitchen table there is a bowl of fruit – a few apples, a small pineapple and a handful of shrivelled, wizened oranges. The Commissioner of Police picks out one of these, holds it in his hand. For a moment it disappears into a boneless knot of flesh, re-emerges on the tip of a forefinger.

'It was oranges such as these that were poisoned.'

'I don't doubt it.'

'Oranges such as these,' says the Commissioner of Police slyly. 'You will not mind if I examine them?'

'Not at all. I imagine you will find oranges like them in every house in the village.'

'That may be so. But I have my investigations to make. Please to excuse me.'

And so as I watch, with quiet amusement, the Commissioner of Police seizes a bread knife and with great precision (but then he is practised) slices the orange into quarters. It contains nothing other

86

than tawny pulp. If the Commissioner of Police is disappointed by this result he does not show it. Standing before me in the kitchen, one hand pressing against the door of the refrigerator, the other palm-down on top of a four-legged stool, he seems strangely complacent, as if the unadulterated orange had provided the solution to some mysterious equation.

'Is there anything else you would like to see?'

'No. I am sorry to have troubled you. I will have a glass of lemonade (he pronounces it "limonard") perhaps.'

Caro is summoned and the glass of lemonade is prepared.

'You are most kind. I am sorry to have troubled you. It will not happen again.'

Thereafter, a mildly convivial air descends upon the kitchen. The Commissioner of Police unbends so far as to place a stray and apparently whole orange upon the table and make a mock-play with his hand of dicing it. Both he and Caro giggle terrifically at this. I manage an uneasy smile. The Commissioner of Police picks over the selection of previously diced segments that lies on the table before him and places one in his mouth. Caro applauds. It is a curious sight – the slim, lanky boy and the waddling little man beaming transparently at one another, surrounded by the dirty plates and the buzzing flies. I decide that it is time the proceedings were brought to a halt.

'You will excuse me, but I have an appointment.'

'Please to forgive me. I am late myself. Where is Ali?'

'He is sitting under a tree in the garden,' says Caro, before I can answer, 'smoking a cigarette.'

'Please to summon him. I am sorry to trouble you. My apologies.'

And in a welter of obeisances and mock compliments the Commissioner of Police is bowed out. I watch him from the window, striding across the grass. He stops for a moment, says something to Caro (who has accompanied him), raises a peremptory finger to summon Ali, who though he has been examining the Commissioner of Police's approach for some time now scrambles to his feet as if suddenly surprised and casts an unsmoked cigarette upon the grass. The figures move off, grow smaller, disappear.

As the afternoon draws in and the sun is the colour of one of the Commissioner of Police's oranges I slip out of the house and walk the mile or so down dusty tracks to Miss Cluff's bungalow. Caro, who is sitting by the door, his head buried in Samuel Butler, does not even look up as I pass. The bungalow appears to be deserted – there is an unsightly cradle of sticky tape over the broken window – but persistent knocking at the door brings Miss Cluff, dressed in a bath robe, with her hair tied up in a knot.

'Mr Castell,' she says ironically, 'fancy seeing *you* here.' I tell her about the visit of the Commissioner of Police. 'Yes,' she says. 'I know all about *that*. You'd better come in.' I follow her into the house: a faint scuffling by the wainscoting, a glimpse of a rodent tail disappearing into the dark bringing back older memories. And then, Miss Cluff's stiff limbs unfurling around me in the fading light, the removal of the bath robe, Miss Cluff's silhouette visible in the space between door and jamb. I do not know whether I enjoy this. I wonder if I, David Castell, my father's son, should be telling you this at all.

Because, because the seconds are ticking away – no that will not do: the metaphor is inexact and besides, it gives too much away. Because there is so much more to tell you that is *relevant*, neither gasping coitus nor shrivelled small talk. There is more to tell, about my father, about the books, especially about the books. So bear with me, please, because there is more of history, of destiny, of chance and design, more searching for this new world to explain.

Returning home at dusk there is no one in the house. Propped up against the door, near the spot where Caro was sitting, I find the copy of Samuel Butler's *Notebooks*: the pages are faintly mildewed. Proceeding into the kitchen and switching on the electric light I discover that the mess of orange pulp and juice has been cleaned up – or partially. Lying on the kitchen table, on a white plate, is a single orange neatly cut into four segments. There is white powder sprinkled on it, like salt. I dab a finger, sniff suspiciously. It is not salt. For some reason I begin to laugh.

10. Books of Brilliant Things

The most important room in my parents' house was, not unnaturally, the library. It was here that my father spent those evenings which he did not devote to freemasonry or local societies and practically all of Sundays. One grew used to seeing him, early in the morning, proceeding from the kitchen through to the hall, carrying a pot of tea on a tray, his arms wedged to his sides by the effort of supporting the two or three volumes he had been consulting over breakfast. Thereafter, he would emerge only occasionally; with affected resignation (when it was necessary to borrow one of my dictionaries), unwillingly (when summoned to the telephone) or rather less unwillingly (when informed that there was food on the table). I spent Sundays in my room.

How my mother occupied herself I was never altogether sure. Possibly she filled gaping hours by means of intense concentration on the mundane. My mother was one of those people who is able to bring a pious sense of resolve to the most trivial activities. This meant that nearly any task assumed practically epic dimensions. She dusted furniture with fervid application, cooked dinners with intransigent seriousness, darned socks with an enthusiasm that suggested the needlewomen at Bayeux.

There was a certain disingenuousness in all this. After a few years I wondered if my father really knew what was going on at all. It was possible to see the process as a sort of mental confidence trick. My mother gave the impression that she had been, in earlier days, one of those people who have a fairly rough time of it intellectually, are sat upon by opinionated fathers and have their intelligence systematically warped by a tribe of boneheaded schoolmistresses. But her intellect was by no means despicable. There were the books, read late at night in bed (a habit which infuriated my father), the opinions on education or politics occasionally expressed, in my father's absence, over the dinner table or advanced in letters to the newspapers. Possibly my father had a lurking suspicion that he had misjudged his wife's character. Throughout my late teens he used to advise me – with apparent seriousness – 'never to marry a clever woman'.

It was possible to see, in fact you could scarcely avoid seeing, the library as symbolic of the intellectual divide that my father imagined separated himself and my mother. When he found her company irksome, or wanted to express his displeasure at some imaginary slight, he retired into it locking the doors behind him. My mother was never allowed in there, not even to clean, so that there were blobs of dust the size of golf balls blowing all over the floor and a great dark stain – resembling, oddly, the map of Italy – on the ceiling, the result of a decade's cigarette smoke. Her exclusion did not simply stem from malice on my father's part. It amused him to construct a fantasy in which the study existed as a sort of grotto of arcana, unfit for inspection by women and children. What my father wanted us to imagine that he got up to in the library was anyone's guess. I knew for a fact that he kept his masonic regalia in there concealed in a drawer. He could occasionally be heard, through the door, intoning masonic ritual to himself.

For a room that excited such discontents and animosities, the library was singularly unimpressive. In the days when the house was built it had, I suppose, done service as a parlour, and indeed there was a giant horsehair sofa in the corner which my father disliked but had never had the energy to remove. It had the resigned, slipshod air of a room that is never properly cleaned, whose windows are never opened. Over by the door there was a small table on which balanced a pile of newspapers with yellowing edges and a whisky decanter. The walls were mostly bare except for a few pictures, prints of Dürer and Bewick, though the highlight of the room's decoration – the *ne plus ultra* so to speak – was a reproduction of an Anglo-Saxon engraving depicting the death of King Edmund. This hung on the wall above the desk. It was here, under the watchful eye of three or four thousand books, that my father sat and busied himself.

The great mass of books – three large bookcases extending from floorboards to ceiling – had to do with matters more central to my father's consciousness. There you would find East Anglian gazeteers, numbers of *Norfolk Archaeology*, a host of forgotten pamphlets picked up in second-hand bookshops, *The Records of the City of Norwich* – two monstrous volumes in red, gilt bindings – and the Victoria County History of Norfolk. The range of my father's local interests was at the same time both indiscriminate and comprehensive. Pushed up against fat books on Saxon field settlement one would find the botanical observations of country parsons, next to annotated editions of the Paston Letters, a Domesday guide to Norfolk and Suffolk. Messent's *Norfolk Churches* and the relevant volumes of Pevsner suggested an interest in ecclesiastical architecture, while a row of paperbacks with titles like *Rum Owd Boys*, hamfisted parodies of Norfolk dialect, confirmed an awareness of the more comic aspects of local life.

There was, in fact, a great deal of the stage East Anglian about my father. Though he affected to deplore local radio programmes in which professional actors assumed garrulous yokel accents and made jokes about turnip-topping, it was obvious that he thought them a necessary prod to local patriotism and would rather have regretted it had they ceased to appear. He had a great fund of anecdotes on the subject of Norfolk eccentrics – 'characters' they were called – men who had not spoken to their wives for twenty years, or were found drunk in ditches or, carrying their enthusiasm for the local football team to fanatic lengths, dyed their hair yellow and green. Witnessing him on the telephone, where his accent grew steadily more broad, or talking to a crony in the street, you could not help thinking that he would like to be regarded as a 'character' himself.

Sunday afternoons at home followed an invariable pattern. Emerging from my room, in search of tea or coffee, I would find my father standing on the stairs, though in such an attitude that it was impossible to work out whether he were coming up or going down.

'Hello, boy. Busy?'

My father always greeted me as if I were a guest of whose arrival he had not been previously informed.

'I've just finished making some notes. I was going to have tea.'

'Well, come and bring it into the library.' Pause. 'There's something I want to say to you.'

The implication – that my father had some terrifically important confidence to impart – meant nothing at all. It was simply a ruse to get me into his room. Once there we might talk of anything: he might ask me to test him on his masonic ritual, a labyrinthine business in which my father figured as someone called Scribe Ezra, or demand to know which books I was reading. This was a rather futile pursuit. My father's ignorance of English literature was practically fathomless, but he had the habit of making some wide assertion which, though not absolutely wrong, could not be modified or refined without recourse to subtleties he was incapable of understanding. Thus he might observe that he had always thought Hardy a gloomy writer, or that Dickens' novels suffered from an excess of descriptive detail. Cravenly, I usually agreed with him, whereupon my father would contrive to look very knowing and pass on, hurriedly and self-consciously, to another topic.

More engagingly, he would talk about himself. Curiously, he did this very well. The rampant egotism that attended pressing, contemporary matters was placed in abeyance as he assessed the past. The events of his life were recounted in a way that combined awareness of his own marginality and a degree of charity to the other people involved.

'Do you know, my old father would have been a hundred years old next month? Dear me, I'm not half the man he was, not a quarter. But he was difficult, there's no denying that. When he was on his death bed, you know, they asked him if he wanted his sister to be sent for – they quarrelled years before – and he told them as far as he was concerned, his sister could go to hell, that there wasn't any reason for thinking that death could patch up hate. He was a remarkable man.'

More often than not the talk turned to his fabulous tribe of relatives. A by-product of Victorian notions of philo-progenitiveness, my father had possessed about a dozen uncles and aunts and something like a hundred cousins, none of whom he had seen for decades. They were luminous, grotesque characters, or perhaps it was my father's descriptions that made them appear so. They had names like Victor and Sid, had kept backstreet grocery shops or been bookies' runners, had run away from the war and been hauled back by the Military Police, got young women 'in the family way' and been forced into cheerless, working-class marriages. My father had discarded them all on the occasion of his engagement.

'They were a poor lot. My father never had any time for them. Envious, not that you could blame them for that: they never had anything. I thought when I met your mother I had to put all that behind me. I didn't want your mother to get involved in all that. I didn't invite them to the wedding. I think,' said my father piously, 'that I did the right thing.'

92

Occasionally he would talk about my mother in a way that suggested he had almost forgotten that I was his son.

'She's an odd woman, your mother. But then she came from an odd family. It used to worry me sometimes that we had nothing in common. But you know, when I thought about it I realized that we had one very important thing in common. *We finished our meals at the same time.* It's a comforting feeling,' said my father, 'to know that you'll finish eating in unison.'

There was a peculiar comfort about these Sunday-afternoon encounters, myself lodged at one end of the horsehair sofa, my father, knees drawn up in front of him, wreathed in cigarette smoke, adumbrating the past. Though, as I have observed, there was a kind of charity extended to the characters who peopled his reminiscences, my father could not prevent a conscious note of triumph from creeping into his voice – an acknowledgement that he had 'survived', had, according to his own lights, prospered and won through.

This winning through was the most integral part of my father's philosophy. That's shown them,' he would remark (it might be of one of my academic successes, the appearance of his picture in the local paper), 'they' being the rest of a predominantly hostile world, mediocre, incurably envious but forced to admit our own unquestionable superiority. The gesture, which I thought otiose and even vulgar, was vital to my father's wellbeing.

But my father was not simply concerned with his immediate family or with my mother's idiosyncrasies. He had more significant truths to impart, here in his study, surrounded by two thousand years of East Anglian history. To put it briefly, my father had certain . . . theories he wanted to explain, certain . . . propositions he wanted to advance, propositions that required a great deal of elucidation lest they be misapprehended by juvenile ears. Why these circumlocutions? My father wanted me to *understand*, and he was prepared to devote infinite labour to making sure that I understood.

My father's theory went something like this:

My mother's maiden name, as you will know from certain hints already dropped across your path, was Spalding. Now, there are a number of derivations of this surname. Along with half the surnames in England it has something to do with the nomenclature of place. The *ingas* suffix is characteristic of seventh-century settlement, meaning 'place of x's people'. So Spalding was 'the settlement of

93

Spalda's people'. Obviously, this is not enough for the inquisitive. Where *was* the settlement of Spalda's people (and who, for that matter, was Spalda)? Spalding, as the geographically minded will know, is in Lincolnshire, not far from the Norfolk border, sixty miles as the crow flies from Norwich, a little way from the Wash and the great mass of sea and fen, half in half out of the water. Not the only Spalding – there are sundry hamlets in Yorkshire and dotted around the Midlands and there is a Spaldwick in Huntingdon – but the only Spalding of any consequence.

And there, you might have thought, my father would have been content. His family, or rather the family into which he had married, came from Lincolnshire. But my father had a probing, inquisitive mind. He wanted exact truths, even plausibly exact truths, rather than sheer speculation, wanted to be sure, *definitively sure*, where he stood in all this, in the progress of history. Having identified Lincolnshire as a nominal base, the *locus familii Spaldingi* if you like, he looked a little closer at hand. Spalding, Spaulding occasionally, when the Spalding in question had social ambitions, is a familiar Suffolk name, not a common one (which would discourage investigation) but familiar. There are Spaldings buried all over East Anglia, in the great graveyard of St Nicholas's, Yarmouth, looking out over the grey sea, in the market-town cemeteries of the Suffolk border – Bungay, Earsham and Ditchingham – under stupendous three-ton slabs of marble, memorialized in gilt lettering, beneath tiny wall-plates in country churches where no one goes, mouldering under sodden fenland grass. My father, who was not a bad amateur antiquarian, soon identified the oldest of these, a certain Nicholas Spalding – merchant and subsequently knight – who had been laid to rest in Beccles in the year 1410, survived by a grieving wife Agnes, *aetat* 63. Beyond this, and the fact that he had three sons, there was nothing.

There was nothing either in the family tree, an impressive and almost certainly forged document, commissioned it was said by a nineteenth-century Spalding who hoped – via the marshalling of much spurious *éclat* – to prove his entitlement to the freedom of the city of Norwich. Unhappily it extended only as far back as the 1580s, and there were some blatant inventions: a Thomas Spalding who was alleged to have been MP for Lowestoft during the Barebones Parliament and – even more fancifully – a Henrietta Spalding who

94

was supposed to have been the mistress of George I. It took only a few moments with the appropriate reference books to disprove this sort of thing.

So what was my father to do? Plainly, the occasion – if it were not to be frustrating, and if the rewards were not to be nugatory – demanded some imaginative leap across the great divide, the historical chasm that separated Nicholas Spalding, merchant and knight, and the darker ghosts of distant, even less pellucid centuries. Because my father had not neglected earlier sources. He had combed the Domesday Book; he had gone even further back, to the early land charters, to the chronicles and to Bede, where he found a great deal on which to speculate and to ponder. And, reading through the Tribal Hideage, in which the great Saxon divisions of territory and influence are set forth, he came upon the tribe of . . . the *Spaldas*. So we were there in this seething cauldron of history, we were there at the start of things, or what my father liked to conceive of as the start of things. We had . . . a *rôle*.

The rôle, unfortunately, was uncertain (I am sorry to bore you with all this history but then, remember, this is a story about history). What had the *Spaldas* done? On the face of it, nothing very much. They had not ruled a kingdom; they had left no list of rulers whose deeds could be posited and whose influence could be assessed; no coins bearing crude impressions of their physiognomy. They had buried no treasure, like Redwald with his great hoard at Sutton Hoo, his silver dishes, the promise of solace in the afterlife. But still my father busied himself, weaving together these threads into a tangled skein of assumption, plausible hypothesis and finally – or so he imagined – *certainty*. The *Spaldas* had come from Scandinavia, and so, you will remember, had Wehha, who begat Wuffa, who gave his name to a dynasty. And there grew in my father's mind a belief that the *Spaldas* and the *Wuffingas* had more in common than mere geographical propinquity. The evidence of place, sifted, noted on sheet after sheet of writing paper, confirmed it. And my father concluded that when the long clinker boats nosed into the Waveney, the Ouse and the Yare, when a few years later Redwald sat in his draughty hall at Rendlesham, pondering uneasily this new magic of the White Christ, the stirrings in Mercia and beyond the Trent, concluded that, concluded . . .

So now you see the roots of this obsession, this preoccupation with what took place in this part of the world, in this cranny of time. Wehha, Wuffa and Redwald. *My ancestors.*

I suppose you think this is all rather fun. My father, and the Commissioner of Police, these goings-on in the shade of the conservatory – how quaint! And the Oxford chapters – what engaging descriptions of the young men and women going about their intellectual business. What *will* happen next? Do I know? Of course, but it's not like that; it's not like that at all. You don't think all this is going to end happily, do you? No, that would be an exceedingly rash assumption. Miss Knox and Miss Cluff: what is going to happen to them? And Mr Mortimer, sly, insinuating Mr Mortimer. What do you suppose is his rôle in all this?

And what about *him*, you are thinking – a perfectly reasonable train of thought. When will he tell us about himself? This speculation about Mr Mouzookseem, these hints about Caro and Miss Cluff, all very entertaining in their way, but we want to know about David Castell, and his part in all this.

Detachment, ironic observation – that's not the half of it. Do you know, there are times, sitting here in the shadow of the evening, thinking about that which is past and that which is to come, when I can scare myself with the quality of my own despair?

11. Du Côté de Chez Mortimer

'I've brought my briar,' said Page, in defiance of an obtrusive NO SMOKING notice, 'and about an ounce of foul shag, and no amount of papists is going to prevent me from enjoying them.'

We were standing in the main hall of the Catholic Chaplaincy beside a table covered with sherry glasses as about us surged a throng of people, all moving very fast – as though they were engaged in some complex, synchronized dance or thought that perpetual movement were a proof of religiosity.

'Remember,' Page had said, 'there'll be girls.' Whatever instinct had led him to connect Roman Catholicism with the female under-graduate population could not be faulted. They swarmed about us: shy girls, whose dresses spoke of convent educations lately con-cluded; strident girls with jutting chins and jewellery from monied, recusant families; eager, bespectacled girls bent upon conversion. As Page let out an unusually spectacular jet of smoke he was accosted by a girl in jeans and wearing a tee-shirt on which had been printed the words JESUS WANTS YOU TO SMILE.

'Please,' she said resignedly, 'will you take that thing outside and get rid of it.'

'What thing?'

'That pipe. Only Father Murphy will be here in a moment and if there's one thing he can't abide it's the smell of smoke.'

'Father Murphy can go to the devil,' said Page blandly.

The girl looked as if she might be about to burst into tears. She turned to me.

'*Please,*' she said, 'tell him to take it outside and get rid of it. We did put notices up and everything and he's the only person who's doing it.'

'I'll talk to him.'

Page, having expressed his public contempt for the request, now proceeded meekly to comply with it. Tapping the pipe out against his knee he placed it in the inner pocket of his jacket. Pipes had lately come to play a major role in the Page mythology; the talk was

97

all of 'foul shags', 'baccy' and 'gentleman's mixtures'. Watery-eyed and choking, Page smoked all these with considerable aplomb.

The main hall of the Catholic Chaplaincy was a wide, high-ceilinged room with white walls and elegant panel-lining, lined with the portraits of notable recusants from Campion to Monsignor Knox. For the purposes of Mr Mortimer's tea party most of the furniture had been cleared away into another room, leaving only sofas and long tables draped with white cloths and a slightly larger table, wedged up against the wall, on which various items of devotional literature were displayed. They were dreary books. They had titles like *Spirit Hands Have Touched Me* or *The Joys of Marriage*, on whose covers deceptively cheerful couples stood looking into each other's eyes. I doubted that they had much of a vogue, even among the earnest young people who laid them out into rows and tried to persuade visitors to buy them. There was about the Catholic Chaplaincy a slightly forlorn, exhausted air. Its staff wore the puzzled yet resentful expressions of those who are doing their best for only minimal reward. There was a great deal of talk about 'strategies' and 'missions', which were intended at some unspecified date rather to touch up 'Oxford' and subsequently 'the world' (in which characteristic they resembled optimistic business prospectuses) but one doubted that Oxford, still less the world, had ever heard of them. There was a great deal of talk too about incense and censers, picturesque vestments; a great deal of advertising of services at unusual hours of the day or night, but one doubted that anyone much admired the former or attended the latter. Books like *The Joys of Marriage* did not cut much ice in Oxford in these enlightened times.

Amongst the array of pamphlets, and in marked contrast to the refutations of birth control, there was a little monograph on the life of Pusey which Mr Mortimer had written and had printed up at his own expense. Its author was standing a little way off down the room in the centre of a group of girls, one of whom was Sarah. As I turned she detached herself from the semicircle of listeners and caught my arm.

'I thought you said you weren't coming.'

'Page wanted to come. Anyway, you're here.'

'Come and meet Mr Mortimer.'

'I've met him,' I said.

Though I had not set eyes on Mr Mortimer for nearly two years – since then our visits to my parents' house had not coincided – it was impossible to mistake him. Alert, confidential, strands of grey hair plastered over the crown of his head, he was in this unfamiliar milieu very much at home, superintending a round of conversation with unobtrusive skill.

'My dear girl. You overvalue the powers of your proselytizing. The great uncaring, immoral masses are still out there. Are they still listening? Do they wish to listen? They come to my tutorials, fuddled with alcohol and sex, and they behave shamefully. I very much doubt whether they wish to listen.'

'They need guidance,' said a small, intense girl who was watching Mr Mortimer with unfeigned admiration.

'Guidance? Precisely – guidance is exactly what they need. But who is going to give it to them? Dear me, who indeed? The Church of England perhaps? I rather doubt it, indeed I do.'

'What the Church of England needs is a firm approach . . .'

'. . . And lots of incense.'

'And copes and albs and birettas . . .'

'And *confession*.'

'Do they?' said Mr Mortimer. 'I very much doubt it. But you must excuse me.'

Mr Mortimer was what is commonly known in Catholic circles as a 'waverer', by which was meant a potential convert whose recession from Anglicanism might redound much to the Church's credit, one who had gone a certain distance but might, lured by appropriate spiritual carrots, go a great deal further. Having halted at a cross-roads whose signposts indicated the approach to Rome, he now awaited the comments of passers-by. This much one gathered from the ambiguous comments about the Church of England and its observances.

Mr Mortimer shook hands with enthusiasm. 'I am delighted to see you. I am surprised that our paths have not crossed before. You have been here a year?'

'Two.'

'I stand corrected. When you have seen as many under-graduate years as I have you will know that a year does not make very much difference.' Somehow in this little speech Mr Mortimer contrived to give the impression that he acted as a sort of *éminence grise*, mapping out the careers of generations of students. He smiled, and gestured with his forefinger towards the group of his admirers who were now deep in a religious argument.

'I wouldn't go to St A's. It's so spiky. Choristers waving censers and so on . . .'

'. . . I wouldn't go to St Ebbe's. It's as much as you can do to get the vicar into a surplice . . .'

'. . . A firm line.'

'. . . A jolly firm line.'

'. . . *Buckets* of incense.'

'These arguments get a little intense for my liking,' said Mr Mortimer. 'I myself incline to a higher form of Anglicanism, without particular concern for stylized ritual. My own vicar, I fancy, rather overplays his hand. But I apologize,' said Mr Mortimer, giving an elegant little flick of his head. 'I gather you are not much interested in religion?'

'Not at all. In fact,' I said, uneasily conscious of the fact that Sarah was hovering at my elbow, 'Catholicism has always struck me as so much pernicious nonsense.'

This was said rather loudly and produced a gratifying response among the six or seven young women clustered around us. Sarah looked slightly pained. However, it was impossible, as I recalled from past attempts, to snub Mr Mortimer. He smiled blandly, indicated displeasure only by switching to another, less controversial subject.

I glanced over his shoulder to where Page, his face unnaturally gloomy, was talking to a girl who I knew to be the secretary of the Undergraduate Catholic Society. At the further end of the room a momentary diversion was caused by the arrival of Fowler who, catching sight of myself and Mr Mortimer deep in conversation, strode immediately towards us. 'No, I haven't got a fucking invitation,' I heard him say to a girl who was dispensing glasses of sherry from a tray.

Fowler had obviously chosen his clothes with some care. He was dressed almost entirely in black, apart from white baseball boots and a thin red tie, sub-fusc jeans surmounted by a studded leather belt. He looked ill at ease, but with an impish glee – as if he thought that though uncomfortable himself he might have the power of making others feel more uncomfortable still. Striding purposefully towards us, as the lines of girls parted obediently to admit him, he contrived to give the impression that he was pushing people out of his way.

Mr Mortimer, who had watched this transit and knew pretty much what Fowler was about, had taken off his glasses – deliberately, I thought. The voices continued to buzz and hum.

'Roddy said that that sort of thing was all very well, but he hadn't got a vocation . . .'

'Tony said that Monsignor Wilson's been giving him all sorts of *queer looks* . . .'

'My confessor said . . .'

'. . . Genuflecting . . .'

'. . . *Gallons* of incense.'

'You're Mortimer,' said Fowler hurriedly, rather as though he were daring Mr Mortimer to deny it.

Mr Mortimer nodded. It was clear that he obtained considerable amusement from Fowler's get-up and the intentness of his address. 'Mr Fowler, it was very good of you to come, very good of you indeed: you obviously have a great deal which occupies your time. You must have something to drink. Some sherry?'

'But I don't like sherry,' said Fowler, managing to imply that it was rather foolish of Mr Mortimer not to know.

'I see. Well, you must have something else then.'

'What else is there?'

'I really don't know. What would you like?'

'I'll have a glass of water,' said Fowler.

They brought him a glass of water, or rather a papercupful. Having taken possession of this Fowler put it down on a nearby table and proceeded to ignore it. Given that Fowler's behaviour was habitually idiosyncratic it was difficult to work out whether he was doing this deliberately. I decided that he was probably unaware of the sensation he was causing: Fowler rather enjoyed being 'taken up' by dons and was usually at pains to appear at advantage before them. A similar thought seemed to have occurred to Mr Mortimer who now replaced his spectacles and wheeled in for the attack.

'And now, Mr Fowler, you are going to tell us about this magazine of yours. The *Radical Review*. A magazine of the arts I believe?'

It was characteristic of Fowler that he could never accept

pleasantries at face value. Obviously 'you are going to tell us about . . .' meant 'let us discuss . . .' It was clear, however, that Fowler regarded this as deliberate misapprehension.

'No,' he said, slightly puzzled. 'I didn't think I was going to tell you anything. I thought you wanted to tell me about some piece or other you wanted to write.'

'It is not customary,' said Mr Mortimer rather sharply, 'to write for a magazine of whose policy one is unaware.'

Fowler glanced nervously towards the door, giving the impression that he was expecting somebody.

'Look,' he said, 'it's called the *Radical Review*, right? That should give you some idea of what stuff we're taking. No bloody poems. No bloody articles about Oxford and the Tractarian Movement. Whatever that is,' added Fowler, failing to disguise a suspicion that he knew very well what it was.

In the corner of the room I noticed Hilary making her way through the throng, glancing ostentatiously to right and left. Fowler turned suddenly and caught my eye.

'Listen,' he said, half to me and half to Mr Mortimer, 'I've got to go and see somebody. I'll talk to you later.' He disappeared, re-emerged suddenly out of a shoal of people, and could be seen warily greeting Hilary.

In one of the periodic redistributions of people and conversation that tended to occur at this sort of party there was a swift shuffling of feet, a moving away on the part of some participants, a moving in on the part of others. I found myself in the centre of a group that included not only Mr Mortimer and Sarah but also Page and the secretary of the Undergraduate Catholic Society.

'So what do you think are the problems facing young people today?' I overheard the girl asking Page.

'*I* am one of the problems facing young people today.'

Mr Mortimer, it transpired, had not been at all put out by Fowler's antics. Presumably his experiences had acclimatized him to undergraduate eccentricity.

'I have met more amiable young men. But how is your father? I regret I have not seen as much of him recently as I would have liked.'

'You can see him next week if you like,' I said. 'He's supposed to be coming up to Oxford.'

Mr Mortimer's attention, which had previously been cursory, now became total.

'Dear me. Is that so? Then I shall certainly make an effort to see him. There are a number of things we might discuss.'

Suddenly I began to feel intensely irritated by Mr Mortimer, a sense of animosity that was increased by the fawning women who surrounded him, the sureness of his position.

'Look,' I said, 'why are you so interested in my father? Last time you practically warned me off him.'

'Your father is a very interesting man.'

'So everyone keeps telling me. You never seemed very interested in his opinions.'

Sarah, I noticed, was looking at me with mild incomprehension. Mr Mortimer, for once, seemed slightly taken aback. 'You had better excuse me. I had meant to talk to Father Murphy about the lecture this evening. There are a number of points still unresolved.'

'What are you talking about?' asked Sarah, who was intelligent enough to divine that by 'the lecture' Mr Mortimer meant his own.

'*Ritual*,' said Mr Mortimer theatrically.

Page came shambling up. He had taken out his pipe again and was twirling it in his fingers. His face had a peculiar, reddish tinge.

'This is pretty awful,' said Page glumly. 'Twenty minutes on the spiritual challenge of life. I think it will take me the rest of the evening to recover.'

'Have you been drinking?'

'Only sherry. God,' said Page, 'the spiritual challenge of life. They make it sound like a cross between *The Pilgrim's Progress* and a forced labour camp.'

'You *have* been drinking.'

'Not so as you'd notice.' To anyone familiar with Page's drinking habits, which to a certain extent I was, this was an ominous admission. It meant that he was quite likely to fall over, or start speaking in Latin. I was reassured, however, by the expression on his face. When drunk he usually became jocose. At the moment he seemed acutely miserable.

'That man Mortimer,' said Page, 'is a crook.'

'What makes you think that?'

'A crook,' Page said, placing one hand on the side of a nearby sofa. 'Can't tell you about it now, but it's not . . . how you think.'

'You're drunk.'

With a tremendous effort Page righted himself and regarded me sadly. 'I wish you wouldn't always go on about how much I've had to drink. Do you know,' Page said confidentially to Sarah, 'he always goes on about how much I've had to drink?'

Sarah, as was usual when people exhibited signs of drunkenness, said nothing but simply looked uncomfortable. 'He's a crook,' Page went on. 'He asks me about you in tutorials. Those tutorials. I can't take much more of those tutorials . . .'

'I think you'd better go home.'

'No. I'm all right. Let's go and talk to Fowler.' Page raised his head, suddenly composed. 'He looks rather as if he could do with it.'

12. Hero Takes a Fall

It is nearly dusk. Looking out of my study window into the failing light I can see Caro sitting, quite motionless, in the middle of the garden. From time to time he will scramble to his feet and walk in a preoccupied manner around the conservatory but for the last half-hour at least he has scarcely moved a muscle. He has been like this all day, and for the greater part of the previous day. For all I know he may have spent the night out there, sitting cross-legged in the centre of the lawn, head buried on his knees, for it was in this posture that I left him late in the evening and discovered him again early the next morning.

There is a simple explanation of this uncharacteristic behaviour. Aziz has gone away. I cannot say that I find this especially surprising – indeed I rather welcome it – but its effect on Caro has been disconcerting in the extreme and the stimulus to a number of distressing scenes. Two afternoons ago I was working in the conservatory when the sound of scampering footsteps over the grass and the furious rattling of the door heralded his arrival, rather out of breath and full of silent anger.

'He has gone.'

'Who has gone?'

'Aziz. He has gone. You have sent him away.'

'I have not sent him away. Why would I wish to send him away?'

Caro, expecting some instant confession, a reluctant admission of guilt, is rather taken aback by this. He peers suspiciously at my desk.

'You have sent him away. You are jealous of us.'

'Do not be ridiculous. What makes you think he has gone away? I saw him not two hours since.'

'I know he has gone away. I know it is because of you. You have broken my heart.' And Caro, who has gone very red in the face, bursts suddenly into tears, holding his knuckles over his eyes and making shrill keening noises.

Investigation revealed a number of inalienable facts, several plausible hypotheses and a fairly obvious conclusion. A search of the garden shed, in which Aziz kept his tools and in which he was assumed to sleep (certainly he was provided with no other accommodation) produced not so much as a pair of shears; the gardening implements had all disappeared, along with the canvas holdall in which Aziz kept all his earthly possessions. A search of the house and its environs revealed that a certain amount of food had been taken from the kitchen and that a pair of blue ankle socks, cut raggedly into shreds, had been placed beneath a table in the hall. The sight of the socks reduced Caro to a state of quite inconsolable misery.

The gardener, summoned to give his account of the departure, was unhelpful: a resigned, elderly man – his face the colour of teak – who seemed contemptuous of enquiry. No, he had not seen Aziz that morning. No, he had not observed him in the village, or playing dice in the bazaar. No, he was not sorry to see him go . . . an unreliable boy who took no pride in his work. No, he was not surprised at his disappearance. It was obvious that he was unhappy. Perhaps (a meaningful glance) Caro had some knowledge of his whereabouts? No, he knew of no relatives with whom Aziz might have gone to stay. Whoever heard of a gardener's boy having relatives? Was this not traditionally the career of orphans and gutter-sweepers from the bazaar? A suspicion of volubility, encouraged by these remarks, proved to be mistaken. Having delivered himself of this statement the gardener would say no more.

'He is a liar,' said Caro, when we were alone again in the conservatory. It occurred to me that there was probably another fairly near at hand. 'To say that Aziz was unhappy. How could he be unhappy? Did I not treat him as a brother? Did I not take him to the bazaar and buy him sweetmeats? We must search. We must search the garden and the road. Do you not see? He may be lying injured somewhere.'

I doubted it. I knew what had happened to the gardener's boy. Bored or disgusted by Caro's advances (he could not have been surprised) he had simply moved on, secure in the knowledge that there were other gardeners, other gardens requiring tenantry. By this time he would be in the bazaar, trading in his gardening tools for opium or tins of Coca-Cola, or, east of the river, promoting himself to other employers: fat, indolent women who would be captivated by his sorrowful good looks and eager to train him as a houseboy, knowing peasants in search of another human windmill adept at scaring crows from the corn. I had no worries about Aziz.

Rather I was concerned with the effect on Caro who since his departure has been nothing less than distracted. To placate him I conducted a perfunctory search of the garden and the quarter mile or so of road that adjoins it. There was nothing there though just outside the gate I discovered a small trowel whose position, on the lip of the ditch, suggested that Aziz had dropped it as he left the house on his way to the village and that a trade in gardening implements might in the next few days be a feature of the bazaar. I did not tell Caro this.

Two hours later, as I sit here staring into the distant horizon, he comes and stands by my shoulder, saying nothing until I turn and notice him, raise my eyebrows in enquiry.

'You promised,' says Caro, 'that you would tell me what you are writing.'

'When I have finished it, *Caro mio*, then I will tell you what I am writing.'

'You are unkind. You have secrets. You write things whose meaning you will not tell me . . . and you send Aziz away.'

'I did not send Aziz away. You know I didn't.'

'You did it to spite me. You could not stand the thought of us together. You have broken my heart.'

Suddenly I feel an almost impossible affection for Caro, as he stands here beside me in the conservatory, his face framed by the curving tendrils of foliage and flower, tears guttering down each side of his face. I reach out and take his arm. He does not respond.

'I did not send him away, *Caro mio*.'

'There is Miss Cluff coming across the grass,' says Caro matter-of-factly, 'and if I do not make tea you will scold me. So I had better make tea.'

For a moment I think that he is making this up. But there are footsteps on the stone, the glimpse of a white sunhat. I release the arm, try to convince myself that I have not seen Caro's glance of reproach.

The afternoon wears on. Miss Cluff and I lie in the shadow of the trees, near the edge of the grass. Thirty yards away, Caro, his eyes

107

fixed resolutely on some constant point high above him, has not moved for an hour and a half.

'So what's the matter with that kid?' asks Miss Cluff for the third time.

Miss Cluff is rather artfully got up in a magenta frock, white scarf and button-shaped jet earrings. She reclines against a tree, regards me quizzically.

'He thinks I sent Aziz away.'

'And Aziz is . . . the gardener's boy, right? Did you send him away?'

'No.'

Miss Cluff casts another glance at Caro, in which pity and prurience are uncomfortably mingled.

'I bet you did. I bet you told him to pack his bags and get the hell out. Isn't that what you did? Jealousy,' says Miss Cluff, shaking her head from side to side. 'Jesus. We once had a newsboy – this was back in Cal – Bobby thought was making eyes at me. You never saw anything like it. It was a pity. He was sweet – the kid, I mean.'

Caro, conscious of the fact that he is being watched and not liking it, gets ponderously to his feet and stalks off in the direction of the house.

'Gone,' says Miss Cluff. 'But he'll be back, I shouldn't wonder.' She gives a tiny twitch to the brim of her sunhat, scratches negligently at her shoulder. 'I always came back,' says Miss Cluff, regretfully.

I have learnt a lot about Miss Cluff in the past few weeks. She is one of those women in whom nearly every activity or object acts as a Proustian stimulus to memory. A hint of rain reminds her of a soggy Florida honeymoon. The English newspapers in my study remind her of her dour, North Country upbringing. I have a suspicion that these associations are contrived, that Miss Cluff – detecting in Caro a resemblance to a former lover, in my house a resemblance to her parents' bungalow – wants merely to remember.

She has knocked about a bit has Miss Cluff, oh dear me yes. Over half of Europe and the Near East in the last ten years, following on the heels of her husband's diplomatic appointments, though the embassy registers knew nothing of Bobby, the foreign ministries only a very little and most of that unfavourable. He was some sort of agent, some sort of government agent that is: a tiny, bustling mole placed by Washington in the topsoil of European policy. Miss Cluff could say no more than that. Probably she did not even care. Miss Cluff had other hobbies to pursue on this whirling grand tour of three continents; to Central America now, where a Fascist regime, covertly propped, seemed in danger of collapsing; to the Far East, where there were intrigues about oil and insurrection; back to England once, where Miss Cluff idled away her days in Harrods, Bobby having suddenly become a fixture at the Ministry of Defence. She had a liking for roulette – nothing excessive, nothing that might jeopardize her husband's career or his expense account, but a liking nevertheless. Baccarat, *vingt-et-un*, stud poker. Miss Cluff knew them all, played them with negligent enthusiasm in half the capitals of Europe; in curious little *salons*, located above Parisian cafés, where the counters are made of frayed cardboard and the croupier is none too sure of his job; in vast Hamburg gaming palaces; in private houses in Mayfair and Belgravia, while Bobby got on with whatever it was that Bobby got on with.

Miss Cluff is consumedly bored by the topic of her husband. He had, it seems, undesirable views on the subject of gambling and though Miss Cluff presumes that he continues to prosper in his career she couldn't positively undertake to say so. When, a few months back, she won an indecently large sum of money in a four-sided contest involving a Bombay financier, the head of an American bank and a member of the Indian government, departure – from Bobby, from that window seat on the transglobal express, as Miss Cluff put it – was the work of a few hours. Miss Cluff was a thousand miles away before Bobby, immersed in some intrigue involving the Indian Communist Party, was even aware that she was gone. You gathered that he did not much regret her passing.

'I always came back,' says Miss Cluff again. 'Well, until last time. Then I came here.'

'You can't stay here forever.'

'Can't I just? You just watch me,' said Miss Cluff with spirit. 'I cleared . . . well, never mind how many thousand it was, back in Delhi. It'll last until, well, until I decide to do something else. And meanwhile, there's that bungalow and there's peace and bloody quiet and a pile of books I've been meaning to read since I was eighteen, and there's you. No, I've got quite enough to occupy me.'

'You don't miss being on the move?'

'Jesus! Travel stopped being a novelty about ten years ago. Do you know,' said Miss Cluff, 'I could never remember where I was, that was the problem. Off a plane one morning, on another in the afternoon. Bobby used to take me to these embassy parties, OK? Well, once he takes me to this party in Madrid – at least that was where *I* thought we were. So, "How are you?" says one of the local Fascists, and I say, "It's great to be back in Madrid." Only we happened to be in Barcelona. That,' said Miss Cluff, 'was when I started to get sick of aeroplanes.'

Sometimes – like the gardener's boy with Caro – I wonder what pleasure Miss Cluff obtains from my company. There is the sex, but then Miss Cluff, judging from her reminiscences, is not too fussy about sex.

'Let's go inside,' says Miss Cluff. 'I could do with a drink.'

We set off across the grass to the back door which hangs open on its hinges. Caro has left another book on the step: it is a mildewed edition of *The Vicar of Wakefield*, somewhat frayed about the edges. I stoop to retrieve it, am aware suddenly of muffled sounds within the house. Caro emerges out of the kitchen. He does not appear to see us, contemplates instead a long, jagged knife which he holds in his left hand.

'What is the matter, *Caro mio*?'

Caro looks guiltily at the knife, at me and at Miss Cluff, whom he is regarding with a sort of wary apprehension. He rolls his eyes.

'You sent him away. You have broken my heart.'

As he speaks Caro is rolling the blade of the knife gently along the inside of his right wrist, holding his arm stiffly out in front of him, as if he were aping the stance of an ancient, bare-knuckle boxer.

'Robbed me of my happiness,' says Caro. He slices deftly at a tiny patch of skin, so that a small trickle of blood begins to course down his arm. 'My *only* happiness.'

'You put that thing down,' advises Miss Cluff from the door.

'Please to keep quiet,' says Caro politely. 'What do you know of this? What do you know of my friend Aziz?'

'Caro . . .'

'I will do it,' says Caro. 'You do not think I will do it, but I will. Then you will know how it was between Aziz and me. I will cut my own flesh and then you will know how it was between Aziz and me.'

'Caro, put that knife down. And then I will explain.'

There is a flicker of indecision in Caro's eyes. 'What will you explain?'

'That there is nothing *to* explain. Put down the knife.'

And suddenly Caro's face begins to crumple. He makes a half-hearted sawing motion at his wrist, thinks better of it, and hurls the knife on the floor with such force that it sticks quivering on the mat. Then he bursts into tears.

Miss Cluff shrugs her shoulders. I try to evade her gaze.

Quarrels, partings, are definitely in the air.

Mr Mortimer's tea party, despite the temporary absence of its host, was reaching its apogee. There were probably a hundred people crammed into the room, clustered around the tables, wedged up against each other on window seats or talking in tightknit, confidential groups. Father Murphy, an elderly Jesuit who resembled portraits of Cardinal Richelieu, had arrived and stood talking to a desiccated youth in a pinstripe suit. There was no sign of Mr Mortimer. Fowler and Hilary stood in the room's exact centre, talking very fast. It was impossible to determine what their conversation was about, but it appeared to be heated.

'There goes Hilary,' said Page, 'making an exhibition of herself again.'

Certainly, Hilary's face, about which dirty hair fell in tangled fronds, showed considerable signs of distress. She was shaking her head from side to side, slapping one hand rhythmically on a carrier bag which the other hand grasped to her waist. There was a look almost of hatred about her which increased with every remark that Fowler made. As with all public disagreements it had the effect of clearing a space around them and reducing the level of the surrounding conversation.

'I can never understand what makes people quarrel in public,' Sarah remarked.

'In their case,' said Page, 'I should think it's a sort of reflex action.'

It did not take long for matters to reach a climax. Whether it was that Fowler had made some especially inflammatory remark or that the expression on his face had become intolerably sardonic, nobody quite knew, but it was as if some sort of electric current, simultaneously galvanizing and calming, had suddenly run through Hilary. She stopped speaking, placed the carrier bag neatly in the

111

space between her feet, and gazed about her almost vacantly. Then, picking up a glass of sherry from one of the tables, she lifted it high above her and with some deliberation poured it over Fowler's head. Strangely, Fowler did not move. He stood, quite motionless, as the brown liquid coursed down his face and seeped into the upper portion of his shirt, a strange gleam in his eyes as though – while regretting the personal inconvenience – he rather approved of what Hilary had done.

Watched by an intrigued crowd of spectators, Hilary turned on her heel and strode out of the room. Fowler produced a handkerchief and began to wipe his face.

'Are you all right?' asked Page.

'Don't ask fucking silly questions.'

'But seriously . . .'

'Get me a towel,' said Fowler. Shortly after this he disappeared to a corner of the room and was, ten minutes later, discovered to have left the building altogether. The carrier bag, which still lay in the middle of the floor, was retrieved and found to contain galleys of the *Radical Review*. Page volunteered to return these.

Shortly after this the party started to break up. The earnest young women began to disappear in ones or twos to evensong in elegant North Oxford chapels, to libraries or to solitary meals. Father Murphy drew his robes around him like the crinoline of a Victorian dowager and departed to celebrate Mass. Fowler, having disappeared, did not return. Though a handful of animated conversations persisted and a number of people appeared to have taken root in the room (an exhausted-looking girl had gone to sleep in an armchair) there seemed no point in staying. Several middle-aged women arrived mysteriously, began to remove glasses on trays and dispose of the paper cups. Page and I lit cigarettes and stood smoking, watching this process of tidying up, while Sarah drifted over to the array of pamphlets and began to thumb through a thick blue book, her mouth forming the words as she read them.

Mr Mortimer came through a side door and walked swiftly towards us. He appeared to have changed his tie. 'It was good of you to come,' he said, ignoring Page. 'A pity your friend had to go. I should have enjoyed speaking more to him.'

'I can't imagine the feeling was mutual.'

Mr Mortimer flashed a sharp, suspicious glance. He had not, I noticed, shaved with particular care. The bluish patches on his chin gave him a slightly sinister look.

'You must excuse me,' he said. 'It has been a trying day. Between ourselves I do not care for these gatherings. You would be surprised at the capacity of Catholic undergraduates to drink sherry, dear me yes. After which they say the most indiscreet things.' He looked suddenly tired, a little flustered. I murmured something about seeing him next week.

'Quite possibly. Your parents are staying at the Eastgate? Then I shall make a point of calling on them. You are not staying for the lecture? You are probably right. Goodbye David,' said Mr Mortimer, 'Mr Page, Miss . . . er.' We left him standing in the middle of the wide hall, his hands extended before him, palms down rather as if he were warming them at an imaginary fire, as about him the women shifted chairs back to their rightful places and began to chivvy the remaining guests from the room.

In one way or another Mr Mortimer's tea party was responsible for a number of events that took place during the ensuing days. The rift between Fowler and Hilary appeared to be total. They did not, as far as I knew, speak to each other again, although Fowler wrote her a number of letters, pleading and rancorous by turns: all of these, however, were returned to him unopened. Curiously, the experience did not seem to depress him though he became – if that were possible – even less sociable as a result, shutting himself away in his room and devoting himself entirely to the *Radical Review*. Indefatigable when it came to self-advertisement, Mr Mortimer did in fact send him some piece of writing, though it was not included in the first issue in amongst the articles on post-structuralism and the Bodhisattva, and went so far as to invite him to dinner. Fowler went, but would say nothing of what took place. Mr Mortimer, obscurely fascinated, continued to leave him messages at the college lodge but one could only speculate at the nature of their relationship.

However, what Mr Mortimer might or might not have said to one member of my immediate circle was slightly overshadowed by what he had definitely said to another. Page's behaviour since the tea party had been erratic. On the next morning he wandered into the college dining hall wearing only his pyjamas. Taxed on this irregularity he claimed that all his shirts were in the wash, but it was

113

felt that the spectacle was not simply attributable to negligence. That evening he got spectacularly drunk in the bar, morose and euphoric by turns, so spectacularly that on walking into Mr Mortimer's tutorial next morning (the Renaissance poets, considered by Mr Mortimer to be mightily diverting) he fell flat on his face and did not get up. Eventually he had to be carried back to the college by a brace of porters.

There followed an exchange of letters between Mr Mortimer and the college authorities, letters that hinged not so much on the fact of Page's collapse (which was undeniable) but on what he was supposed to have said to Mr Mortimer immediately before it (which was debatable). Mr Mortimer had been mildly shocked by the incident. 'I couldn't possible describe it,' he told me afterwards. 'In fact it was positively indescribable. Lying there,' said Mr Mortimer, emphasizing his words distinctly, 'like something out of Breughel. And the things he said. I couldn't possibly tell you them.'

I did not press him. Oddly, Mr Mortimer appeared to resent this want of interest.

The college authorities declined to act with any severity. There was, after all, no law against falling down drunk in front of Mr Mortimer. It was thought, however, that Page might profitably be transferred to another tutor. But Mr Mortimer had been busy writing letters and having confidential chats with other members of the faculty, most of whom resolutely refused to teach him. Meanwhile, as the dons argued and Mr Mortimer fulminated, Page loafed round the college, smoked quantities of tobacco, and remained sober for approximately two hours out of each twenty-four.

'I simply don't understand how anyone could be so unpleasant,' said Sarah later that evening as we sat in my rooms drinking coffee.

'If you mean Fowler it's happened before. You've seen it happen before.' She had.

'I don't mean Fowler, I mean you.'

'I thought my behaviour was exemplary.'

'Don't be stupid. Insulting remarks about Catholicism and then asking Mr Mortimer why he was so interested in your father.'

'It matters quite a lot to me what Mr Mortimer sees in my father.'

I had been subjected to a number of similar interrogations. It did not seem worth going through the reasons why I disliked Mr Mortimer, why I thought his wavering steps in the direction of

Catholicism simply opportunism, why I distrusted his obsessive interest in my father. I shook my head.

'I mean,' said Sarah, 'have you actually read that book of his?'

'No.'

'That didn't stop you sneering at it.'

'Pusey. Ango-Catholicism in the nineteenth century. Did Newman lower down a stuffed dove on Easter Sunday? It could be a shade more relevant.'

Sarah did not say anything. She was regarding me thoughtfully. When I placed a hand on her shoulder, she silently removed it.

13. Take Me to the River

Disappearances, the *dirzi* used to assert, seldom came singly: an ancient saying but one which latterly, applied to straying cows and mislaid children, had lost much of its effect. Nevertheless, it was used again, and to very great effect, was reiterated all round the village in the light of the news that emerged a day later, news whose magnitude was unprecedented and whose implications were alarming. The *dirzi*'s stock rose dramatically. Generally, his remarks had come to be regarded with derision, even by the credulous. But when you have remarked persistently that disappearances tend to be catching, and when the disappearance of a gardener's boy is followed by the spiriting-away of no less a person than the Commissioner of Police . . . Well! There was a sudden groundswell of support in the *dirzi*'s favour. That same evening he advised no fewer than seven pregnant mothers-to-be on the sex of their unborn children and diagnosed three cases of syphilis. All of which tended, obliquely, to confirm another of the *dirzi*'s sayings: that every earthquake will make at least one man happy.

The disappearance of the Commissioner of Police became apparent at midday, when he failed to arrived at the village gaol to inspect a cache of prisoners newly arrived from east of the river. This in itself was not unusual. Frequently, he failed to arrive at the gaol by two and on one occasion had not been there by five, but given the particularity of his instructions to understrappers and to the village headman who arrived after lunch it was thought politic to despatch a constable to his bungalow. The constable returned half-an-hour later in a state of some bewilderment. He was not an observant youth. He had not noticed, for instance, that the covering of faded pink forms had been removed from the door, nor that there were axe marks about the handle; merely that the door was half-open and that the Commissioner of Police, repeatedly importuned, did not reply from behind it. 'It is most unusual,' he reported. 'There positively no sign of him.'

Strange occurrences, the *dirzi* was fond of saying, usually had a reason behind them. After a further hour had elapsed a deputation set out for the bungalow, composed of three constables, the village headman and a number of idlers scenting diversion. They did not find the Commissioner of Police, but they found much else that was noteworthy. The axe marks on the door handle, the absence of the pink forms produced a shaking of heads ('It *most* unusual'), a clicking of tongues and a reluctance to venture further. But it was mid-afternoon now; an interested crowd had begun to gather. The editor of the *Sentinel* was there, licking his pencil and itching to interview the village headman. A police constable, greatly daring, pulled the door open to its furthest extent and peered inside.

The Commissioner of Police was not known for meticulous house-keeping but it was clear that what lay inside the bungalow was not merely the result of negligence. For a start there was a dead chicken lying just beyond the door, its head neatly severed, and a quantity of dark blood oozing out over the coconut matting: beyond this a heap of crockery – smashed cups and fractured plates. These discoveries, relayed to the waiting crowd, prompted the most lurid speculations. Dead chickens! Blood! Smashed crockery! It was confidently pre-dicted that a search of the bedrooms would produce nothing less than the body of the Commissioner of Police dangling from a meat hook, or cut into quarters and hidden beneath the mattress. Enquiry brought more prosaic results. The door of the Commissioner of Police's bedroom, forced open, revealed only an unmade bed and a twisting, serpentine pile of soiled linen. What had happened? The Commissioner of Police's clothes were still in his wardrobe. His watch – a giant lump of metal like a cauliflower – was still lying on the bedside table, along with other more confidential items. There was an ashtray on the chair which contained a single cigarette, half-smoked, suggesting that so abrupt had been the Commissioner of Police's departure that he had not had time to finish it.

Aberration? Lunacy? Abduction? A Commissioner of Police had been kidnapped six months ago some miles away, east of the river, by rebels or insurgents, nobody quite knew, and found down a well with his genitals stuffed into his mouth. There had not been a ransom demand. Reminded of this and other shocking outrages that had befallen public servants, the little group of men became thoughtful. The goverment ought to be alerted. The government would undoubtedly send troops, but even this was preferable to the

117

spectacle of the Commissioner of Police, head down in a well, with his mouth stuffed . . .

The flies buzzed. The array of faces outside the door became positively kaleidoscopic. Finally the village headman proposed a search of the kitchen: 'It may be there someone there.' At this faces brightened. The kitchen! That was certainly the place to search! What might not be found in the kitchen? There was a purposeful stampede across the obstacle course of broken crockery, down a small flight of stairs into the evil-smelling den where the Commissioner of Police did his cooking.

Here they found something more momentous – or rather two things (it was fortunate that the *dirzi* was elsewhere). One was the head of the Commissioner of Police's favourite goat, staring exopthalmically from a shelf. The other was a small, snivelling girl who was discovered wrapped up in a blanket, lying half in and half out of a cupboard. Slapped, cajoled, humoured and finally threatened, the girl revealed that she had been hidng in the cupboard since late the previous evening. There followed an exhaustive catechism.

What was she doing in the house of the Commissioner of Police? She was the Commissioner of Police's mistress. What was she doing hiding in the cupboard? She had been frightened. By whom? By the men who had come last night. Which men? Strange men, not from the village. Strange men, with loud voices and staring eyes. They had burst into the Commissioner of Police's bedroom, when, when . . . had dragged him from his bed and beaten him with flails, told her that her throat would be cut if she so much as left the house. Evil men. They had taken the Commissioner of Police's tea service – a gift from his uncle in the government – and trampled on it, had seized his goat and slaughtered it before him. They had . . . called her names she would rather not repeat. Wicked men. They had dragged the Commissioner of Police into his kitchen and forced him to cook food which they had then fed to his chickens. They had asked the Commissioner of Police numbers of questions – about the village, about its inhabitants. They had stuffed his mouth with rags to prevent him crying out. And then they had gone, taking him with them, wrapped in a sack. There had been noises of a cart moving off, and then silence.

There was not a great deal that could be done. The Commissioner

118

of Police's house was put under guard and the fragments of the tea service swept up and placed in an earthenware jar. The girl was allowed to go, the crowd ordered to disperse, which it resolutely declined to do. Messengers were sent here and there, east of the river, to adjoining villages, to obscure hamlets where dull-eyed peasants – unaware, perhaps, that there was such a thing as a Commissioner of Police, still less that he had been kidnapped – shook their heads with perfect indifference.

It was all to no avail. It was as if the Commissioner of Police had ceased to exist. There was no ransom note, no hint as to his whereabouts. A government official arrived in a motor car, asked several vaguely worded questions, remarked that it was all very distressing and departed. He made no mention of the appointment of any successor.

And that was that. Within a week all memory of the Commissioner of Police appeared to have been erased from the popular consciousness. Though his disappearance was occasionally used as a means of dating momentous occurrences, he was never otherwise referred to in conversation. Monstrous and unnerving, the event seemed assimilable only by a conspiracy of silence. The Commissioner of Police's house was allowed to fall into disrepair. The tea service remained, unregarded, in the earthenware jar but gangs of youths came and hunted his chickens all over the coconut matting, stole items from his wardrobe, so that for a time it was possible at the bazaar to see here a hat, there a tunic, or a jacket swathed like a tent over some undersized urchin. This practice, frowned upon as disrespectful, was eventually discontinued.

Thereafter, no tangible evidence of the Commissioner of Police's existence remained. His mistress went to live with the village shoemaker, something of a social climb-down, and no longer cared to speak of him. The enforcement of law became altogether less stringent. From which it might be deduced that the passing of the Commissioner of Police was not much regretted. And meanwhile the dust rose in distant puffs along the horizon, the pinpoints of light still flickered, unnoticed, except perhaps by the *dirzi* who – mindful that pride comes before a fall – kept his silence.

Shortly after these momentous events, some instinct compelled me to walk down the river bank to Dr Feelgood's. In the distance the outlines of the Cree Wharf formed a squat hump, rising to prod the purple sky. There was nobody there, though a pile of cut logs stacked a little way from the porch indicated recent activity. The door hung half-open: as you approached you were conscious of a terrific smell of damp which became quite overpowering when it closed behind you. In the half-light, made more shadowy by shuttered windows, it was barely possible to see. A beam of torch light, however, revealed familiar pieces of furniture: the two long tables, their tops covered in shiny, peeling plastic, a sofa, the high-backed chair on which Mr Mouzookseem used to sit and conduct his business. Chairs and card tables lay strewn all over the room as if the Queen of Brobdingnag had suddenly become enraged by her dolls' house and decided to redistribute its furniture.

Mice swarmed everywhere. Oblivious to the glare of the torchlight they ran over the sofas and under the chairs, spilled out of cushions, squirmed like an undulating furry carpet all over the floor. Solitude, or the lack of any human disturbance, had had a predictable effect: thousands of pairs of glinting bead eyes, shining out of the dust, chairs that appeared to disintegrate when you placed your hand on them, reduced and dissolved into layers of scampering fur. The floor seemed strangely uneven: it was only when you stooped down and ran a hand along the floor-boards that you realized that the unfamiliar ridges were caused largely by mouse dirt.

There was a fair amount of rubbish lying in the corners of the main room – tablecloths, a pair of shoes – and a number of signs of the haste in which it had been vacated: unwashed cups on the table-tops, half-empty bottles, their rims thick with dust, on the serving hatch which had served as a makeshift bar. Beyond the wicker door all was as it had been three months since – a cornucopia of news-print, tattered paper, stuck to the walls and stiff with lacquer. I picked a sheet up from the floor: it was a copy of the *Times of India*, dated 1951.

The torch, held high in the air and slanted downwards, cast enough light to allow a systematic examination. Passing slowly over the columns of faded print, monitoring the archaic typefaces, it was possible to feel a certain amount of regret for the demise of Mr Mouzookseem, a sensation increased by the tangible reminders of his past. It would have been appropriate now had there been voices from the other side of the door: 'Sir, you are incapable. I regret I must ask you to leave. Come, Aisha, a hand here with the gentleman. What a weight! He had better stay there on the floor – no one will mind,' etc. etc., the clink of bottles and skittish laughter as well as the rustlings and squeakings and the sounds of unregarded mice. It was as if Dr Feelgood's existed not, in its present state, as a series of empty rooms full of rotting lumber but as a series of mental pictures, like Breughel brought up to date: fat peasants lying asleep with their heads on the table, the Asian sluts giggling as they sat off duty drinking Seven-Up on the veranda. Mr Mouzookseem haggling with shifty-eyed men over the supply of contraband spirits. These were characteristic images, but they existed elsewhere, were invested – time having moved on, become roseate and illusory – with a spurious glamour that precise recollection might not have allowed.

They, or at any rate the first image, had also been responsible for an incident which, as it took mental shape, seemed to have distinct bearing on all that followed, the incident of the brandy. As I have remarked, Dr Feelgood's was the only place in the village where you could get brandy, or almost the only place, and Mr Mouzookseem, seeing that he operated a one-man cartel, rather fancied himself as a connoisseur. In fact, he operated a spectacular confidence trick whereby the menu at Dr Feelgood's – a tattered sheet of paper with the items scrawled on it in red ink – advertised various grades ranging from 'quality' to 'superior'. All this, as I have also remarked, was patent nonsense – there was not so much as a thimbleful that did not come out of earthenware jars marked 'No 1 Special Export' – but it gave Mr Mouzookseem illimitable pleasure to pour this liquid into balloon glasses and sniff it suspiciously, a trick that occasionally deceived simple people.

Though Mr Mouzookseem claimed that he got his brandy from reputable sources (there was even talk of 'merchants') everybody knew that it was smuggled in from across the river by a local criminal called Nazeem Salman, a man famous in the village for possessing four wives. Whereupon contention arose. Because the Commissioner of Police liked brandy, despite being the nominal exponent of its prohibition, went so far as to make overtures to Salman for its supply on a regular basis. Salman, understandably, was put in something of a quandary, brandy having only a limited availability in this part of the world. He was anxious to humour Mr Mouzookseem, as a regular and generous customer, but he was also concerned to mollify the Commissioner of Police who had hitherto turned a blind eye to various irregular activities but might not, if thwarted, continue to do so. So, for a time, a compromise was effected, or rather, Salman (being a fair man) decided to double-cross both of his customers at the same time. Each consignment was split in half and both Mr Mouzookseem and the Commissioner of Police fobbed off with excuses about smashed bottles and peccant customs officials. It soon became clear, however, that demand was exceeding supply. Mr Mouzookseem had a shrewd idea that he was being traduced. The Commissioner of Police, meanwhile, developed an insatiable appetite for brandy. Tempers became strained. At one point somebody broke into Dr Feelgood's and stole two jars of No 1 Special Export. Mr Mouzookseem retaliated by bribing the editor of the *Sentinel* to write an anonymous article attacking drunkenness amongst government officials.

Finally, Mr Mouzookseem, who had caught which way the wind was blowing, and did not in any case believe the stories of smashed bottles and corrupt excisemen, came to Salman with a proposition. It was a dangerous task that he was engaged upon and poorly rewarded, given the extent of his domestic commitments. In exchange for a regular and undivided supply he would increase Salman's remuneration and give him in addition a cow and two chickens. The Commissioner of Police got no brandy that month. But the Commissioner of Police was not a stupid man. Informed that an entire consignment of No 1 Special Export had fallen overboard during a hazardous river-crossing, he offered to release Salman's brother-in-law from the town gaol. Financial gain and family loyalty fought an inconclusive battle and family loyalty might still have won, had not Mr Mouzookseem – who had a shrewd inkling of what was going on – suddenly upped his offer by three chickens and a goat. Again the Commissioner of Police went brandyless.

And so the business went on as Salman assembled quite a collection of livestock and greeted his relatives from gaol, until it assumed a more obvious aspect, became merely figurative. By which I mean that at this stage nobody really cared about the brandy, which was scarcely worth this exertion. Quite simply, it was symbolic of a clash of wills.

After three months of lame excuses and diminishing supplies the Commissioner of Police lost his temper. Salman, sent for and arraigned on the Commissioner of Police's best carpet, was presented with a simple yet compelling option: either all supplies of brandy came henceforth to the Commissioner of Police's bungalow, or the Commissioner of Police would cease to connive at the entire range of Salman's illegal trading activities. That just about did it. Salman had other lucrative lines that he did not wish to jeopardize for the sake of a few jars of inferior liquor; the line in dud contraceptives, the line in slabs of American chocolate. Though Mr Mouzookseem, driven in desperation to extravagant lengths, promised whole flocks of poultry, lakes of whisky and even hinted at the procuration of an elephant, Salman remained adamant. He had given his word to the Commissioner of Police and he dared not break it. Not even, Mr Mouzookseem suggested, for even more staggering allurements? No, Salman rather thought not. A thousand apologies, honoured Sir, but the next consignment of earthenware jars would, much as it offended his sensibilities, be delivered to the back door of the Commissioner of Police's bungalow.

And there, you might have thought, the matter would have been allowed to rest. Six earthenware jars were duly delivered a few days later, in the small hours of the morning. Counted, prised open and inspected some hours later by the Commissioner of Police's subordinates, they were found to contain syrup of figs. The open feud between Mr Mouzookseem and the Commissioner of Police dated from that moment.

In the top left-hand corner of the room the beam of torchlight revealed something that previously, a small islet adrift in a sea of print, I had not noticed. It was a small fold-up map of the world – one of those maps which exist in diaries and with the aid of simple origami can be extended to cover several square feet – curling at the edges and secured to the wall with rusty tin tacks. It was a rather elderly map. Looking at the outline of Africa you discovered names like Tanganyika, Zanzibar and Dutch East Africa. Quite a quarter of it was shaded red, denoting, as a colour-code obligingly explained, 'the confines of His Majesty's Empire', and there were dotted lines intended to represent the principal shipping routes. But more curious than this, more curious even than the whimsical embellishments – the miniature dreadnoughts in the channel, the lines of camels stretching across the Sahara – was a series of large crosses printed here and there, in black ink across the continents.

They appeared to follow no very clear pattern: a handful in Western Europe, a larger concentration in the Middle East and then extending further across the globe, an outcrop in India and Pakistan (though the name Pakistan appeared nowhere on the map), a few in even more outlandish places, in Burma, Borneo and Java. Several of the crosses had been linked together so that there was, for instance, a thin grey line connecting Delhi and Peshawar, another joining Haifa and Tunis.

What did they mean, these curling lines, the periodic crosses along their trajectories making them look for all the world like thin strands of barbed wire? For the moment I allowed myself to imagine that they were in some way connected with Mr Mouzookseem, existed as another fold in the voluminous garment that was his past.

Outside it was growing dark, the receding sun a great red stain in a dusky sky. Emerging from the front door it was possible to detect sounds of movement near the clump of trees adjoining the river bank. Two figures began to draw near, yet with an air of caution about their movements. I extinguished the torch, stepped backwards into the shadow of Dr Feelgood's and strained to catch the approaching voices.

'Yes, I am aware that there is somebody there. A *person*? I daresay it is a person. What else could it be? A police officer? Very likely. I should not be surprised if he runs away, they are all cowards these policemen. You think he may have heard us? With the amount of noise you are making I should consider it a certainty.'

I switched on the torch, held it up to my chin like a microphone so that they should see my face. I heard Mr Mouzookseem mutter something to his associate. The figures drew level.

'Oh, indeed. A thousand apologies – I thought you were a policeman. I was on the point of instructing Ali to hit you.'

Al, to whom Mr Mouzookseem nodded cursorily, was a gaunt, unsmiling man about a foot taller than his master. I gathered that he would not much have regretted the mistake.

'I'm very glad you didn't.'

Strangely, at first Mr Mouzookseem seemed to regard our meeting as the most natural thing in the world, as if we were old acquaintances who had chanced upon each other in the bazaar. He did not enquire what I was doing. Mr Mouzookseem had not changed outwardly. Only a certain incompleteness about his hands and a slightly wary expression suggested that all was not quite as it had been.

124

'You are revisiting – what is the expression – your *old haunts*? I am very pleased to see you. What a coincidence that I too should be here.'

'You're the last person I should have expected to see.'

Mr Mouzookseem grinned knowingly, displaying a row of discoloured, peg-like teeth. 'And why should that be? You have been listening to bazaar gossip. You have heard that fool of a *dirzi*.'

'They said you had gone . . . east of the river.'

'They said a great many things, I do not doubt. What is there east of the river? Idle peasants with fat wives and brown grass. Nothing there for me. No money. And Aisha saying she would go back to her grandfather. Her grandfather! Was it not so, Ali?'

Ali, his gaze fixed firmly on the ground beneath his feet, gave the merest suspicion of a nod.

'He is not a talker, Ali. I find that a useful quality. But you have had your problems here, is it not so? Fires. Poisonings. Or is this *dirzi*-talk, bazaar rumours? Tell me.'

I told him. Mr Mouzookseem, however, listened with only perfunctory attention. From time to time he would shift his gaze back in the direction of the village and mutter something indistinct in muffled tones to Ali. When I came, however, to the story of the Commissioner of Police and his kidnapping he expressed the keenest interest.

'Kidnapped! I would not have believed it. What an extraordinary occurrence – it gives me great pleasure to hear it.'

'You is a wicked man,' said Ali, without obvious irony.

'Possibly. They took him away you say and no more was ever heard of him? Astonishing! There was no ransom demand? They did not ask that the beggars should be let out of gaol? That is what usually happens. No, I thought not.'

I watched Mr Mouzookseem's face as he said this, but his response appeared to be transparently genuine. Possibly he had some suspicion of this, as he was at pains to pass on to another topic.

'No Commissioner of Police? Dear me! Trouble too, I shouldn't wonder. But what is this? Ali and I come here, expecting mice and empty bottles and we find only you. It is most surprising.'

I saw that Ali was carrying something in his left hand, a brown container, bound with rope and secured with a strap. He placed this on the ground, shielding it with his legs, almost, I thought, as if he would not like me to ask what it contained.

'I shan't disturb you.'

'You do not disturb us. No, that was not what I meant. But I am curious to know why you are here? Perhaps you will tell me?'

There was in Mr Mouzookseem's voice a shade of truculence, combined with mild bewilderment. I considered asking him point-blank about the cloakroom, about the piles of tattered newsprint, about the map. But there was about the two of them a tangible sense of unease, the impression that they wanted to be elsewhere, a hint that my reply ought simply to supply reassurance and not branch off into areas requiring labyrinthine explanation.

'There was a rumour that the place had been sold. I thought I'd come and see if there was anyone living here.'

Mr Mouzookseem nodded in a way that suggested he saw through my dishonesty and, to an extent, welcomed it.

'There is no one living here. Mice and rotting floorboards are all that is here. Perhaps one day *I* shall be here again. Who knows? We shall see. And now Ali and I must be off. There is much to do.'

As he spoke there came the sound of voices, borne on the wind, coming from the direction of the village. Mr Mouzookseem jerked his head sharply to one side for a moment and considered it. Then he gestured to Ali.

'Much to do. We shall meet again, Mr Castell. Who knows? Perhaps we shall meet again here. I should not be surprised. Come, Ali.'

I watched them disappear around the side of the building, Mr Mouzookseem proceeding with quite elephantine caution over the uneven ground. At the corner he halted and extended his hand up at right angles to his torso in a grotesque wave. Then he was gone.

Curiously, the encounter served neither to raise him nor to lower him in my estimation. The picture of Mr Mouzookseem that I had assembled in my mind – 'Aisha, more brandy for the gentleman' – was capable of withstanding the sight of him, furtive and ill-at-ease, standing in the gloom before Dr Feelgood's. The image, once conceived, was incapable of being altered, quite ineradicable. Mr Mouzookseem existed forever as a fat, esurient potentate, in an atmosphere of brandy, girls and fractured conversation; just as home was my father's study, the bonfires burning at the end of the garden; university, Miss Knox curled up in her armchair, leafless trees, Page showing his teeth as he smiled, and winter afternoons spent gazing out over darkening quadrangles.

14. Down There on a Visit

Though my father derived inexhaustible pleasure from my presence at Oxford he did not much enjoy visiting me there. Twice a year he and my mother would travel up by car, book rooms at a hotel – it might be the Eastgate or it might be the George – and occupy themselves with two or three days' low-spirited sightseeing, culminating in a meal for myself and such friends as I cared to produce in a restaurant off the High Street where the menu, and my father's appreciation of it, never varied. I found the experience a trying one: the visits to the college library where my father, ostentatiously silent, thumbed through medieval chronicles, the afternoon teas which my parents insisted I give them in my rooms, the morose walks by the river, brought mounting unease. There was an undeniable feeling of relief when they had gone.

It was not true, however, to say that no one enjoyed my parents' visits. On the contrary, my friends enjoyed themselves enormously. My father had a definite vogue among my immediate circle at Oxford, encouraged by my habit of reading his letters at lunch or recounting his more outrageous pronouncements to a wider public. The news of his arrival habitually brought a steady stream of visitors. Page would come and attempt to provoke my father with opinions on immigration; Fowler study him with the detachment of a zoologist who has discovered some obscure and valuable species of fauna. My father held varying opinions of my friends. Page, whose formal dress and deferential air impressed him, he rather admired. Fowler, in whose nonchalance he detected only rudeness, he held in utter contempt. Still, it was probable that my father found in these occasions, the tea parties enlivened by anecdote and tenacious opinions, a more attractive aspect of university life.

The problem was, I suppose, that my father's conception of what Oxford was, or what it should have been, belonged to another age; to the novels of Beerbohm and Compton Mackenzie. It pained him that the proctors no longer stalked the streets imposing curfews, that the undergraduates dressed no differently from students at any other university, that ancient quadrangles were now dwarfed by purpose-built accommodation blocks; pained him that nobody wore gowns, that bastions of gentlemanly prejudice had admitted women. Out of humour with the present my father sought in Oxford contact with the past. Deliberate archaisms – the striped boating blazers, the finalists, clad in subfusc, trooping down to Schools – delighted him, yet he had to search hard to find them. There had come into existence a demotic, modern city no key to which was contained in the pages of *Zuleika Dobson* and *Sinister Street*. Consequently, my father came to Oxford with the air of a man determined to find fault. One grew used to a daily catalogue of subtle depravities: the urchins playing football outside New College choir school, the shirts airing from windows in Peckwater Quad, the American tourists thronging the porch of All Souls. We had moved on, into a gaudy, shriller world.

But my father's place in the ebb and flow had not remained stationary. It is typical of children to imagine that their parents' lives have remained inviolable and unchanging, so much so that it takes something like divorce or serious illness to make you realize that they alter in the way that anybody else's life alters. My father's life had in the last few years undergone several notable developments. For a start, having reached the age of sixty he had retired from his job. The absence of insurance, absolution from the necessity of adding codicils to policies, did not seem to depress him. My mother too had resigned her position at County Hall and enrolled in a degree course at the University of East Anglia. It was impossible to say whether or not my father approved of this step. It was, no doubt, highly creditable that my mother should wish to take up academic study. My father enjoyed describing the extent of her endeavours to friends and would, when she graduated, enjoy the degree ceremony very much. Meanwhile, he continued to distrust clever women.

My father had not been idle in his retirement, though here, as with other aspects of his character, it was impossible to be precise about the nature of his achievements. Rather than devote himself to freemasonry or good works, both of which acitvities had previously taken up a great deal of his time, he decided to devote himself exclusively to his studies. Since the early disagreements with Mr Mortimer and the investigations into the etymology of my mother's name, my father's interest in East Anglian history had broadened immeasurably. A great many more books had been squeezed into his study, a great many more sides of paper covered with my father's slapdash, spider-crawl handwriting. He claimed, or so I gathered from infrequent letters, to have developed a completely new theory of early East Anglian history in which the rise of the Spaldas played a disproportionate part, and had even written a book about it.

Characteristically, having revealed this much my father would reveal no more. I gathered from my mother that there was some problem about the manuscript, that in at least one very important part it was not yet finished. Another suggestion was that it had been sent to the Oxford University Press, but that no decision had been reached on whether it would or would not be published.

They arrived on a cold Saturday morning towards the end of November. A gale was blowing in Front Quad, sending the leaves scurrying in small eddies about the feet of anyone who walked across it. The sky threatened rain. My parents looked peevish and resigned, spoke of car trouble on the way down, in a way that contrived to hint at mechanical failure while leaving no doubt that it had been caused by my father's appalling sense of direction. They did not come alone. In fact, they brought Mr Mortimer with them.

The effect of this trio in the doorway, sitting together on my sofa a few minues later, was disconcerting and had a predictable effect on conversation. Several confidences which I had been itching to impart were automatically jettisoned by the sight of Mr Mortimer, pink and beaming, fussing over the cups of tea which I handed first to my mother and then to my father and himself. He was at pains to assure me that his arrival had not been premeditated.

'Such a coincidence! Dear me, I was out walking in the High Street – as you know I have a number of small concerns which occasionally incline me in that direction – when I imagined that I saw your father. And dear me, do you know it *was* your father. Your mother too' – here Mr Mortimer inclined his head – 'and they invited me to accompany them.'

'Curious,' I said.

'Yes, it *was* curious,' said Mr Mortimer affably. He looked about him. 'Such an *elegant* set of rooms.' A wave of his hand apostrophized the off-white panelling, the mass of press cuttings which I had tacked to a notice board above the fireplace. 'It is very seldom that I penetrate into an undergraduate's rooms, but do you know, when I do I am rarely disappointed by the decoration.'

This was spoken in such an arch tone of voice that I felt certain it would provoke comment. However, my parents remained silent. Beyond greeting me they had not said anything since entering the room: they were both the sort of people who are happy to leave conversation to more accomplished performers. I had not seen my parents for some months, since August in fact, and now took the opportunity of studying them closely. My mother looked just as she always did, although her hair, which had begun to grey at the edges, gave her an air of benignity which had not previously been evident. The change in my father was most marked. He wore a pair of trousers even more stained and shabby than usual and a dowdy russet sports jacket. He did not look well. There were creases in his face, a pronounced sagging of skin which had not been there before. As I watched he turned and said something in an undertone to my mother.

'Dear. Your father was wondering what we were going to do about lunch?'

'Come and eat in hall. It's Saturday – there won't be many people lunching in. And then we could go and have coffee in the bar.'

Mr Mortimer looked at me with a glance that, translated, meant, 'I know your little game, and don't think I don't.' My father nodded.

'I'm not very hungry. I was just telling your mother I wasn't very hungry.'

'You can eat just as much or just as little as you like.'

Presently Mr Mortimer excused himself to visit the lavatory. I took an opportunity to ask about the book.

My mother inclined her head nervously in my direction, her way of indicating that one had said something imprudent.

'The book?' said my father slowly. 'It's come back. Not that you knew it wouldn't. I half expected it. It doesn't matter.' The expression on his face suggested that it mattered greatly. 'I suppose whoever read it didn't agree with it. I suppose they do these things properly.'

'I suppose they do.'

'What do you think about it?' said my father sharply, turning to my mother and contriving as he did so to knock his empty coffee cup on the floor. There was an awkward silence. Though my mother had obviously been asked the question before, it appeared (with equal obviousness) that it still disconcerted her. My mother had an ambivalent attitude towards my father's achievements, a suspicion that she ought to defer to him, tempered with a more general feeling that one ought to be sparing in one's praise. I suspected that my father slightly resented this gentle indulgence.

'I thought it was very good. I thought it was rather dense though. You know dear, your father will rather go on about things.'

(There was no doubt about it: my father *would* rather go on about things.)

We were interrupted by the return of Mr Mortimer, rubbing his hands together and diffusing a vague smell of soap and water. My mother, who was about to make some further remark about the book, stopped suddenly. We all looked at Mr Mortimer with the guilty, complicit air of people who do not want to be overheard.

Mr Mortimer was unabashed. 'Dear me, I was just thinking. You mentioned lunch. Perhaps you would care to come and lunch with me at Merton? I cannot promise anything epicurean – cold meat and so forth – but it will not be frugal.'

Those lunches at Merton! I could imagine those lunches at Merton. The exquisite boredom of them: the long polished table and the creaking of the college servants; Mr Mortimer making discreet small talk and being sniffily knowledgeable about the wine. There would be baskets of stale bread on the tables, trays of cold meats (about which Mr Mortimer would no doubt be a connoisseur) and afterwards, tiny cups of bitter coffee. My mother shook her head.

'I think we'd better eat here. It will only mean coming all the way back. Merton's rather a long way isn't it?'

Mr Mortimer began to say something that may have been 'taxis' but my father cut him short.

'No, we won't. It's very kind of you, but no. Besides, there's something I want to say.'

This was obviously some sort of prearranged signal. My mother rose to her feet and announced that she intended to look at the college library. Mr Mortimer volunteered to accompany her. Outside it had begun to rain: through the narrow window, which provided a slanting view of the quadrangle, I watched him raise an umbrella with pedantic efficiency. I was left alone with my father.

131

'Cigarette?'

'Do you know,' said my father, 'I think I will? Your mother thinks I've given up. I *have* given up,' said my father defiantly, helping himself from the packet. He had a preoccupied air, suggesting that whatever he wanted to say was not yet fully formed in his head, looked once or twice around the room, examined a magazine that was lying on the table, replaced it.

'How's that young woman of yours?'

'If you mean Sarah, she's very well. She said she'd come round after lunch. She said she particularly wanted to see you.'

My father's attitude to the young women to whom he was (infrequently) introduced verged on the prurient, an excuse for remarks that were wildly indiscreet and incorporating reminiscences of his own colourful bachelorhood. But he did not rise to the bait.

'You're not thinking of getting married?'

It is impossible to convey the complexity of tone that my father managed to inject into this remark; a mixture of apparent seriousness, marginal irony and truculent good humour. I, too, decided not to be drawn.

'No.'

'Good,' said my father, entirely straight-faced. 'I'm very pleased to hear it. I tell you, boy, the greatest mistake you can make is to get married too early. Not that you should wait too long either. I sometimes think,' said my father, 'that I shouldn't have waited so long with your mother.'

Comment seemed otiose. My father paused to see what effect this pronouncement would have and then set off on another tack.

'What do you think of Mortimer?'

The opportunity to deflate Mr Mortimer finally in my father's estimation was irresistible. I remembered the conversation on the stairs, Mr Mortimer's bald head luminous in the electric light, whispered confidences. Yet it struck me that there was almost something plaintive in the question, that my father had illusions about Mr Mortimer that he would rather not have mocked.

'I don't think it's for me to criticize your friends.'

'You don't like him do you?' said my father. 'I don't blame you, I suppose. In fact I think if I were your age I shouldn't like Mortimer. Do people like him here?'

'Not really.'

'I don't suppose they do, do they?' said my father vaguely. He bobbed his head in the direction of the door.

'Page can't stand him.'

'There aren't many people,' said my father, half-approving, 'whom that young man can stand.' He stood up, plunged his hands into his trouser pockets and leant against the back of the sofa.

'I won't take your friends out to dinner this evening. I don't feel up to it. And I daresay you'd rather be doing something else anyway.'

'That's not true,' I said, 'and you know it.'

'Is it? I'd like to think it is,' said my father. He looked unaccountably sad; a fat, elderly little man, rather too conscious of the probable destiny of fat, elderly little men. Nothing else was said until the return of Mr Mortimer and my mother, about whom there seemed a certain confederacy. Mr Mortimer made a great show of placing the wet umbrella in the wastepaper basket and then stood over it, hands aloft, as if he had just performed some sort of conjuring trick. My parents exchanged glances.

'We'd better go and queue for hall,' I said. 'If Mr Mortimer will excuse us.'

Mr Mortimer would. 'I shall go to the lodge,' he said, 'and summon a taxi.'

Outside in the quadrangle the rain continued to fall. A few bedraggled figures scurried under arches or stood in the lodge waiting for the downpour to cease. Twenty yards away, Fowler, carrying a pile of books under his arm, was walking intently in the direction of the library, quite oblivious to the water that cascaded over his face and neck. For some reason that I am not entirely able to remember – it may have been that I wanted to leave a note for somebody on my door or that I did not relish the prospect of reintroducing Fowler to my father – I instructed my parents to set out for the dining hall, where I would join them in a few minutes. Consequently, having lingered briefly in the passage I was able to watch their progress over the quadrangle.

There was in the exact centre of the quad a circular patch of grass whose position meant that a journey from my room to the distant arch of the dining hall required a certain amount of circumnavigation. Strangely, at the edge of the grass the group composed of my father, my mother and Mr Mortimer subdivided. My mother and Mr

133

Mortimer trailed at a snail's pace round the right-hand side of the lawn. My father, hands plunged deep into his pockets, head bent a little against the wind, strode off round the left-hand side and, having reached the arch, stood watching my mother and Mr Mortimer approach. There were a number of other figures beneath the arch, a couple of girls clutching box files, a handful of people waiting for lunch. My father made an incongruous figure in the group. Surrounded by the jeans, the chattering girls, grey hair plastered symmetrically to his scalp, I noticed that he was smiling grimly.

15. Don't Worry about the Government

On the night of my chance encounter with Mr Mouzookseem, an explosion occurred in the bazaar, sometime after twelve o'clock, causing only limited damage. A number of vending stalls, flimsy contrivances of wood and cloth, were blown into the air and descended to form scattered piles of debris, and a tray or two of fruit converted into a glistening pile of pulp, but the injury to life and limb was negligible. Such of the house owners around the bazaar as possessed windows found them blown out, or rather in, as the glass tended to spray in cascades over sleeping occupants, causing a number of superficial wounds. An old woman had a heart attack but no one, least of all the bazaar traders concerned with the retrieval of property, was particularly worried about *that*. The *dirzi*, convinced that the end of the world was at hand, was found on his knees outside his house confessing to exotic sins.

Beacons were lit in the bazaar and a small crowd gathered to gaze at the devastation, examine the rivulets of shattered glass and listen to the harangue of a local politician. Who had done this wicked thing? A silence. Was there any enemy of the village, any low reprobate (he would not say peasant) who would want to do this wicked thing? According to the tumult of accusation and counter-accusation there were a great many.

Somebody remembered the village shoemaker's recent public quarrel with certain of the bazaar traders over their refusal to grant him a stall. The politician, a little, elderly man, four feet six inches in height but monstrously fierce, announced himself tolerably convinced of the shoemaker's guilt and was roundly cheered by his audience (including the shoemaker who, unnoticed in the crowd, declined to confront popular prejudice). Several people set off in a body to the shoemaker's house where they threatened his wife, who was by now rather used to this sort of thing, threw stones at his chickens and ended up by setting fire to his roof. The conflagration remained unextinguished for some hours and the crowd enjoyed itself enormously.

The grey morning light permitted more sober reflection. The glass was swept up into piles. The body of the old woman was brought out and gravely examined. The *dirzi* looking somewhat sheepish, remarked that it was an outrage. What was to be done? And then somebody remembered that a government inspector was due to arrive later in the day to examine certain sanitary arrangements connected with the bazaar. Spirits rose. The politician, who had a quite proper contempt of government, suggested that they should interrogate all known malcontents with a view to summary punishment but he was overruled. Instead a catalogue of damage caused by the explosion was prepared and the village settled down to await the arrival of the government official.

He never came. Whether he had been detained, or had forgotten the appointment, or whether his visit existed simply in the popular imagination was never established.

As the day wore on the crowd dwindled away, first in ones and twos, and then in disgruntled, acrimonious knots, like children to whom some special treat or diversion has been denied. The politician remembered a previous engagement; stumped off to inflame a rival village on the subject of taxes. The *dirzi* was sommoned to somebody's deathbed. The village headman went back to tending his cattle.

Eventually there was only a handful of bored, resentful men standing in the patch of bare grass before the bazaar, shading their eyes against the sun, watched by a group of uncomprehending children. Until, after the hour set for the official's arrival had passed, even the children went away and only the men remained staring, a little self-consciously and with resignation, down the empty street.

As spring turned slowly into summer, the villagers became increasingly uneasy, worried by what was in their eyes a quite unusual phenomenon. It was simply this: government, or higher authority generally, seemed to have forgotten about them. When the official had failed to arrive to inspect sanitary arrangements relating to the bazaar it was first assumed that he had merely been delayed, or that there had been some confusion about the date of his visit, but when a week had passed it began to be doubted whether he would ever arrive at all. The new sanitary arrangements – something to do with the speedy disposal of refuse – were almost immediately forgotten and the bazaar relapsed into characteristic squalor.

Normally the absence of an official to carry out some perfunctory inspection would have alarmed no one. Unfortunately there had recently emerged other signs of negligence on the part of the government. The local police constables, bereft of their leader, clamoured that their salaries had not been paid. The travelling veterinary surgeon, who arrived at intervals to inspect sick cattle and treat cases of fowl pest, had not been seen in months, with the result that about a quarter of the village cattle had died. But more alarming than the absence of visitors (who, as they tended to ask awkward questions, were regarded as a nuisance) was the absolute absence of communication.

'It most unusual,' remarked the *dirzi*, who had appointed himself a sort of unoffical spokesman on this and other matters, to anyone who would listen. 'Where is they pink forms the Commissioner of Police would get? The forms asking how many cattle-thieves and pickpockets? Where the Commissioner of Police for that matter? Before if this happen they send troops and line up the men in the bazaar and ask questions. But there is nothing. I tell you, it would not happen five years ago.'

'You is right,' whomever it was he was speaking to would reply. 'And my Romesh, he that work in the gaol, say he have had no money in months. It all happen since that good-for-nothing Commissioner of Police go.'

Before long a suspicion arose that this was nothing more than an elaborate confidence trick on the government's part, that this negligence was intended to lull the village into a false sense of security, after which harsher measures could be introduced as a means of quelling resulting licentiousness. 'You wait,' advised the canny. 'They seeing what sort of people we is. They think we make merry hell down here, what with no Commissioner of Police, and then before you know it they send soldiers. But we too clever for that.'

Consequently for a time a semblance of normal life was maintained. But the villagers lacked resolve. There was an outbreak of petty theft, blatant, obtrusive theft which the police constables, whose salaries had still to be forwarded to them, declined to do anything about, and a riot in the bazaar. After this nobody minded very much if soldiers were sent. Each morning the main road leading to the village was anxiously scanned. Nobody came.

The irony of the situation was inescapable. Normally the villagers regarded government as a more or less unwarrantable imposition, an excuse for the levying of taxes and the asking of awkward questions about the sale of livestock. Confronted with the fact of its absence they became fretful: where once the government had been blamed for its intransigence it was now blamed for its inaction. As the *dirzi* put it: 'It not good enough. How they think we manage our own affairs? We is only simple people. It would not happen five years ago. Somebody steal a melon in them days and they send soldiers.'

Eventually there was a putting together of heads, a conferring, a discussion among the villagers as to suitable courses of action. What was to be done?

Somebody suggested that a deputation should be sent to the neighbouring village to enquire if they were experiencing similar problems, but this proposal was heavily defeated. 'You gives them people an inch and they takes a yard. Before you know where you is all the cattle get stolen and then where are you?'

Warily insular, the villagers declined to acquaint anyone else with their difficulties. Perhaps, suggested somebody else, a deputation ought then to be sent to the government or to one of its representatives? This proposal was warmly approved – a deputation had practically been appointed – when it was realized that nobody knew exactly where the deputation ought to be sent. The villagers were careless in their dealings with the outside world. They knew that until a short time ago, the tax collector arrived with unfailing regularity but they did not know where he came from, still less who had sent him. They supposed that he came from the cities. They had heard about the cities. The travelling salesmen, the refugees fleeing from war and uncertainty, had told them about the cities but they did not know where they were, still less in which direction one travelled to find them. In this respect the village resembled a permeable membrane, but permeable only from the outside. Though people might occasionally try to get in, it was only rarely that somebody attempted to get out.

At length somebody remembered the existence of a local tax collector, local to the extent that he lived fifty miles down the river, who had visited the village two years back to investigate a case of smuggling. Presumably this man knew something about the workings of government, would be able to provide some explanation of the apparent inactivity, would at any rate be able to reassure, provide some fragmentary guidelines for action.

The deputation padded off, watched by an admiring, optimistic crowd. It came back three days later, only a little wiser than it had been when it set off. The tax collector no longer lived at the village fifty miles down the river. The villagers disclaimed all knowledge of him, had, when pressed, grown hostile, thrown stones and finally driven them away. The deputation had, however, managed to garner one useful shred of information: 'They say no taxes collected there in three months. And no vet either. There not many cattle left down there. We didn't see any.'

It was all most alarming. Travellers who arrived in the village, and they did so only infrequently these days, were taken to the area of waste ground before the bazaar and interrogated. Morose, vacant men, beggars and pedlars mostly, they were almost without exception unable to shed any light on the situation. One or two of them claimed to have seen detachments of soldiery on the roads, to have observed 'whirlibirds' – by which expression they meant helicopters – in the sky, but none of them could say what this portended. There was trouble abroad, they said vaguely. They could not understand the villagers' resentment at the absence of tax collectors. ('You do what you damn like now, and no one to stop you. You not think of that?') But the villagers had thought of that. Strangely it was not a course of action that appealed to them. Given the choice of limitless licence, they recoiled.

Miss Cluff increased her visits now to the rate of one or two a day. It was not unusual for her to arrive just before lunch and stay until the early evening. She was nervous, much given to cigarettes, to staring out into the wide horizons with faint unease as if she expected whatever fears obsessed her to take tangible shape out there in the empty sky. We sat drinking wine in the garden and did not talk much. Miss Cluff attempted to help Caro with his reading, but after a couple of days admitted defeat.

'It's not that he has problems in making out the words, not that. It's the questions he asks. Jesus! Right now it's Trollope, *The Warden*, OK? So it's "What's a bishop? What's an archdeacon?" And then when you've told him, "Why doesn't the archdeacon tell the bishop to go and screw himself?" Isn't there anything more up-to-date you can give him to read?'

'I gave him a copy of *Metamorphosis*. He seemed to think it was rather puerile.'

'You're telling me. He asked me about that. Did I seriously think a man could turn into an insect? Did I know of any cases where men *had* turned into insects? I never was any good at explaining allegory,' said Miss Cluff, 'certainly not to literalists like Caro.'

Generally, when Miss Cluff did speak it was simply to relate speculation that she had picked up in the bazaar and from her servants.

'They say there's trouble, political trouble. Soldiers on the roads. Trouble back west.'

'Who says?'

'My houseboy for a start. Won't go back to the village after seven in the evening because he says the roads aren't safe.'

Through the window of the conservatory I could see Caro playing patience, studying each card intently as he placed it on the table in front of him.

'So what's going on?' said Miss Cluff, giving a little confidential grin.

'I don't know. I gather the tax collector failed to arrive last week – they come fairly regularly you know – and at first everyone thought he'd been delayed or was ill or something, but then they asked at the other villages down the river and found that nobody had paid a penny of tax in months.'

'You take my word for it,' said Miss Cluff sapiently, 'when governments forget to collect taxes then there's something very peculiar going on. It makes you wonder whether there still *is* a government.'

After this Miss Cluff became unusually good-humoured. Plainly the prospect of armed insurrection and the absence of authority failed to disturb her.

'We were in some African banana state once when they had a coup. Bobby had something to do with it I guess – I never found out what. Anyway, we were at a government reception when the news broke, talking to the minister for education, a sort of ape who probably couldn't have worked an abacus let alone all the computers the Yanks were sending him. There was an announcement over the tannoy and suddenly all these black men in pinstripes are running out of the room. The minister for education went *green*, jumped into a taxi and whistled off in the direction of the bank.'

Caro came out of the conservatory, looked uncertainly about him, saw Miss Cluff and smiled.

'I will make tea,' he announced. 'It is time that we had tea.' He turned to me. 'Your friend would like tea?'

'Fine,' said Miss Cluff. Caro bobbed his head and disappeared into the house.

The abortive reading sessions had raised Miss Cluff in Caro's estimation. Whereas he had formerly regarded her presence as both irritating and inexplicable – an extra chair in the garden, a second bottle of wine – her interest had dissolved his animosity. This change in attitude had been marked in a number of ways. Some time before he went so far as to make her a cake, a floury megalith, a foot square, smeared with chocolate sauce. Miss Cluff had not felt able to eat any of this but she had approved its design. Caro was appeased and, had I not prevented him, would have made another even larger cake. After this he limited himself to casting brief, admiring glances in Miss Cluff's direction or asking ingenuous questions. 'This Miss Cluff,' he would say, 'does she have a husband?' 'I believe so, but thousands of miles away.' 'Thousands of miles away, you say? That is very interesting. And what did you say was her first name?' 'Julie, *Caro mio*.' 'Julie,' he pronounces it with an Hispanic lilt, 'that too is very interesting. I shall remember that. I do not think I shall make her another cake. I shall certainly make her something else, but not perhaps a cake.'

However, the promised gift did not materialize. Though on one occasion Caro announced that he intended to construct a special curry and brought back numerous herbs and spices from the bazaar which he laid out in little heaps on the kitchen table, eventually something else emerged to claim his attention and the dish was never made. The green peppers, which Caro had purchased the previous day, quickly went rotten in the heat and had to be fed to the chickens. The bunches of herbs, now shrivelled and friable, were thrown away.

16. Party Chambers

Fowler's parties were known throughout Oxford as the type of entertainment at which anything might happen. The reason for this was not clear. The few that I had attended, dull, self-conscious gatherings, demonstrated that their appeal derived from the reputation of previous parties held long ago, long before most of the guests had arrived in Oxford. Although nothing ever happened, the possibility that something might happen sent a continuous electric current through the room so that every gesture or pronouncement produced nudges and pleasurable thrills of anticipation. It was considered something to have been asked and these parties, at which nothing ever happened, at which nobody got drunk, at which there was rarely even the letting-off of a fire-extinguisher, were the subject of interminable inquests in which quite ordinary behaviour was somehow made to seem exceptional. When Page and I, rather irritated by a particularly dreary evening and suspecting the existence of a myth, made some enquiries we discovered that earlier parties had not been without incident. Staircases had been demolished, the police had been called, fires had been lit: in short, they had been the focus for some pretty general depravity. It seemed that we had done Fowler an injustice.

Though the majority of the guests enjoyed themselves enormously, went away convinced that they had been part of some luminous event, it would be true to say that the host did not enjoy them at all. Fowler regarded the giving of parties as a social obligation which he could not very well avoid, whose evasion would redound very much to his discredit. He did not trouble to hide his disdain for the type of people he invited: 'Nice of you to come,' he would say to newcomers, '*fucking* nice.'

But there was a sardonic gleam in his eye that made more perceptive guests writhe with nervousness. It was not to be expected that Fowler would invite to his parties people he actually liked. The guests came from all over Oxford and the Home Counties, were of all ages, social groups and dispositions. A carful of hippies, pale long-haired anachronisms from the Iffley Road, curious middle-aged women of foreign extraction with their hair done up in buns, a don or two: they had only one thing in common – Fowler hated them.

At the house in Museum Road it was eleven o'clock in the evening and lights blazed from uncurtained windows. The sound of music, faint yet insistent, could be heard coming from an upstairs room.

'I suppose we needn't stay long,' said Sarah.

'I suppose not.'

Fowler came slowly down the stairs, a half-open bottle of wine cradled under his arm. At parties he presented himself only rarely to his guests, shutting himself away in a room at the top of the house and emerging at intervals to superintend the proceedings. We exchanged nods.

'There's a fucking great lot of people up there,' said Fowler. 'I don't know any of them but they seem to have been invited. If you see Page, tell him I want to talk to him.' He was wearing, in addition to the usual arrangement of white shirt and subfusc trousers, an uncharacteristic bow tie and dark sunglasses.

Upstairs perhaps as many as twenty people were gathered in Fowler's room. In the corner there was a small pile of the *Radical Review*, the top two or three copies slightly askew. The guests, scrutinized en masse, seemed neither foreign nor familiar. Page was talking to a pursy little man in a dinner jacket. As we entered the room he detached himself and came over.

'This is frightful. I can't tell you how glad I am you've come.'

'How long have you been here?'

'Two hours. Three hours. The usual thing with Fowler's parties. You come early hoping that something will happen and of course nothing ever does happen. So you just start getting drunk.'

He turned and picked up a copy of the magazine. 'Have you seen this? It's awful rubbish isn't it? Fowler spouting on about Post-Sexualism, whatever that is. Do you know what it is?' He threw the magazine on the floor. 'Does anybody here know what Post-Sexualism is?'

A slight tremor passed through the company, which stirred collectively like troubled dreamers. Nobody said anything. Page sat on the floor and put his head on his knees. 'I've got something I want to tell you,' he said.

The little man in the dinner jacket came up.

143

'Would your name be Fowler?'

'No. He's downstairs somewhere.'

'Oh dear. I had hoped to have a few words with him. He sent me an invitation and a copy of this.' He indicated the copies of the *Radical Review*. 'I wanted to talk to him about it.' The little man looked at me inquisitively. 'Are you anything to do with it?'

'There's a piece of mine in it.'

'The Post-Structuralist as Bodhisattva?'

'No. That was Fowler.'

'Oh dear. Never mind,' said the little man sadly. 'Perhaps I shall be able to speak to him later.'

Moving around the room one was able to detect the characteristic elements of Fowler's parties. The stale, sweetish smell of cannabis hung in the air. Girls sat in tight, crook-backed groups on the floor having earnest conversations. The music, rhythmic yet atonal, throbbed and juddered. A friend of Fowler's, a tall, grotesque boy named Micalef, was dancing with jerky, unco-ordinated movements alone by the record player. Sarah came up and put her hand on my arm.

'I think I'd better go.'

'Stay a bit. Half-an-hour,' I said. 'I've got to talk to Page.'

I suppose it was at this time that I finally realized it was all up with Sarah, despite the frequent attempts at self-deceit, the whispered assurances. I stood watching her for a moment, ill at ease, but inwardly preoccupied. It wanted only a few days to the end of term and she had much to occupy herself with. Whereas other people devoted vacations to relaxation and the completion of unfinished work, Sarah naturally devoted them to foreign travel. This Christmas it was India, an expedition on which I had flatly refused to accompany her. She was thinking of India now, or so I imagined, of air tickets and dusty, overcrowded Bombay trains.

'I'll see you tomorrow then.'

She kissed me lightly on the cheek, gave a glance that was half-annoyed, half-regretful and then was gone. Curiously, confronted with the realization of futility, here in the smoky atmosphere of Fowler's room, surrounded by a kaleidoscope of neutral faces, I felt nothing, even a kind of relief. Only tomorrow, faced with the propsect of an interminable Oxford Sunday, would it start to rankle.

Page, meanwhile, had risen to his feet and was looking vacantly around him, straining to eavesdrop on one of the several nearby conversations.

'I don't think much of this stuff.'

'Well have some of *this* stuff. I haven't felt so mellow in ages.'

'I don't think I feel very well.'

'God, you're not going to be sick again are you? Please God, don't let her be sick again.'

Page beckoned me over to him. We sat side by side, propped up against the wall, drinking from a bottle of red wine that Page produced from his inside pocket, wrapped in brown paper. Glassy-eyed, the sweat pouring down his white, angular face, he was nevertheless coherent.

'Look, I wanted to talk to you . . . I don't think I'll be around here, not in Oxford . . . much longer, but that's not the point.'

I nodded dully. For some reason it did not seem worth enquiring why Page was not going to be around in Oxford for much longer.

'It's about that bloody man Mortimer,' Page went on. 'Or rather not about Mortimer; about your father mostly. That book he wrote, the one you're always going on about, the one about East Anglia, the one he sent to the University Press.'

He took another pull at the bottle, blinked slightly, put his head very close to mine.

'Well, it was rejected. The syndics rejected it. All very well, you might say. After all, think how many books the syndics are asked to comment on each week? But did you know that Mortimer's one of the syndics?'

'I'd heard something of the sort.'

'Mortimer's one of the syndics. And he wrote them a letter, strongly urging them against publication. I've seen it,' said Page bitterly. 'Bloody fool will leave his correspondence lying all over his desk so the undergraduates will be impressed. *He wrote to them and he told them not to publish it.* I'm sorry,' said Page. 'I thought I'd better tell you.' He put his head on his knees again.

This party of Fowler's seemed reminiscent of earlier models. Micalef stood on a table ripping sheets out of a copy of the *Radical Review* and letting them fall slowly to the floor. A pale, listless girl was being persuaded to take off her clothes. Fowler was nowhere to be seen. I decided to leave.

There is in any case not much more to tell you about Oxford. Though my career there had another six months to run, though there were other parties, other conversations which might be thought to have a bearing on what came afterwards, other incidents involving Fowler, Sarah and a huge supporting cast, it seems in retrospect that all that was significant had already happened. It will not interest you to know that I idled away my time and performed execrably in the examinations, or that I applied myself with hectic diligence to my studies and achieved spectacular success (neither of which suggestions representing, by the way, a true picture of what went on in those six months).

My parents' visit, the conversations with Page and Sarah, the nagging feeling of purposes working themselves out in defiance of human will (my will) suggested some sort of climacteric. The future, the immediate future, advised patient resignation. Walking back through the deserted quadrangle to my room, the wind rushing through the passageways, brought back familiar images – the cliff-top figure watching the retreating ships, uneasily anticipating what might next appear over the horizon. Lodged here in limbo, the past so confused and unresolved as to be unquantifiable, the future unpredictable owing to the unravelling of present threads, one could feel only unease, and a little resentment.

The next morning revealed that at Fowler's party something indeed *had* happened, not unique (something very like it had happened once before) but of sufficient magnitude to invest Fowler's parties with an even more enviable reputation. At two o'clock in the morning Page put his arm through a window in the lavatory and would have bled to death had not Fowler, prompted by the noise to investigate, applied rudimentary first aid and sent somebody to summon help. They got an ambulance and Page – his face, according to Fowler, as white as bone china – was taken away to hospital where, despite the rudimentary first aid, he very nearly died. An investigation by the college authorities established nothing more than the fact that Page was drunk and that the incident was not accidental. Fowler never forgave Page for this. Such was his discomfiture that he never, so far as I recall, gave another party.

Upon his discharge from hospital, Page was given a year off by the college authorities, who deduced mental as well as intellectual instability – a year from which he never returned. Eventually he passed into college folklore, a figure to be brought out, polished and commented on ever more fancifully when the talk turned to college eccentrics. Mr Mortimer wrote a spirited letter to the college, regretting the whole business and there was an article in the university newspaper about the prevalence of undergraduate suicides. What Page thought about all this was never established. I never saw him again.

17. The Will of God

As I write the wildest rumours are circulating in the bazaar, the most implausible speculations being devoured as if they were invisible food and you might grow fat on fancy. Caro has been down to the village three times and on each occasion has returned bearing yet more improbable news. You would not believe that . . . It would have been thought impossible that . . . But no, I must compose my pen. I must try to tell you what actually happened.

Deprived for some months now of any outside interference in the running of their affairs, the villagers had viewed this negligence simply as misfortune. The taxes had not been collected; livestock had been left to die in the fields; the surrounding area had been plagued by petty thefts and niggling, motiveless acts of violence. However, as no one was prepared to do anything about it, it could scarcely be expected that matters would improve.

Now the villagers seemed curiously resigned to this lapse into sluttish antinomianism, into a world where nothing was ever done and nobody cared whether it was done or not – a resignation that was practically gleeful. 'It is the will of God,' they said.

'I is not going to question the will of God,' said the *dirzi*, with some hauteur, when it was suggested his rôle as a seer and visionary obliged him to offer guidance. 'You gets back to your fields and stop worrying yourself about things that don't concern you.' Nevertheless, the *dirzi*'s confidence in an all-seeing, benevolent deity whose general concern was the welfare of humanity, and whose specific concern was the welfare of the *dirzi*, was somewhat undermined. He could be seen occasionally at dusk returning from the fields, his prayer mat dangling behind him, a morose and solitary figure. 'I wonders sometimes,' he told acquaintances, 'whether I is cut out for this line of work. Is things going on here that I do not understand.'

The *dirzi* was no wiser than anyone else in the village. Yet gradually, as the weeks passed and no word came from higher authority, apprehension was replaced by a growing conviction that the village could get on perfectly well without it. It was hard to detect the origin of this idea, even less easy to determine its exponents, but before long it became clear that a number of the standard procedures of village life were being reapplied. A veterinary surgeon appeared, apparently from nowhere, and began to restore various of the village livestock to health. A number of villagers swore that their taxes had been collected and that they had to pay interest in respect of former evasions. This was very strange. The police constables began arresting people again, usually for the most trivial reasons and on the flimsiest of evidence. 'Why is you doing that?' a mother would demand, as her son was frog-marched to the town gaol. 'Who tells you to do that, I like to know?' To which the constables would reply: 'Never you mind. We has our orders. And you come too, perhaps, if you not careful.' Plainly there was a new power abroad in the land.

Eventually it was discovered that the village headman had allied himself to the editor of the *Sentinel* and the remaining constables and formed a committee to manage the affairs of the village: hence the summoning of a vet, the enforcement of law and order and the levying of taxes. The village headman's explanation of this course of action was a simple one. 'There is all that money around. They has been saving it, all of them. And this village still got to be run you know?' A few malcontents tried to remonstrate but the police constables, their salaries brought up to date, were not having any nonsense.

Public opinion, inflamed by the *Sentinel*, rather approved of this step. It was felt that the committee, by their insistence on the levying of taxes, had demonstrated impressive civic awareness. In fact the response was sufficiently emboldening for the committee to press ahead with a series of judicious measures designed to promote the public wellbeing. They instituted a curfew ('what all them people want to walk round the streets for after it dark?') and they enforced the admittedly slack regulations relating to the sale of liquor with enthusiasm.

After this, public response became markedly less enthusiastic, but the die appeared to have been cast. The committee announced that it intended to consider some imaginative schemes whose implementation could only be for the public good. These were not without interest. There was the scheme to close certain of the village roads and open others in the hope of creating a freer flow of traffic.

149

There was the scheme to build a fence round the village in the hope of excluding undesirable elements. Had the village headman and his associates been allowed complete licence for an extended period there was no knowing what they might have got up to. There were certainly fairly well-developed plans to proclaim the village a republic, with its own parliament and postage stamps. However, this petty if imaginative local despotism was suddenly thrown into turmoil by a totally unexpected event.

The government had fallen! This was the explanation of the months of neglect, of absent tax-collectors and negligent veterinary surgeons. There had been a revolution! A civil war! At the very least an inordinately bloody coup involving the wholesale slaughter of government ministers!

The rumour, which originated with a passing vendor of sweetmeats, gained credence when the *dirzi* returned next afternoon from the fields carrying a large, rusting lump of metal. It was a mortar shell. Its discovery whipped the villagers into a state of hysterical frenzy, an attitude the committee did its best to defuse: 'Is a lot of nonsense. If the government falling who make them fall, eh? You tells us that,' they said, uneasily. Later, when the rumours became too insistent to be ignored they said: 'So what if the government falls? We is running our own affairs now you know.'

When there were definite sightings of soldiers some miles down the river bank and once the sound far away of gunfire they said nothing at all. The villagers, obscurely, were rather cheered by the news. It might mean soldiers, it would almost definitely mean looting, the temporary disturbance of settled patterns of existence, but it would undoubtedly bring an end to uncertainty. It would also, as several people pointed out, mean an end to schemes involving fence-building.

Yet the villagers wanted confirmation. Expeditions set out east and west of the river in search of evidence of fighting. Groups of men stood in the bazaar monitoring the night sky in case it should contain flashes of distant explosions. It was all in vain. The expeditions found not so much as a cartridge case. The night sky remained opaque and silent.

At last a group of men arrived in the village, strange silent men dressed in dirty uniforms and carrying rifles, who sat on the ground near the bazaar in exhausted, confidential huddles. Strangely they committed none of the outrages traditionally associated with soldiers. They bought food from the bazaar, asked permission to draw up water from the wells. When the village headman approached, trailed by a handful of nervous police constables, they hung their heads respectfully. He must excuse their sudden appearance. They would not stay. In any case they were expected back west. The village headman, swiftly disguising his relief, acted with considerable shrewdness. 'That all right. You boys stay as long as you like. We not even charge you for the water. Back west eh? What happening there?'

The soldiers were surprised by his ignorance. Had he not heard that the government had fallen? That there had been war? That the country was in the hands of the New Revolutionary Congress? The village headman looked uncomfortable. 'I hears very little,' he said. before the soldiers left he asked them: 'Is you boys government or this Revolutionary Congress?' 'Revolutionary Congress,' they said. It had escaped the village headman's notice that several of them had scarlet stars sewn onto the shoulder flaps of their jackets. 'So what,' enquired the village headman, 'is this Revolutionary Congress going to be doing?'

But the soldiers did not know. They assumed, they said, that there would be some official communication, that new officials would be appointed. 'Is a great day,' they told the village headman. 'Now we is all free. Equal! You ought to organize a celebration.'

'I sees what I can do,' said the village headman morosely. Needless to say, no celebration was organized.

The soldiers left on the following day. At first the committee was inclined to disbelieve their story. 'We is doing nothing hasty,' they said, when questions were asked regarding the raising of curfew. 'For all we know they is making that up.'

The soldiers had not been making it up, however. Three days later a messenger arrived, resplendent in a bright blue uniform, bearing a large pink envelope addressed to the village headman. The letter it contained was a very long one: most of it was quite inexplicable. There was a great deal about the Revolutionary Congress and its principles. A page was devoted to an excoriation of the fallen government.

'A lot of hot air,' remarked the village headman. 'They not be troubling us, you see.'

But the document incorporated both principle and practice. The Congress, it said, was aware that numerous villages were suffering hardship caused by the absence of government officials. Consequently, new officials were in the process of being appointed. A new Commissioner of Police would be arriving in the region within the week.

The village headman was frankly incredulous. 'I does not believe it,' he observed to anyone who would listen. The police constables were crestfallen, but sceptical. The majority of the villagers, impressed by the pink envelope and the polysyllables, were astounded and on the whole in favour. 'Anything is better,' they said, 'than that headman collecting money that do not belong to him.'

Only the *dirzi* was unmoved. 'It is the will of God,' he said.

18. New Dawn Fades

Life in London, though it brought new acquaintances, fresh ways of looking at things and a diminution of rôle and immediate influence, also resurrected older connections. After Oxford the city still acted as a magnet for the clever, the ambitious and even for the indifferent. It appeared that one could do anything with unavoidable publicity or nothing with absolute anonymity.

This discovery, that one could find familiar faces lurking in every alleyway of metropolitan life, though initially startling, became eventually a predictable and even welcome addition to routine. The student journalist seen leaving offices in Fleet Street; the undergraduate actor found busking in the Strand: such sightings seemed not to be the product of coincidence but an inevitable coming together of ambition on the most suitable stage. Predominantly the effect was diverting. It was pleasant to test new experiences in the company of old acquaintances. The literary party, the newish film, the bachelor dinner: all these provided a keener thrill when witnessed in the company of somebody one already knew. For they could be added to the stock of existing lore, fitted neatly into lists of places visited and people seen, were footnotes in effect to a palimpsest commenced some years earlier.

Ultimately, however, one grew bored by the familiar juxtapositions, the unvarying social events, declined invitations to football matches and drinks parties where the talk consisted unfailingly of stale college gossip. The immediate past, looming again before one, seemed slightly jejune.

There were four of us in the flat, a number my mother and, for that matter, less irregular visitors thought excessive. Yet the rooms were spacious and their occupants discreet so that it was only in the early morning (when one wanted to use the bathroom) or the early evening (when one wanted to use the kitchen) that proximity became irksome. My flatmates seemed to have few friends – a characteristic I shared – but those they did were seldom invited round. There was a general feeling, unspoken yet implicit, that while gregariousness was all very well it did not do to live with gregarious people. We were a quiet little colony whose gossip revolved around books, wine and the prospects of the English cricket team.

Life after Oxford, initially confusing, settled down into a predictable and largely congenial pattern. My departure from the place, coincident both with a national slump and personal irresolution, led to a period of unemployment. These fretful, inconclusive months were dominated – or so it seems in retrospect – by a series of near misses or (depending on your point of view) narrow escapes. I nearly sat for All Souls, nearly went to study 'Creative Writing' at an obscure provincial university, nearly became a traveller for a raucous and philistine firm of publishers.

Though I might have been disconcerted by the world's lack of interest in my abilities, my father was frankly appalled. He took to bringing the envelopes containing elegantly worded rejection letters to me as I lay in bed and standing over me as I opened them.

One morning, in desperation he produced a tenuous but influential connection, an Uncle Roger whose lustre in the business world was such as to enable him to direct innumerable appropriate words into suitable corners. Uncle Roger turned out to be a fat, cigar-smoking fifty-year-old, who wore a cheap suit and had an office in Pimlico in which he appeared to do no work at all. His manner, however, was infinitely reassuring.

'Now, my dear sir,' he seemed to say, 'what is it that you want to be? A financier? Then perhaps I might introduce you to the governor of the Bank of England. A lawyer? Then possibly you might care to dine with some learned friends of mine, Lincolns Inn barristers all of them, this evening? A publisher? Excuse me one moment and I will telephone Lord Weidenfeld.' All this accompanied by furious puffs at the cigar and an apoplectic rolling of the eyes.

It took only half-an-hour's conversation to establish that Uncle Roger was a fraud but it was amusing – amusing for a week – to listen to his recitations of the number of friends who owed him favours and to attend a few, perfunctory, interviews with down-at-heel businessmen who looked you up and down and found you wanting in the same instant. None of them came to anything. I gathered, indirectly through Uncle Roger, that I lacked resolve. Faced with this indifference his attitude was still magnificent.

'Now, my dear sir,' he seemed to say, 'you have shown yourself idle. You have shown yourself unwilling to grasp opportunities when they are offered to you. But never mind! I have confidence in my abilities, if not in yours, so let us see what I can do.' As it turned out, he could do nothing.

Fortunately at this juncture something else came up. I had managed, in the intervals of haunting Uncle Roger's dingy offices off Warwick Square, to place a few newspaper articles, do a little writing for the weeklies. This, at any rate, was evidence of promise. Eventually I obtained a job as a junior copywriter in an advertising agency whose premises were situated to the north of Oxford Street. Here I sat and wrote cheerful little jingles about a variety of tinned food – for such was the 'line' that the agency followed – walking there and back each day from Victoria in the belief that the exercise would do me good. They were formative months.

Though the present seemed predictable and assimilable the past continued to obtrude in a way that could occasionally become disturbing. Paradoxically, undergraduate contemporaries one had liked the least, or from whom one had grown away, seemed the most anxious to keep in touch. People with whom one had exchanged barely a dozen words in the last year contrived ingenious ways of securing addresses; wrote newsy, interminable letters. They were pursuing traditional careers: lurching away on the backs of safe jobs in accountancy; undertaking teacher-training courses; doing something in the City. The tone of their letters suggested that they did not much enjoy it, that they found life outside the university a disappointment, a continual struggle to keep pace with glamorous contemporaries, a little fraught and slightly enervating.

All this is brought home, lodges insidiously in one's consciousness, one Saturday morning when the post brings letters both from Fowler and Sarah. Saturday morning in the flat constitutes perhaps the most enjoyable time of the week. Toby, the landlord, is at his cottage in the country. Dennis and I usually take the opportunity to eat a lesiurely breakfast in the drawing room. We are doing this now, lying sprawled on armchairs in our dressing gowns. Outside the rain falls in the square. Dennis too has received a letter which he is holding between finger and thumb rather as if he expects it to burst into flames.

'My God,' he says, 'it's from Luciano.' 'Luciano?' 'Luciano,' says

Dennis, 'who was round here last week. The one who pinched Toby's cigarettes. Lovely, langourous Luciano.'

Dennis is one of those fortunate men who look about ten years younger than their actual age, in his case – approximately – forty. At the right time, in the right sort of milieu and after the judicious application of lotions, he can occasionally be taken for twenty-five. Given the nature of his tastes this is an enviable attribute.

One speaks of milieu, yet Dennis's is uncertain. You might see him perhaps in a fashionable night-club, or drinking in a Chelsea pub. It is his intention, almost invariably realized, to keep the various parts of his life in watertight compartments. Not unnaturally this exclusiveness extends to his acquaintance. The bar proppers at the Queen's Head would be mildly suprised to learn of the teaching job (in a flagitious comprehensive) that exhausts his weekday energies, the habitués of Heaven and Rosa's Club astonished to learn of the youth-club work and the Sabbath attendance at Mass.

'What does Luciano say?' I ask. 'He says he doesn't love me any more,' says Dennis. 'What do you expect if you will carry on with wop waiters at the Savoy?' Dennis does not say anything. Beneath the self-absorption he does not seem particularly depressed.

I turn to my own correspondence. The letter from Fowler contains little that I do not already know. In the year or so since my departure from university his fortunes have been at a low ebb. He had failed to complete his thesis. His grant had finally run out; he spoke of vague literary plans.

'Interesting?' Dennis enquires. 'Marginally,' I say. 'Anyone I know?' 'No,' I say. 'No one you know.'

The introduction of friends to Dennis habitually brings understandable problems. In fact there has been a regrettable coldness between myself and an old college associate dating from the occasion when Dennis described him, in his hearing, as 'a languid-eyed lovely'. I scan the other letter which, among much breathless information – Miss Knox is a painstaking correspondent – proposes a visit.

Dennis re-emerges from behind the door, dressing gown flapping at his heels, a pint bottle of milk a third full in his left hand.

'Bloody Toby,' he announces, 'has gone down to the country again and taken all the tea spoons with him.' I suggest, indelicately, a portion of his anatomy that Dennis might use to stir his tea. 'Shocking youth,' says Dennis. He props the newspaper open on his lap, begins to work his way shortsightedly through the columns of smudged print. 'So no more Luciano?' I ask.

'That's right,' says Dennis, not looking up from the newspaper, 'but, my dear, don't trouble yourself about it.'

The morning wears on until the tea is cold and the toast leathery. Prompted by a photograph in the newspaper Dennis begins a speculative monologue on the subject of a girl called Suzy, the latest of an assortment of young women currently favoured by the landlord. 'I mean,' he says, 'she is enormous. *What do they do to each other?* I have this vision,' says Dennis, 'of Toby with his head trapped between those blubber thighs, slowly asphyxiating . . .'

I leave him seated by the fireplace, go back to my room, sit on the unmade bed and re-read Miss Knox's letter.

19. More Tales from the Riverbank

For several days the villagers – intrigued and excited by the prospect of the new Commissioner of Police's arrival – posted lookouts along the dusty dirt-track that led to the main street. Further afield, a mile or so from the outskirts, small boys were bribed to sit in tree-tops and monitor the distant horizon. They were given whistles and ordered to blow them if it seemed that anything, any vehicle, any person or any animal, were approaching.

Anxious to ingratiate themselves with the new official, and with an eye to the pronouncements of the New Revolutionary Congress, the villagers had prepared a modest yet enthusiastic welcome. Lines of bunting had been decked around the wooden coverings of the bazaar stalls. Trestle tables had been set out on the patch of waste ground in front of the bazaar and covered with an array of exotic fruits and such liquor as could be procured without affronting the sensibilities of the village headman. In addition, the *dirzi* had assembled a small group of young women in white robes and colourful headdresses and armed them with bunches of flowers which they were instructed to scatter when the new Commissioner of Police made his appearance.

The village headman, not unnaturally, refused to associate himself with the proceedings, confining himself to stumping round the bazaar examining the preparations with marked disapproval.

'What you want to do that for?' he asked the *dirzi* who, having assembled the young women was now rehearsing them in a welcoming song of his own composition. 'You is making one damn fool of yourself.' To the people who were preparing the fruit and lining up the trestle tables with painstaking symmetry, he said: 'What good you think that do? How you know he like fruit, eh? He might think you trying to poison him.' The village headman was the only person who laughed at this joke. His reputation, anyway, had lately undergone something of a decline.

'What it got to do with you?' asked the villagers. 'We tell you one thing. You not last long when the new Commissioner of Police come – that for certain.' The village headman, who had a sneaking suspicion in the back of his mind that this might be the case, did not say anything.

Three days passed during which public interest first held constant, flagged, was revived by the exhortation of the *dirzi* and then vanished completely.

'He will come tomorrow,' said the *dirzi* at the end of the first day. 'I feel it in my bones. We must be up early to make sure he not catch us unawares.' At noon on the second day he said: 'He has been delayed. He will come this evening, tomorrow morning. I is not certain.' Late on the afternoon of the third day he said: 'I do not understand this. What it say in that damn letter anyway?'

But the letter, when a search for its whereabouts was undertaken, seemed inexplicably to have disappeared. The village headman, taxed with its destruction, protested his innocence. 'I know nothing of letters,' he remarked. 'What I want to go tearing them up for I like to know?' 'But it addressed to you,' said his interlocutors. 'What you do with it, eh?' 'I does nothing,' said the village headman. 'I do not know what you talking about.' After this he shut himself up in his house and refused to come to the door.

Meanwhile the villagers' careful preparations began to look rather lacklustre. The exotic fruits, left in the sun, grew overripe and began to suppurate. Several small boys evinced an interest in the lines of bunting and removed it for some private purpose. The group of young women, rehearsed almost to distraction in the *dirzi*'s welcoming song, grew bored of sitting in the sun exchanging small talk while the *dirzi* fussed and exclaimed over their costumes, and drifted away. There were of course a number of false alarms. Having been issued with whistles the small boys could not, as they sat perched high in the tree tops, forbear to try them out. This happened several times, after which the whistles were confiscated and the small boys instructed to shout instead. 'And if you shouts when there no good reason you be in big trouble,' the *dirzi* told them. There was no shouting.

On the morning of the fourth day the lookouts were removed and the small boys told to go home. 'He is not coming,' said the village headman, encouraged by recent developments to venture out of his house. 'What I tell you, eh?' The *dirzi* refused to admit his own discomfort. 'He coming all right. He not suit himself to fit our convenience you know.' 'We sees about *that*,' said the village headman cheerfully.

Consequently, when late in the afternoon of the fourth day puffs of dust out on the dirt track indicated that a vehicle was approaching the village there was nobody there to see them. The first that the *dirzi* knew of the impending arrival was when a small boy ran up as he sat in a field contemplating the meagre body of a dead bird.

'There a cart coming down the village street,' gasped the small boy. 'You better come quick. There women in it too.' '*Women*!' exclaimed the *dirzi*. 'What you saying? You better not be playing games with me boy.' 'I is not playing any games,' said the small boy, affecting an injured tone. 'I seen them. Men too, but women sitting in the back. You better come.'

The *dirzi* jumped to his feet, seized his prayer mat and sprinted into the village with an alacrity that belied his years. Reaching the bazaar he found that a small crowd of villagers had gathered in front of the trestle tables, anxiously scanning the main street.

'It true what they say then?' gasped the *dirzi*, who was somewhat out of breath. 'There a cart coming. The Commissioner of Police?' 'It true,' said the villagers. 'And women in it too, by all accounts.'

A hurried attempt was made to restore various of the preparations that had been made to greet the Commissioner of Police's arrival. Such of the exotic fruits that had not succumbed to the sun's rays were brought out and arrayed on the trestle tables. Two strings of faded bunting were retrieved and draped about the tops of the bazaar stalls. The *dirzi* despatched messengers throughout the village and managed to assemble three of the young women, though not alas wearing their white robes.

By the time that these activities had been completed the vehicle was barely seventy yards away, as on either side expectant villagers began to line the road. It was a large cart, drawn by two oxen, with perhaps a dozen people sitting inside. As it drew nearer, a bell, manipulated by one of the passengers, began to clang with monotonous persistence. Afterwards it was never properly established whether the *dirzi* sank to his knees out of exhaustion or out of a wish to show respect to a representative of the government. Whatever the reason a number of the villagers were encouraged to follow suit and within seconds there were at least two hundred people abasing themselves in the dust, heads lowered, eyes cast down upon the ground. There was a silence, broken only by the creaking of the cart, the mild chatter of its occupants. Slowly the cart came to a halt. With equal slowness, the *dirzi* raised his head.

Then he let out a gasp of astonishment. There were a dozen people sitting in the cart. Standing aloft in the driver's seat, dressed in a blue uniform with a silver-buckle belt stemming the tide of his stomach, was Mr Mouzookseem. Behind him, their heads craned forward to form a circle of faces, were five or six of the Asian sluts and a number of men never before seen in the village, dressed in the uniforms of police constables. A low murmur ran through the crowd, a tumult of assertion and counter-assertion. 'I has never seen anything like it. What is things coming to?' 'A *prophet*. Did I not tell you he could predict the future?'

Standing by the side of the foremost bazaar stall, the villagers bowed down before me like flattened corn, it was possible to conduct a minute examination of Mr Mouzookseem as he stood aloft in the cart, hands folded over his chest, a peculiar smile playing over the corners of his mouth. In addition to the blue uniform he was wearing a pair of black boots, which lent him a slightly sinister appearance. There was a large scarlet star pinned to his breast. The Asian sluts, I noticed, were chastely got up, wore sober dresses and resolutely declined to giggle. Plainly somebody, probably Mr Mouzookseem, had impressed upon them the seriousness of the occasion.

For some time nothing happened. The villagers relapsed into silence. Mr Mouzookseem stamped his boot once or twice on the rim of the cart, but seemed content to let somebody else make the first move. The *dirzi* struggled slowly to his feet and spoke in a quavering voice.

'You is the new Commissioner of Police. That is it, eh?'

'I is the new Commissioner of Police,' said Mr Mouzookseem loudly and mockingly, showing his teeth. 'The Commissioner of Police of the New Revolutionary Congress.' He paused, addressed the *dirzi* in a slightly lower voice. 'From now on I am running this place.'

They brought a pair of steps and placed them by the side of the cart so that Mr Mouzookseem could descend without discomfort. The crowd flocked about him as he inspected the arrangements that had been made for his welcome.

'What a surprise! You have prepared a celebration in my honour? Where is it? This is it? I am gratified. Did I not say, Ali, that I doubted whether I would be welcomed back? I am most gratified.'

The exotic fruits, or what was left of them, were proffered for Mr

161

Mouzookseem's inspection but he declined to sample them. Confronted with the two lines of faded bunting he appeared to be slightly put out. 'You could have done better than this,' he said. 'I suppose there was nothing available? Well, it does not matter.'

The three young women, at a sign from the *dirzi*, struck up the welcoming song, but Mr Mouzookseem shook his head. 'We will have none of that,' he said. 'No music, please.'

Trailed by the police constables and the Asian sluts, watched by the wide-eyed crowd, Mr Mouzookseem proceeded on a tour of the bazaar, turning over pieces of silk that were laid out on the narrow trays, chewing occasionally on a piece of fruit that some anxious bazaar trader pressed into his hand. Pausing in front of one stall where there lay a small pile of wizened oranges he was heard to laugh very loudly. Judging the time right for sycophancy the *dirzi* began to laugh as well. Mr Mouzookseem turned sharply on his heel.

'Please to desist from this frightful noise,' he commanded. 'And you people, get about your business; get back to tending your fields and your children.'

But the crowd continued to watch as Mr Mouzookseem made his way with laborious efficiency around each of the bazaar stalls. It was growing late now, the ground before the bazaar a mass of slithering shadows as the villagers jostled each other to obtain a better view. The edge of the crowd drew backwards as Mr Mouzookseem approached, moved forwards again as he passed by. The villagers looked ill-at-ease and anxious. 'What is he doing?' they demanded of each other. 'What so interesting about the bazaar?' 'You wait,' advised the pessimistic. 'There something happening here and we is never going to hear the end of it.'

At length Mr Mouzookseem stopped in front of the last stall, declined the handful of figs which its owner offered him, and began to talk very loudly. His tones suggested that he thought some explanation of his arrival in the village was in order. He spoke in a peculiarly high-pitched voice, one hand fingering the scarlet star on his tunic.

'You think it strange that I should be the new Commissioner of Police? You are probably right. It *is* strange. But life is strange. There has been a revolution, yes. Far away governments have been falling, soldiers have been fighting.' Such was Mr Mouzookseem's excitement that he began to pronounce 'have' as 'haf'. 'You are all free, free I tell you. There is no more *tyranny*,' said Mr Mouzookseem in a final, dramatic conclusion.

After this the crowd dispersed. Mr Mouzookseem got hold of the *dirzi* and conducted a private conversation with him along more prosaic lines.

'You know what I mean by all that?' The *dirzi* blinked. 'It means you people don't trouble me and I won't come troubling you. That way we'll all get along fine.' 'I understands,' said the *dirzi*. He and Mr Mouzookseem retired to the town gaol and did not emerge for some time. The bazaar swiftly became deserted. The remainder of the exotic fruits were taken away and fed to the pigs.

'You are an ignorant people. A tree falls down,' said Mr Mouzookseem waving his hand expansively, 'and you think the end of the world has come. It rains and that dam'fool of a *dirzi* tells you all babies born blind.' The *dirzi* shifted uncomfortably at this public dismissal of his talents. 'Things,' said Mr Mouzookseem, and there was a hint of mischief in his voice, 'are not all they seem. Mouzookseem the brothel-keeper, you think, Mouzookseem the brandy-seller, not Mouzookseem the Commissioner of Police, the friend of the New Revolutionary Congress. But what does it matter? I tell you anything and you are so stupid you believe me. But life is strange . . .'

20. Terminal Jive

And so the day of Miss Knox's visit arrives, a Sunday towards the end of summer but with a keen breeze sweeping through the squares, sending morose sunbathers scurrying intermittently back to their houses, making Victoria station – where Miss Knox's train demands to be met – a cavern filled with rushing wind so that the dust swarms against your legs, rushes up and stings the backs of your hands. Miss Knox, found standing in front of the confectionery kiosk, is apologetic.

'I'm sorry you had to meet the train,' she says, 'but I knew I'd never be able to find your flat.' 'It doesn't matter,' I say, giving her an appraising glance, finding that everything one expected, the pebble spectacles, the fringe, is still there; that the mental portrait one had preserved of Miss Knox remains complete, untouchable.

We set off down the long expanse of Victoria to a side gate that takes you back to the road, with Miss Knox, a curious irregular gait making her resemble a species of human cork, casting nervous little glances of which she thinks I am unaware. It is confusing, disturbing, but after a little while pleasant to make remarks which recall, somewhere, remarks made before, to exclaim mutually at some expression of Miss Knox's coined two years previously which has lodged naggingly in the subconscious, pleasant to hear Miss Knox observe that it is good to see one again, pleasant also to return the compliment, whereupon Miss Knox relapses into a thoughtful silence. I have already devised ways in which the afternoon can be spent.

'We could go for a walk,' I suggest, 'or we could go back to the flat and have tea.' 'Who's going to be at the flat?' asks Miss Knox. 'Dennis probably.' 'Then we'll go for a walk,' says Miss Knox, who has heard from somewhere, from God knows what source, of Dennis.

And it is agreeable to wander down through the wide Pimlico squares, thread one's way through the lines of parked cars down to the river, agreeable to loiter through smaller, dirtier streets in the shadow of the Westminster Council estates and stand looking out over the water to the distant shores of Battersea as the trains rush overhead and conversation is punctuated by the rattle of shaking metal.

It is less agreeable to hear an account of all that has occupied Miss Knox's time in the past year, to listen to an estimation of the character of Tim, the chemistry student Miss Knox met in India, to register mentally all the reasons why his company is so infinitely preferable to one's own. There is a great deal about Tim, his spectacular intelligence, his power of bringing Miss Knox 'out of herself', a process of which Miss Knox evidently feels herself to be very much in need.

'It's a good relationship,' says Miss Knox, eyes darting from behind her spectacles as if I might be about to disagree. 'So was ours,' I say. 'That was a long time ago,' says Miss Knox defiantly. After this exchange conversation is only hesitantly resumed.

Across the river, through the gates of Battersea Park, Miss Knox detaches herself and goes off to examine a flowerbed. I watch as she bends over it, monitor the strange, shapeless blue frock that for as long as I can remember has been a fixture of Miss Knox's summer wardrobe. The breeze is whipping up now, the patch of grass on which we stand deserted except for a monstrous dwarf child playing vacantly in the dirt; Miss Knox's hair, disarranged, flying over her head in myriad tangles. I smoke a cigarette, watch Miss Knox stride self-consciously towards me, turn again and look at the river.

Predictably the talk turns to mutual acquaintances, Miss Knox's friends, who have dispersed to the four corners of the country pursuing a variety of useful occupations: teachers, lawyers, journalists: middle-class children dutifully accepting their birthrights. 'It must be so nice,' says Miss Knox wistfully, 'to be settled.'

It emerges that Miss Knox has enrolled herself in a course designed to provide her with the means of teaching English to foreigners. 'Does that mean you want to work abroad?' 'I don't know,' says Miss Knox vaguely. 'I don't know what will happen.' There is a pause. 'I've missed you,' says Miss Knox. I do not reply. 'Something quite important's going to happen. I thought I'd come and tell you about it.' 'How important?' I ask. 'Reasonably important,' says Miss Knox. 'I'm becoming a Roman Catholic.'

165

Given past conversations this does not seem especially surprising but I go through the motions of expressing astonishment. 'I've been having instruction from Father Murphy,' says Miss Knox confidentially. There is a pious, irrational gleam in her eye. 'And other people of course. Mr Mortimer was very helpful.' 'He hasn't come over himself then?' 'I don't think so. He says modest Anglo-Catholicism is more his line.' I have a brief vision of Mr Mortimer elaborating his spiritual dilemmas at the tea party at the Catholic Chaplaincy. 'He asks about you,' says Miss Knox, who is plainly determined not to let the topic of Mr Mortimer slip from her grasp, 'and about your father. He's not very well is he?' 'He's not,' I say. 'I'm sorry,' says Miss Knox.

We cross back over the Albert Bridge towards the Embankment where the sun gleams palely on the surface of the water, past a small file of Chelsea pensioners moving sedately in the direction of the Park.

'What do you think about it then?' asks Miss Knox, turning and twisting her fingers together in a white, knuckleless knot. 'About what?' 'About my becoming a Catholic?' says Miss Knox deliberately, suspecting feigned incomprehension. 'I don't see,' I say, 'what my opinion's got to do with it.' 'Still,' says Miss Knox, 'I'd like to know.'

It does not seem worth trying to undermine Miss Knox's self-confidence. Considering the proposition, turning over the scene of Miss Knox making her oblations at some popish altar, I realize that I do not care. 'I think it's a great idea,' I remark, but cautiously, so that there shall be no hint of disingenuousness. Miss Knox seems rather relieved. 'I'm glad,' she says. She gives my arm an affectionate little squeeze. This does not improve my temper.

The gesture imposes a spurious feeling of intimacy, of shared opinions and common experience. There is an exchange of smiles; Miss Knox as she speaks gives little jumps of pleasure, claps her hands together, looks at me shrewdly.

'You haven't changed,' she says. 'How can you tell?' 'Just intuition,' says Miss Knox, as we wander down the Victoria Embankment, casting occasional glances at the river. 'Your intuition,' I say. 'Oh yes,' says Miss Knox. 'You remember that magazine you used to write for, the *Radical Review*?' 'Could I forget it,' I say, thinking of the term's grant, never repaid, that went into the printing of the second issue. 'Well,' continues Miss Knox, 'I saw Fowler last week in Oxford.' 'How was he?' 'He seemed rather down. He never finished his thesis you know. I think he shares a house down the Iffley Road somewhere. I felt rather sorry for him.'

Suddenly I feel an intense hatred for Miss Knox, absolute contempt for her incurable optimism, her sympathy, her complacent estimations of other people's characters.

'It would have been a lot easier,' I say, 'if you'd hated me.' Miss Knox looks mildly perturbed by this, fresh from a world where such emotions are inadmissible. 'I couldn't do that,' she says. 'Anyway, what do you mean?' But it is impossible to tell Miss Knox to her face the thoughts of the last thirty seconds. I murmur something about disguising emotions. 'You're strange,' she says cheerfully. 'I always said so.'

Back in the direction of Pimlico the streets are inexplicably choked with cars and there are children playing haphazardly on the pavement. 'You'll come and have tea?' I ask. 'Sure,' says Miss Knox. 'I'd like to see where you live. I always think,' she continues, 'that you know so much more about a person if you can see where they live.' There is an almost childish sense of absurdity about Miss Knox as she says this.

We climb the two flights of stairs to the flat, come upon Dennis who is standing just inside the door, putting on his coat. 'Hel-*lo*,' says Dennis, with exaggerated courtesy. 'How very nice to see you.' 'We were just going to have tea,' I say, hinting to Dennis that he is welcome to stay. Dennis refuses to rise to the bait. 'You'll have to excuse me,' he says. 'I shall be late for Mass.' There is a strong suspicion of aftershave about him. 'You haven't got ten pounds have you?' 'I thought you were going to Mass,' I say maliciously. 'That's all very well,' says Dennis, 'but I have to meet someone afterwards.' The ten pounds is handed over and Dennis departs at speed, so that the sound of his footsteps can be heard echoing on the stairs.

Miss Knox and I retire to the kitchen where crockery is piled up in the sink and there are copies of the *Guardian* lying all over the floor.

'Lived in,' says Miss Knox. She perches on a stool, legs dangling in front of her, watches me as I make the tea. 'This Catholicism business,' I say, 'what did Mortimer have to do with it?' Miss Knox looks wary. 'Not much,' she says. 'He asked me if I wanted to discuss it with him. I said yes. He's a very intelligent man,' says Miss

Knox defensively. 'He advised me to do it. He said it wasn't a step he could take himself, but it was a step he thought I ought to take.' 'And you thought he was right?' 'A confirmation.' Miss Knox rattled her tea spoon against the side of her cup. 'I often wondered,' she says, 'just exactly what you had against Mr Mortimer.' 'It would take too long to explain,' I say. Miss Knox allows the subject to drop.

Tea drunk, cups washed up and left to drain on the rack, we proceed to my room where Miss Knox eyes the unmade bed, the books propped in ungainly piles against the wall, with amusement. 'You *haven't* changed,' she says.

'Outward appearances,' I tell her.

And it is still pleasant, pleasant up to a point, Miss Knox having consulted timetables, made efficient calculations with her wristwatch, to offer to escort her to the station, pleasant to wander again through the empty square where pigeons cluster in great brooding flocks and there is a distant view of towerblocks set against the horizon.

'I don't suppose,' says Miss Knox, 'that we shall see each other again for a while.' 'I don't suppose we shall,' I say. 'I'm going abroad,' says Miss Knox, still feeling that some explanation is needed. 'Spain. France. I'll send you a postcard.'

On Victoria Station Miss Knox puts her arm on my shoulder. 'It's been good to see you. I think a lot about you,' she says. 'Give my love to Tim,' I say. 'I'll do that,' says Miss Knox, declining to take offence. She reaches up and kisses my cheek. 'There,' she says. 'And now I must go.'

I watch briefly as she walks off towards the ticket barrier, stay until the blue frock recedes from vision into a jumble of porters and American tourists, turn away.

It is most unpleasant to return to the empty flat, sit abstractedly watching television and trying to read a novel that one of the weeklies has sent in for review, positively disagreeable to have to attempt to stem a cascade of memories that eventually form a sort of log-jam in my head, by which I am aware of their existence but cannot bring myself to examine them and let them float individually away.

At half-past-ten Dennis returns, a smell of alcohol added to the reek of aftershave. 'Your friend gone?' he asks. 'A flying visit,' I say.

'She had something to tell me.' 'I bet,' says Dennis, 'that you took her off into the bushes and *molested* her.' 'You,' I tell him, 'are an immoral, unregenerate queen.' 'Flattery,' says Dennis, who rather enjoys these sorts of insults. We smile at each other uneasily, with mock complicity.

When I return home from the bazaar, my intention being to acquaint Caro with the amazing news of Mr Mouzookseem, I find him in the front room silently flinging clothes into a large shapeless bag.

'What are you doing, *Caro mio?*'

'I am leaving,' says Caro sullenly. 'I am leaving you and I am not coming back.' He hurls a shirt into the bag, bends down and scrabbles amid a pile of socks. 'Look! See! I am packing my clothes . . .'

'They are my clothes,' I say, and indeed they are. I can see my best sports jacket protruding from the neck of the bag. Caro does not reply, but continues to hurl garments into the bag at breakneck speed. I watch him for a moment.

'Where will you go?' I ask him.

'That is none of your business.'

'You might at least tell me where you are going.'

'I am going to Miss Cluff's,' says Caro gravely, 'to *Julie*'s. She understands me. She will take care of me.'

I place my hand on the bag. 'You are going nowhere.'

'Please to remove your hand,' says Caro, seizing hold of it. 'I am going and there is nothing you can do to stop me.'

We tug for a moment at the bag, which eventually falls to the floor and deposits socks, shirts and ties all over the carpet. Weeping with rage Caro bends to retrieve them. I stand back, irresolute, watching his shaking back, his smooth forearms going nervously about their business.

'You'd better go then,' I say.

'There is food in the kitchen,' says Caro over his shoulder, 'and the beds are made. But there is one more thing I must tell you. I have read what you have been writing.'

'You know and I know, *Caro mio*, that you cannot read.'

Caro gets to his feet, slams the bag on the table in a cascade of socks and undergarments. 'You are wrong,' he shouts. 'I can read. I have taught myself to read – I and Julie. I have had no help from

169

you, but I have learnt. I have read your writing. And it is lies. All of
it is lies!'

'It is not lies, Caro.'

'All of what you have done before I know nothing of,' says Caro.
'But what you have done here I do know of. And it is lies. All of it is
lies!'

He goes out of the room, dragging the bag behind him. There is
silence, absolute silence. Not even the generator hums.

Within twenty-four hours of his arrival in the village the new Commissioner of Police announced several measures which were
designed to endear him to the majority of the villagers. The curfew
was abolished; the village headman placed under house arrest and all
regulations relating to the import and distribution of liquor
suspended until further notice. The *Sentinel* survived to print a
single issue, given over entirely to Mr Mouzookseem's arrival and
the merits of the New Revolutionary Congress, and was then
banned. A great deal was heard in these initial days of the New
Revolutionary Congress. One of the Asian sluts made a tour of the
village distributing scarlet stars and Mr Mouzookseem stuck leaflets
on every housefront in which its philosophies were encapsulated for
such as cared to read them. Needless to say, nobody did. After a few
days the leaflets were removed. The scarlet stars, mislaid, sold,
rusted in the sun, were not replaced.

Having allowed the villagers the spectacle of his arrival and one or
two further occasions on which he announced the new regulations,
Mr Mouzookseem retired from public view. The day-to-day running
of the village's affairs was left in the hands of the police constables
and a deputy commissioner – a novel appointment made, apparently, on Mr Mouzookseem's personal initiative. The *dirzi*'s elevation
to the post caused widespread amazement. 'What he do that for?' the
villagers asked one another. 'What the *dirzi* know about cattle
thieves, eh?'

The only person who was not amazed was the *dirzi* who, dressed in
a brand new uniform, strutted round the bazaar at all hours of the
day and night and made himself generally insufferable. He did not,
however, remark that it was the Will of God.

One other event occurred that might have been thought remarkable. A deputation of men was sent to Dr Feelgood's armed

with brooms and buckets of cleaning fluid. It was rumoured that Mr Mouzookseem occasionally visited the site to superintend whatever was going on. Eventually a poster appeared on various walls and trees around the village announcing a grand reopening night at which liquor would be served free of charge. The villagers regarded Mr Mouzookseem with a new respect. If this were the actions of its officials, to what other acts of benevolence might not the New Revolutionary Congress extend?

21. Great Eastern Land II

The news that my father was seriously ill did not come as a surprise. He had been ailing in quiet, unspectacular fashion for some time, rising late in the morning, retiring early in the evenings, disconcerted by his obvious exhaustion.

When I had seen him three months previously he had remarked, 'I'm tired. It's your mother running round to that damned university.' He had looked fretful and a little distracted, worrying about the arrangements for the club and society meetings with which he was still connected. On several occasions, confronted with trivial domestic concerns he had said, 'I'm getting too old for this sort of thing.' I failed to notice because I had always thought him indestructible.

The last few months had produced convincing proofs of his immortality. His friends had begun to die, intermittently at first and then with alarming regularity – the boys he had played football with on the Norwich estates in the 1930s, the colleagues who had bored him to distraction in the insurance office all those years – and my father became an inveterate funeral goer; a survivor, one of those solemn little men in black hats who stand outside churches with other little men in black hats so that you can almost imagine them thinking, 'It won't be me next: it'll be the other fellow.'

In the end my father quite got to enjoy funerals. He bought himself a black tie: there was talk of a new dark suit to replace the threadbare one he had worn at work, and I am fairly sure that he was negotiating for a pair of black gloves. My mother put her foot down about the gloves.

My father's attitude to his increasing frailty was uncharacteristic. He had never been the sort of parent who diagnoses tuberculosis from a slight cough: as a child one was, literally, not allowed to be ill. His own ill-health produced only resignation.

They telephoned me at work and told me he was dying. It is odd how one reacts in such situations. I can only remember turning to my Managing Director and telling him that I should probably need to take a week's holiday and then afterwards walking to buy a railway ticket at the travel agent's, feeling mildy disappointed because it would mean missing a party I had been invited to at the weekend.

Liverpool Street Station, early on a December evening, brought cause for reflection: familiar landmarks recalled previous journeys, journeys home from Oxford, of which this formed a laborious second leg, journeys back from unsuccessful metropolitan job interviews. Looking out from the carriage window of a stationary train, beneath the wide Victorian arches and the overcast sky, it was possible to rehearse the route: the jumble of blackened brickwork, asphalt car parks and the backs of grimy houses, leading on into the Essex suburbs, Shenfield, Romford and Ingatestone, and then away into the distance on the East Anglian line.

It is a hundred and eight miles from London to Norwich as the crow flies, slightly further as the train runs, two hours, two and a half if you want to venture as far as Yarmouth, the most easterly station in England. A curious journey, a strange mixture of concrete and clay, of city and country, of things going on and things not happening at all.

Travelling out of Liverpool Street your first impression is that London goes on for ever. It is not until the train reaches Romford, a quarter of an hour out, that one is truly conscious of there being countryside on either side of the track, though even this effect is reduced by an awareness of the firefly lights of Dagenham and Upminster away in the distance. And then, open country: white-painted houses jutting out from behind the trees and ploughed fields edging up to the track. This is East Anglia: dull you might say, intolerably dull, for where are the hills and valleys, the plunging contours that lend variety to landscape? Not here among the square churches, the tiny lanes trailing off to God knows where, the files of scrubby trees leading down from the track, becoming progressively smaller as they go. Look out of a carriage window, here for instance where Essex becomes Suffolk, when the train crosses the Stow just out of Manningtree, and you will see why my father was so incurably fascinated.

But there is more, much more, out beyond Ipswich where the line veers north west through the Suffolk market towns and the fields recede under the sombre sky. It is a landscape of wire fencing and stunted larches, pools of water, the overspill of the Ouse, of the Waveney seeping over the flat earth, an atrophied land. A land in which history reaches up at you, stares you in the face. Because the features of the landscape, the layout of the fields, the wedges of woodland along the horizon, the horizon that seems to fall away for ever, have not changed in a thousand years, in fifteen hundred years, since the days of Wehha, who begat Wuffa, who gave his name . . .

Field settlement, you must realize, is extremely ancient, parochial boundaries equally so. The church in the middle of the field near Diss, in which no one ever worships, its roof half-decayed and its windows smashed in, distributed about the floor in little fragments of purple glass, is probably thirteen hundred years old. Not, however, that it has always been like that. First, I should speculate, it was a pagan temple in which livestock were sacrificed to ancient, elemental gods, then – thanks to Redwald – it would have been simply a Christian altar, then perhaps a wooden shack, then (almost definitely) two hundred years later when the Danes were in the area, a heap of charred rubble, subsequently – rebuilt and refurbished – a modest stone structure tagged with the name of some local saint, and then, finally, extended by a local merchant anxious to secure the wellbeing of his soul by restoring its fabric, doubling the vicar's stipend and having twelve old men to pray for him after his death. Because history, remember, is a ragged business. This is how things happened in this part of the world, in this part of time, or rather we can only speculate, speculate as my father had done about what he saw around him, wanting to *explain* it and simultaneously his own role, his position in the scope of things.

There is not much more of this to tell. Time is running out anyway, the seconds are ticking away and I have written more, perhaps, than I ought to have written, much more. It is always the same. One begins with the intention simply of stating the facts and then a curious compulsion supervenes, one's pen runs away in an inky marathon, exhibits a life of its own, becomes uncontrollable.

Sometimes I stop for a moment and put down my pen, neatly blot the page in front of me, and wonder what you will make of this. After all it is a long time, fourteen hundred years near enough since Wehha begat Wuffa, who gave his name . . . two centuries since Parson   Woodeforde   cast   from   him   the   duplicitous   yet sweet-tempered Betsy White, half a millenium since Sir John Fastolf sat in his draughty halls at Caistor, watching the wind careering over the flats and the great boats drawn up on the shale. There is always wind, you understand, in Norfolk, for what is there to prevent it? The north wind sweeps down from Jutland and there is no landmass, there are no hills to divert it, simply the flat earth and the wet fields from Lynn through Norwich to Great Yarmouth.

But I urge you not to forget this, not to forget that it matters. We are defined by our past. Woodforde, John Paston, Wehha, Wuffa and Redwald, my father immersed in his spider's web of ancestry and connection; we are all a part of this; we are as one in the great mass of fact and fancy, plausible hypothesis and whimsical speculation (and who am I to differentiate? It will not be long before you find *that* out) that is the past, East Anglia, so called because of the East Angles . . . the Great Eastern Land.

22. At Dr Feelgood's II

It was generally agreed that Mr Mouzookseem's behaviour at the reopening of Dr Feelgood's did him the createst credit. To the crowd of villagers, half drawn out of curiosity, half lured by the free liquor, he was politely condescending. He shook hands; he asked the odd, perfunctory question, nodded when some compliment was paid, but it was clear that he was not prepared to enter into any deeper conversation. With persons of note, however, with the *dirzi* and the veterinary surgeon, his manner became positively deferential. This attitude was widely approved as being illustrative of a proper sense of priority. As the *dirzi* remarked: 'He not standing on ceremony, but he do know who is who.' Had Mr Mouzookseem treated village notables with hauteur or met baser elements with bonhomie he would have forfeited a large part of his respect.

The arrangements for the reopening proceeded from a conviction that Dr Feelgood's, like Todgers, could do it when it tried. A red carpet had been produced from somewhere and spread out inside the door. Brightly coloured Chinese lanterns hung from the ceiling so that the main room was bathed in queer, tinted light. Neither of these ornaments produced the effect that Mr Mouzookseem had intended. The red carpet in particular was regarded with suspicion. Being prudent and superstitious men the guests declined to step on it and at any time during the evening you might have seen a villager hopping over the scarlet square when he imagined that nobody was looking.

If Mr Mouzookseem was annoyed by this abuse of his hospitality he did not say so. He moved silently and without ostentation through the crowd of people, stopping occasionally to refill his glass or exchange a word with one of his subordinates. 'I is thinking you ought to make a speech, perhaps,' the *dirzi* suggested at one point early on in the proceedings, but Mr Mouzookseem shook his head. 'What do I want to make a speech for? These people have come here to enjoy themselves. They do not want to go hearing speeches.' 'Is only a suggestion,' said the *dirzi* humbly. Privately he did not particularly care whether Mr Mouzookseem made a speech or not.

Yet though Mr Mouzookseem thought it unnecessary to make a speech and protested that his guests had come merely to enjoy themselves, it was clear that for him at any rate the evening had a symbolic value. From time to time he would retire to an armchair that had been placed at the end of the room, a little apart from the row of tables and sofas, and sit contemplating the spectacle, his chin resting abstractedly on his hand. There was something about his attitude that discouraged the villagers from approaching him. A number, thinking to prosecute business interests, had brought gifts and documents proving their entitlement to various trading privileges but Mr Mouzookseem waved them away. 'Plenty of time,' he said, 'for that another day.'

Discomfited, the villagers retired, though a number of them left their gifts, mostly baskets of fruit, at his feet – a stratagem that was ostentatiously ignored. Public opinion tended to vindicate this approach. The *dirzi* sniffed contemptuously as he surveyed the piles of oranges and bananas. 'We all do know what that means,' he remarked. 'Some people have no respect.' In the end one of the Asian sluts removed the baskets to another room. The bazaar traders, conscious that they had been guilty of some social indiscretion, began rather shamefacedly to apologize.

Though the rebuke was felt to be appropriate, seeming even to augur well for the commercial prosperity of the village (no one liked the bazaar traders who were inclined to be autocratic and raise prices) its effect was to dampen spirits. As the editor of the *Sentinel* remarked to the *dirzi*: 'I not like it at all. All very well telling us to enjoy ourselves, but he sit there looking as if we doing something wrong.' 'He a little nervous,' said the *dirzi* who was conscious of a similar feeling of unease, 'that all. It mean a lot to him you know, opening up this place again.'

Something of this feeling communicated itself to Mr Mouzookseem. After several conversations with the handful of Asian sluts a battered gramophone was brought out and plugged into a socket in the wall. 'This liven things up, you see,' remarked the *dirzi*. 'I not know about that,' said the editor of the *Sentinel*. However, he consented to beat his foot upon the floor in time to the music.

Unfortunately the record player had much the same effect on the villagers as the square of red carpet. Several of them stuck their fingers in their ears and could only with difficulty be persuaded to remove them. Nevertheless, there was a general easing of tension. A few people began to dance, quietly and with deliberation, in the centre of the room. As I watched, Caro emerged through the door, leading Miss Cluff by the hand. Miss Cluff, dressed in a magenta frock, smiles sardonically as she catches my eye. Caro, plainly, is embarrassed.

'I did not expect to see you here,' he says, looking out of the corner of his eye at Miss Cluff. 'Nor I, you, *Caro mio*.' 'I do not want to upset you,' says Caro. 'I do not want for all the world to upset you, but Julie does not wish to speak to you.' 'I am not upset, *Caro mio*.' 'That is good then,' says Caro.

By means of some electric gadgetry the Chinese lanterns had been induced periodically to change colour. Caro and Miss Cluff danced beneath them, their arms clasped tightly about each other.

The bringing out of the gramophone had clearly appeased Mr Mouzookseem's sense of obligation to his guests. Seated in his chair, hands resting on his lap, he appeared to take no further interest in the proceedings. Nobody, least of all the *dirzi*, was deceived by this. 'You wait,' he advised, fancying he knew human nature, 'never mind that he not want to make speeches. Something going to happen, you see.'

The *dirzi* was not the only guest to congratulate himself on his prescience. A rumour circulated to the effect that Mr Mouzookseem was planning some extravagant finale to the evening, that a conjuror was being brought in from east of the river who would produce coloured handkerchiefs from empty boxes; that a troupe of dancing girls was shortly arriving to complement the activities of the Asian sluts. 'He up to something,' predicted the *dirzi*, who was rather depressed that he had not been taken into Mr Mouzookseem's confidence. But although Mr Mouzookseem had numerous conversations with the Asian sluts and on one occasion disappeared from the room for several minutes, there was no sign either of the conjuror or of the dancing girls: it was decided that these were a deliberate concoction on the part of the *dirzi*.

Moving to the far end of the room, away from the lanterns and the small group of lumbering dancers, it seemed possible to gain a further insight into Mr Mouzookseem's mind – an insight that proceeded from décor. Though the reopening of Dr Feelgood's was intended to instil a sense of continuity, to reassure the villagers that former modes of existence could be restored without hurt or inconvenience, it was clear that there had been substantial changes. The walls of Dr Feelgood's had been repainted, not, as was customary, in feeble emulsions, but in strong vivid colours. The faded linoleum, which had been a fixture for as long as one could remember, had been replaced by shiny matting; rickety tables gave way to more solid contrivances with plastic tops. It was hard not to believe that these alterations, though they might have satisfied an urge that was simply decorative, did not also reflect the change in Mr Mouzookseem's status, that the plastic chairs and the expensive paint had a deeper and symbolic significance.

23. Victims of the Past

He was dead by the time I arrived. Norwich station, grim and dark with the wind rushing along the platforms, produced only Uncle Roger who, it transpired, had been ordered to fetch me. Confronted even with human mortality, he contrived to be magnificent. 'It has been a very sad business,' he said at one stage during the journey home.

As we approached the house he said: 'It was damned tricky getting down here for this, I don't mind telling you.'

My mother, who opened the front door, said: 'He's dead. He died half an hour ago. You'd better come and see him.' She seemed exhausted, but not otherwise distressed.

We climbed the stairs together and crossed the landing to the main bedroom. My father was lying in the exact centre of the double bed, his eyes closed and his arms folded across his chest, hair – completely grey now – neatly parted in the centre. His face, though white and shrunken, was strangely serene. 'Did he know?' I asked. My mother considered this for a moment, smoothing her hand nervously down the sides of her skirt.

'I think he must have done, though we didn't tell him anything. But when they send you back from the hospital you must know that it's because they can't do anything and need the beds. He asked about you.' She extinguished the bedside lamp that had illuminated my father's face. 'It was a pity that you couldn't get here in time.' We stepped back onto the landing. 'Your room's not ready I'm afraid,' said my mother. 'But there's a sleeping bag on the bed. You'd better use that. Do you know, that's one thing I'll always remember about your father. He'd never use a sleeping bag. We once took one on holiday with us, years ago before you were born, and he wouldn't sleep in it. There was a terrific row about that.'

Uncle Roger was magnificent at dinner. 'My dear people,' he seemed to say, 'in life we are in the midst of death. We must keep our spirits up. We must not repine.' He drank half a bottle of wine and told stories of my father as a young man. My mother listened with polite interest. I could see that her mind was elsewhere. 'Your mother's taking it very well,' Uncle Roger confided at one point when she left the room to fetch some item from the kitchen.

When, after the meal was over, he began an involved account of a car trip that he and my father had undertaken to Lincolnshire, she announced that she was going to bed. 'You must excuse me,' she said. 'But there's a great deal to do tomorrow. I shall see you both at breakfast.' Thereafter Uncle Roger became confidential. 'A difficult man to get on with sometimes, your father,' he remarked more than once. 'Why . . .'

But whatever relevations Uncle Roger could impart on this subject seemed scarcely pertinent. There was a rumour, faint yet perceptible, that he and my father had had some major disagreement in their dealings with each other and that the relationship had never really recovered. I left Uncle Roger sitting by the fire with the remainder of the wine, still magnificent in his grief, and went to bed.

Pondering the remarks of my mother and Uncle Roger it was possible to arrive at a view of my father that was not dissimilar to theirs. He had been a truculent man, convinced that the best means of dealing with the negligent was to have 'a bloody good row' with them, but the truculence had been the result of something more than shortness of temper. My father had been an ambitious man, whose ambitions had been incompletely realized, a competitive man who had not grasped the most effective means of competing, an anachronistic man who, looking at the world *sub specie aeternis* and not liking what he saw, had deliberately sought his pleasure in the arcane and the archaic.

Something else had taken place at Dr Feelgood's which proved on reflection to be an integral part of all these developments. There were no mice. No tails whisking beneath the sides of ramshackle sofas, no bead- eyes peering like jet buttons from apertures in the wainscoting. This was not immediately noticeable. The eye, dazzled by the novelties of décor, took some time to register the absence of scurryings and hurryings, of squirming nests beneath the matting and faraway rodent squeakings. Though one might examine wainscoting in search of bolt holes, scan the floor for evidence of mouse droppings, no trace of them remained: a disturbing phenomenon for which the Chinese lanterns and the red carpet scarcely compensated . . .

*

They buried my father in a small church on the outskirts of the city where he and my mother had occasionally worshipped. There were a great many people there; the representatives of half-a-dozen charitable institutions, bowling clubs and masonic lodges, a large number of curious people whom neither my mother nor myself had ever seen before. A group of my father's discarded relatives arrived, the men wearing ill-fitting suits and the women covered in shiny jewellery. 'We saw it in the newspaper,' they said, explaining their tenuous connection to anyone who would listen. They sat at the back, ostentatiously, but a little overawed by the display of lustre and *éclat* in the front pews. It had been my father's ambition – frequently reiterated – to be remembered by the excellence of his funeral, and that ambition was achieved. Uncle Roger read the lesson. My mother shook hands with a great many elderly gentlemen she had not met before and would never meet again. Everybody agreed that my mother took it very well.

On the morning after the funeral I came into my father's study to find a small dapper figure sitting in the chair beneath the engraving of St Edmund. It was Mr Mortimer.

'What are you doing here?'

Mr Mortimer seemed somewhat flustered by my appearance. Clad in a dark suit, surmounted by a sober bow tie, a shade plumper than when I had seen him last, he was profuse in his apologies.

'Dear me. I am afraid that your mother may not have informed you of my arrival. I had hoped to be here yesterday but there was a meeting from which I could not satisfactorily absent myself. A sad business,' said Mr Mortimer. 'But one wants to make oneself useful. Knowing my interest in your father's line of work your mother asked if I would come and sort through his papers. And do you know,' said Mr Mortimer, 'that is exactly what I am doing at the moment?'

He gestured with his hand at the bookcases, which were vastly disarranged, and at the desk on which lay an edifice of books and papers.

'A man of varied pursuits, your father,' said Mr Mortimer carefully, 'but there is some interesting stuff here, some very interesting material.' Plainly Mr Mortimer relished nothing so greatly as the prospect of rearranging the papers of a dead acquaintance.

The cloakroom, illuminated only by the flickering light from under the door, revealed that refurbishment had not been confined to the main room of Dr Feelgood's. Turning to examine the folds of tattered newsprint, to consult some tangible reminder of Mr Mouzookseem, I discovered only a whitewashed wall. There was no sign of the map with its assembly of crosses, the connecting lines that had spoken of past journeys and arrivals. I placed my hand against the pale surface, hoping perhaps to find an indication that the newspaper still existed, that it had possibly been painted over. There remained no trace.

Why should Mr Mouzookseem wish to erase his past, so lovingly preserved, so painstakingly arrayed in a tide of print, in a testimony to his existence? Inexplicable at first, the problem quickly admitted solution. In the corner of the room, half-hidden under a pile of sacks and some empty bottles, there was a wedge of tattered paper. Excavation revealed the greater part of the world, curling at the edges, Surinam and China lodged in uneasy juxtaposition, stained with some deep, indelible ink. It could only be concluded that Mr Mouzookseem had destroyed the record of his past . . . because that past had never existed.

Seeing Mr Mortimer in my father's study, searching with his precise mind for 'interesting material' amongst the voluminous output of a lifetime brought back older memories: Mr Mortimer's sly winks as my father spoke of the problem of the Spread Eagle, the warning delivered on the stairhead, the first stirrings of resentment.

'What are you going to do with all this stuff?'

Mr Mortimer patted the small heap of books on the desk indulgently. 'Dear me. At this moment I scarcely know. I have made only the most cursory examination. Some of it will I imagine go to libraries. Your mother has kindly suggested that I choose a few volumes for myself. The majority will, I fear, have to be disposed of.'

'As far as I'm concerned it's staying here.'

'I fear,' said Mr Mortimer, 'that that will not be possible.'

'Look,' I said, 'I don't know if you have any conception at all of what was going on in my father's head . . .'

'Oh yes,' said Mr Mortimer. 'As a matter of fact I had an exact conception of what was going on in your father's head.'

*

They raided Dr Feelgood's shortly after midnight. The music had grown so loud and the guests so animated that it took some time for the villagers to realize that the piercing whistles and the whirling figures who suddenly emerged onto the dance floor denoted something more than overexuberance. Curiously, this intrusion coincided with the absence from the room of Mr Mouzookseem. The *dirzi*, on whom responsibility for the gathering immediately devolved, said: 'What do you think you doing? This is a private party you know, not one of your dam' cat-houses.' Later he said: 'Is not me who running this. You give me two minute and I get the owner.' Shortly afterwards he said: 'I tell you I not knowing him. In any case I only arrive five minutes since.'

It was all to no avail. Though search parties were sent to the upper rooms of the house there was no sign of Mr Mouzookseem. The police, surly, inquisitive men, lined the villagers up in rows and began to search them. Somebody (it was never subsequently established whether this was a policeman or a villager hoping to curry favour) put his foot through the record player. The music stopped.

Standing in the cloakroom, listening, as the *dirzi*'s depositions became first self-righteous, then respectful and then entirely craven, it was possible to reflect on the symmetry of recent events. In fact there was a certain inevitability about the proceedings, about the information which the *dirzi* – more by luck than judgement – managed to extract from his interlocutors. 'Who is he? He the new Commissioner of Police, you not know that? You in trouble when he come back. If I were you I go away now . . . You say he *not* the Commissioner of Police? I do not understand. We got a letter from the New Revolutionary Congress, they that won the war . . .' The information that followed, relayed in the *dirzi*'s quavering tones, did not in the light of previous revelations come as a surprise. 'You say government win war? Nobody tell us. We get letter saying there New Revolutionary Congress, Congress that send Commissioner of Police . . .' Eventually the *dirzi*'s voice was drowned by a welter of accusation and counter-accusation and the sound of glasses being thrown on the floor.

Voices behind the door advised the urgency of immediate problems. The *dirzi* was becoming plaintive. 'I do not understand. It say in letter . . . No I not read letter. I is only a simple man, you understand.' Mercifully, whoever had redecorated the cloakroom

184

had not troubled to alter the exits and entrances. Beyond the window the night air beckoned. It was time to leave. Into the dark air, the same backyard, wreathed in the shadows of piles of timber, on through the watery grass. There was mist coming up from the fields, pale, nebulous mist, so that the outlines of the Cree Wharf, black and solid in the distance, disappeared from time to time amid the swirling vapour. Back down the path it was possible to detect the sound of shouting. A small procession of people, moving two by two and apparently under some constraint, had begun to emerge from the door of Dr Feelgood's.

There was a silence. In the garden, beyond the window, it was possible to make out wisps of smoke rising from a small fire that was burning beneath the trees. As I watched, my mother emerged out of the smoke carrying a plastic bag which she proceeded to drop onto the flames.

'I knew all about it,' Mr Mortimer went on. 'You forget, I knew your father for a great many years. Oh dear me, yes, I knew all about his interests. I discussed them with him fifteen years ago, and then I stopped. And do you know why I stopped?' said Mr Mortimer. 'I stopped because I lost interest, and because he was *wrong*. Those theories about the Spaldas, about your history – they are quite fanciful. They are very amusing, and they show an admirable grasp of source material, though your father had no idea of how to distinguish between a fact and a hypothesis. In fact I would go further. Your father, much as it pains me to say it, did not want to distinguish between a fact and hypothesis. He was obsessed,' said Mr Mortimer, 'and like many obsessed people he did not wish to accept the evidence of his eyes.'

'You're lying,' I said.

'I am *not* lying,' said Mr Mortimer evenly. He pulled off his spectacles and, drawing a handkerchief out of his jacket pocket, began calmly to polish them. 'What possible reason would I have for lying? Your father was an inquisitive but unscholarly man. He had a lot of fanciful theories about history, his history, our history. At first I tried to talk him out of them. And then, being a prudent man, I desisted. After all, what business was it of mine?'

'You forget,' I said, 'that I studied all this as well.'

'Yes, you did, didn't you?' Mr Mortimer placed his spectacles on the bridge of his nose, gave an enigmatic little glance. 'And dear me, you would have been much better off not doing so. There are, believe me, much more profitable lines of study. But I warned you. I took you aside and I *warned* you about all this. And precious little good,' said Mr Mortimer, 'it seems to have done you.'

'What was there to warn me about?'

'That you don't take liberties with the past. That you don't tamper with it for your own ends. God knows,' said Mr Mortimer, 'that's all your father was doing. Creating something out of something else that wasn't there. I warned you about that; I warned you explicitly and deliberately and you chose to ignore me. Which is why this unpleasantness arose in the first place.'

'I don't believe you,' I said. 'And if I did believe all the nonsense about taking liberties with the past I wouldn't imagine that your role was completely disinterested.'

Mr Mortimer looked pained. I believe he thought for a moment that I might hit him. Then he sat down again in the chair.

'I really must ask you to go,' he said. 'I have a great deal to do. You had better ask your mother if you disagree. But it is all true, I'm afraid it is. *Taking liberties with the past*,' Mr Mortimer intoned solemnly. 'That's all it was. Something which really ought to be allowed to speak for itself.'

I had heard this before; in wide, oak-panelled rooms with the sunlight shining through high windows, enunciated in quavering, cultured tones, imparted by other Mr Mortimers in high-ceilinged lecture theatres before a sea of vacant faces. A former tutor of mine had written a whole book about it. *The past is what you make of it* I had once cunningly proposed in an essay and got a complacent, saurian smile, a disconcerting refusal to be drawn. Mr Mortimer fought without camouflage.

There did not seem to be anything left to say. I left him in the library, busily working amid the pile of books and the guttering wastepaper basket.

Mr Mouzookseem disappeared without trace. Though a warrant was issued for his arrest and though substantial rewards were offered for information leading to his capture, no inkling of his whereabouts ever came to light. So outraged were the villagers by the deception practised upon them they declined even to speculate: a silence which, though thought by the authorities to betoken complicity, stemmed from a general conviction that Mr Mouzookseem was better forgotten. Had he been a notorious brigand, or committed picturesque murders, tongues would undoubtedly have wagged. Deceit ensured that he was removed from conversation, if not from memory.

Although no hint of Mr Mouzookseem's subsequent activities ever emerged, a certain amount of information filtered through which related to past accomplishments. Such was his notoriety that a government department set about composing a file. However, the hope that evidence of cumulative depravity might follow provided quite illusory.

It was established that Mr Mouzookseem's origins lay comparatively near at hand, barely a hundred miles down the river in fact, though his early activities were obscure. Born the son of a small landowner, who had been arrested for debt and died in prison, Mr Mouzookseem had held some trifling government office – it may have been something to do with the veterinary arrangements relating to pigs – until dismissed for peculation of a kind too spectacular to be ignored. There had followed a career of more or less illegal activity (here boundaries, much less Mr Mouzookseem's adherence to them, were inadequately defined) whose staples were prostitution, contraband liquor and fraud. A prison sentence for running a protection racket indicated that he had not been unambitious. Yet his activities had remained modest. He had possessed no private army. He had never attempted to interfere in politics. An insular man, he had never attempted to transfer his activities to foreign parts. As far as the authorities were concerned this was rather a point in his favour: the pursuit of malefactors was invariably complicated by connections abroad.

A new Commissioner of Police, recently arrived in the village, though piqued by Mr Mouzookseem's evasion of justice, was reassured. Such information as he had obtained indicated that he could be certain of one thing: Mr Mouzookseem would not return.

And that is nearly it. After a discreet interval – it might have been six months or a year – my mother married Mr Mortimer and went to live with him in Oxford. The unkind said that he had married her for her money but this, seeing that my father had not left her any, seemed improbable. I did not attend the ceremony, which took place in the chapel of Mr Mortimer's college, though reports indicated that Mr Mortimer's bearing was exemplary. In any case, I was busy with other plans. Shortly afterwards Mr Mortimer published his *History of Early East Anglia*, which drew a number of respectful notices in the Sunday and weekly papers.

Though there had originally been some suggestion of keeping up my parents' house as a second home, it was eventually sold to a jobbing plumber who parked his vans in the gravel drive and converted my father's study into a sun lounge. I visited it once, when the family was out, and wandered down the side path to the garden. However, the jobbing plumber's imagination had run to external as well as internal detail. There was a swimming pool in place of the patch of waste ground where my father had constructed his inept bonfires and even the lavender rockery – on which my mother had expended so many hours of patient labour – had disappeared.

Of all the villagers affected in one way or another by Mr Mouzookseem's defection it was the *dirzi* who felt the keenest hurt. A conviction lingered that his relation to Mr Mouzookseem's fictitious administration had deeper roots than he cared to maintain: the resultant social ostracism pained him deeply. Initially the *dirzi* had attempted to make some capital out of his status as Mr Mouzookseem's deputy but after the Commissioner of Police had informed him that the appointment was wholly bogus and might still render him liable to prosecution, he was concerned to distance himself from the previous regime. The villagers were unconvinced. The *dirzi* found his offers to tell fortunes fell upon deaf ears, that his attempts to predict the future met with universal derision. Compelled eventually to lower himself to weather-forecasting for peasant farmers, he became a morose and solitary man, preferring to wander alone in the fields and contemplate the inanimate rather than subject himself to the unfortunate remarks of the bazaar idlers.

The *dirzi*'s depression did not stem from the fact that his abilities had been called into question: he was not a vain man. Rather it proceeded from an awareness that his good nature had been abused, that his disinterestedness had been met merely with guile, confusing for a man who had previously acted with discretion and success in the affairs of human kind. Perhaps, the *dirzi* thought, his motives were misconceived? The flat fields and browsing cattle, even the dead birds whose graves he dug, placid and unthreatening, assured him that this was so. There were times, the *dirzi* thought, as he gingerly conveyed the moribund pigeon into its tiny hollow of earth, when you should not put your trust in human beings; a maxim that the gods advised but which pundits all too frequently tended to ignore.

It is nearly dark here in the empty house as I sit by the open window, conscious of the light fading over the fields, down to the sinewy curve of the river. Outside it has begun to rain, so that the occasional droplet of water falls onto the windowsill, courses in a tiny rivulet down the wall. It is at times like these that I miss Caro's company. But Caro has not been seen in the village for some days. He continues, so far as I am aware, to assist the authorities with the enquiries into the affair of the poisoned oranges.

I switch on the desk lamp, flood the table-top with yellow light. The page, neatly blotted, encourages me to pick up the pen once more. Because the minutes are ticking away, there is not long to go before it will be time to forsake these notes, this explanation of all that has happened, to go down to the river, haul suitcases, negotiate passages. When a position becomes untenable, my father used to say (he had a fondness for military metaphors) retreat from it. But not quite yet. There are one or two other things to write.

Two nights ago I had a dream, one of those curious dreams in which reality twists itself in such a mild and subtle manner as to alarm you only at its climax, present you finally with an Alice in Wonderland world full of perverted logic and warped perspectives. It recalled distinctive images – the cliff-top figure monitoring the retreating ships – but for the fact that there *were* no retreating ships; merely calm, unruffled sea. I consider it as one among a series of sharp, pungent dreams that crackle in my head, populated by familiar faces. Mr Mouzookseem smiles, my father closes the book he holds up to his face, Miss Knox's eyes swim behind aquarium spectacles. I snap my fingers. The figures recede.

Outside the rain continues to fall. Watching the slight movement in the air, hearing the wind gust against the roof, the muffled blows of air hitting wood, I can imagine that it is raining everywhere, dark arrowheads of rain falling all over the world. It is nearly time to go now, down to the river, baggage strapped across my shoulders, but meanwhile it is pleasant to consider this tumult of water, a universal pouring forth of the heavens, imagine that it rains over the wide East Anglian fields, rains on the bones of Wehha, Wuffa and Redwald (my ancestors, *certain*), on the rows of Spaldings hard underground in St Nicholas's churchyard, out towards the coast and the long arm of the Breydon Water; that there is nothing but fog settling comfortably over the damp grass like a blanket, beneath the great wide sky.

The wind rushes through the open window, disturbs the pages on the desk. I shuffle them dextrously together, pinion them with a paperclip, secure in the knowledge that eventually someone will discover them, that they will be read. I peer up at the lamp, catch a glimpse of my face's reflection, not unpleasing in the eerie light, switch it off. Outlines of furniture recede into darkness. The clock ticks as I sit considering the sheaf of foolscap, the threads of circumstance no longer assimilable, a past which is neither mine nor yours, has no beginning and no end, whose explanation lies not in the living but in the dead.

Flamingo

Flamingo is a quality imprint publishing both fiction and non-fiction. Below are some recent titles.

Fiction
☐ Innocence *Penelope Fitzgerald* £3.50
☐ The Seven Ages *Eva Figes* £3.95
☐ La Douleur *Marguerite Duras* £3.95
☐ The Game of the Pink Pagoda *Roger Moss* £3.95
☐ Swansong *Richard Francis* £3.95
☐ Loving Roger *Tim Parks* £3.50
☐ Incidents at the Shrine *Ben Okri* £3.50
☐ Monkeys *Susan Minot* £3.50
☐ Dog's Life *James Rogers* £3.50
☐ Great Eastern Land *D. J. Taylor* £3.50

Non-fiction
☐ Rain or Shine *Cyra McFadden* £3.50
☐ Love is Blue *Joan Wyndham* £3.50
☐ Nine-Headed Dragon River *Peter Matthiessen* £3.95
☐ Rites *Victor Perera* £3.50
☐ Love Lessons *Joan Wyndham* £2.95

You can buy Flamingo paperbacks at your local bookshop or newsagent. Or you can order them from Fontana Paperbacks, Cash Sales Department, Box 29, Douglas, Isle of Man. Please send a cheque, postal or money order (not currency) worth the purchase price plus 22p per book (or plus 22p per book if outside the UK).

NAME (Block letters) _____

ADDRESS_____

_____

_____